# Messenger

A Novel

For Mary,
Thank you for your
deep reading of
Messenger. May you
receive the message
you need most!
Love + blessings
Liz

Liz Keller Whitehurst

ISBN: 978-1-954614-43-7 (hard cover)
978-1-954614-44-4 (soft cover)

Edited by: Amy Ashby

Published by Warren Publishing
Charlotte, NC
www.warrenpublishing.net
Printed in the United States

*For Wilson and Joy*
*who believed*

# Messenger's Composition Book

*Call me Messenger. Don't be afraid. Don't be anxious or worried.*

*Everything's gonna be okay.*

*You want to know, know, know. Want me to write it all down. Well, I like to write. Ooooh, I love this notebook! Lots of clean, blank pages. They smell so good. You think you're pinning me down, honey, but you're in for a surprise. Everybody is. Oh well. If it'll make you happy. Here goes.*

*You want to understand what's going on here—what I've been trying to do? Well, you know how in books or stories writers will use lots of symbols instead of saying what they really mean? Something stands for something else? This won't be like that. I'm going to tell you what's what. But don't expect too much. Look, you can't figure it all out, no matter how hard you try. Let's just say the swerve's a hint—a wink—a little nudge along the right path.*

*This is how it's done: you wait and wait. You won't know it's coming. You wake up one morning. It's sunny or it's cloudy. You get up early or snooze for a while. Doesn't matter. The day will seem like any other. What I mean is, you will have no idea anything's about to happen to you. That just around the corner, on your way to work or to the store, the message will come. You'll realize everything that's happened in your life—whether you ate pancakes or oatmeal every morning for five years as a child, whether you like blue, whether you're right- or left-handed—every single thing you've ever done or thought or experienced will come into play.*

*You might feel happy or elated or afraid or terrified or want to cry or laugh or scream. Doesn't matter. It's like having a baby. Ready or not ... here it comes. And it's yours now—forever. So if you're smart, tuned in, or whatever you want to call it, you'll watch for it all the time. You know the end of the story even if you don't know the particulars. Or the big W: when.*

*Doesn't matter how much you wish for it or want to get it over with, depending on your temperament, doesn't matter. Until the time is right, no amount of fretting or sweating will make it come. So don't begin that game at all. Your message will arrive when it's good and ready.*

*Okay—let's put it another way. You know that message everybody's been waiting for their whole lives? They've looked for it in the mail, email, text, letter, in every book or magazine they've ever read. On billboards. In others' faces.*

*Well, I bring that message. That's my job. It's up to me. That's why I came. It comes through me for you. When you least expect it, when you give up and stop looking, that's when you'll get it. It'll explain everything, answer those questions that wake you up in the night in a cold sweat, turning, longing, watching the hours tick by.*

*So here you go.*

# PART ONE
# HIDE AND SEEK

Six months earlier

*This is what started it all.*

# Alana's Notebook

## Transcript of Marty's Facebook Video

*Marty: Lots of people have replied to the photo I posted of the mystery woman who gave me a message. They want to hear my story. Okay, so here goes.*

*I'm heading to work, see? It's a perfectly ordinary day. I know because when I think back, try to put it all together (like when you drop a glass and it breaks, you better find all the pieces, or you'll step on a slice barefoot in the night), I couldn't find anything—no warning. No tip-off. No clue. Nothing.*

*Nothing's on my mind that day—just tired. Dreading work. All my problems plucking my nerves. Money, my parents' bad health, my wife's mad at me again. My hair's definitely falling out. Every day—more hair in the shower drain. Kid's failing algebra for the second time; dog keeps peeing in the same places on our tiny patch of lawn. All these dead circles of grass staring up at me. The usual.*

*I get out of the car and hurry down the street and there she is. This woman. We'd call her a "bag-lady" back in the day. I don't really pay attention to her—too much else going on all around—people, noise. Listening to that god-awful bing on my phone telling me I've racked up a hundred new emails to read when I get to work. So I'm about to pass her without really seeing her. You know, I try my best not to make eye contact with these people—give them a little privacy in their shame.*

*I jump when I feel her touch me. I'm shocked and then, like they say—electricity. She hands me something. I feel my hand clutch it. It's just a dirty piece of paper. Okay, I figure—must be one of those things they give you in exchange for money—flyer, newspaper, whatever. But it isn't.*

*At first, I shove it in my overcoat pocket till I get to the next wastebasket. I pull my hand out, ready to drop the paper in, still not paying attention until my eyes rest on the words. It's not a copied, printed thing. It's handwritten. And for some reason, I start thinking how you don't see that anymore. Everything's printed, copied—or not on paper at all. So it wasn't the words, at first. I didn't focus on them. It was the curiosity that a message—no, a note, handwritten—sparks in you. Your heart leaps somehow. You can't keep from wondering—is this it? Is this the one?*

*So I finally read it. And when I do—how can I tell you? It's like time stops—like all those moments in life. When the doctor calls, "It isn't cancer." Or the car door slams in the dark night when your daughter's late coming home. Or your wife's text: "I still love you." Those moments are really very short but take up a lot of room in a lifetime.*

*This was one of those. Not long. Not profound.* **TAKE A CHANCE. FOLLOW YOUR DREAMS.** *I know it doesn't sound life changing or earth-shattering.*

*But listen: really, it is.*

*I was making some big decisions in my life at that time. After I got the message, everything reconfigured for me. It lightened me up. Reminded me of who I am. It was just what I needed.*

*So what do I do? Well, quite naturally, I go back. I want to find her and thank her and ask where all this is coming from. Like, where's she getting it? Who's sending it? It's obviously not from her. I go back to the exact same spot near the wastebasket, in front of the chicken place on Eleventh.*

*But she's gone. Completely. Without a trace. I walk around the block, look everywhere. Nothing. I even go into the chicken place to ask if they've seen her. "Ah—yeah. Old? Red cap? We're always chasing her off," the young kid, his polyester uniform too big, awful acne, says. Then looks at me like I must be crazy.*

*Well, I don't give up easy. I keep walking those streets, determined to find her, to figure out what gives. Finally, way down First Avenue, I catch a glimpse of her red cap. I run toward her, stop, and snap a photo through the crowd. When I pull my phone back down, she's gone. I don't know if she turned down a street or disappeared into thin air. The photo is terrible, but it at least captures something about her.*

*So there you go. I think I can say without a doubt, this is the strangest thing that has ever happened to me. I keep my message in my wallet and look at it every day, just like I have since I got it. But I can't even remember exactly what the woman looked like, even with the terrible photo. Except for her eyes, which were this strange golden color. Doesn't matter, I guess. My message was for real.*

# Alana's Notebook

*THIS IS IT! Just what I've been looking for. My big break! WHAT A STORY!*

*This Marty is getting a lot of Facebook replies from people all over the city who say they received a message from her too.*

*But I can't find her. Even though I walk the streets, hang out where people say they got their messages. She definitely gets around. I can't find a pattern, either with who gets a message or where they get it. I stare at the grainy photo Marty took of her. She's turned three-quarters of the way around, with just her profile visible. Her body looks thick, heavy—but that's probably because she was wearing loads of clothes. Red stocking hat. Definitely an older woman but impossible to tell how old. Not much to go on.*

*Who are you?*

*I messaged Marty after I watched his video. He told me to check out this coffee shop at First Avenue and East Third Street and ask for Ed, the manager. A tall, thin Asian guy, some tattoos. Marty had talked with him about her but hadn't gotten very far. "I really think this Ed knows more than he'd tell me—like who she is and where to find her. Ask him."*

# ALANA LOOKING FOR ANSWERS

Alana headed down First Avenue, glanced into the eyes of dozens of people who hurried by in the opposite direction. A sad old man with baggy skin around his eyes held a sign that read, "Do you have a heart?" He'd drawn a heart below the question mark. People pushed baby strollers, carried skateboards, walked their bikes, then locked them in the racks along the street. Alana stopped random people, asked if they'd ever seen the mysterious woman.

She passed an Ace Hardware store, feet and back-rub shops, a clairvoyant. Optimo Cigars, McDonald's, Karma Bar (where smoking is permitted, the sign announced), and the Three of Cups Sicilian Restaurant. Other restaurants and bars. She smelled greasy Italian food, the earthy, claustrophobic smell of dirty people too crowded together. She cringed at a pile of dog shit. She scanned far down each street for a glimpse, a brushstroke of bright red in the middle of all the iron gray, the low-hanging clouds in the fall sky, the air itself. Cold. The concrete held the cold relentlessly. She'd never get used to New York's cold. But there was no red stocking cap to be seen, either up close or on the horizon.

Alana found the coffee shop Marty had told her about and spied Ed behind the counter waiting on customers. He wore his thick, jet-black hair a little long and a short-sleeved black tee. *He's not much older than me,* she figured. *Hot, but in a sweet way. Not too full of himself.* Watching him, Alana noticed Ed gave each person his full attention. He didn't hurry.

Alana was thrilled nobody else had come in behind her while she waited. When she got to the front of the line and their eyes met, Ed paused a beat before asking for her order. But Alana wasted no time and dove right in with questions about Messenger.

"Why are you looking for her?" Ed asked, a little aggressively.

"I just want to write a story about her and the messages she's been giving people. This guy, Marty, posted a photo of her online, asking if anybody had seen her. Lots of people replied, and a few said they saw her here." She wished Ed would at least look at her while she talked instead of wiping down the counter. "People wanted to know more about Marty's message, so he posted this video. He said the message changed his life. I'm just wondering what you know about her."

Ed got her coffee, then shrugged when Alana pressed him for more information. He stared down at the mermaid and the retro anchors tattooed on his forearm. Alana waited, noted a spareness to him. Clean-shaven. Not a wrinkle in his T-shirt.

"I don't know what to tell you," he finally said. "She comes in here some, okay? You think she tells me anything? No. Nothing. I'm the last person to judge. I just like her. She helps people. She needs a place to hang. I let her use the bathroom. Plus, I'm the manager. I can give her free coffee if I want to. I don't need to answer to anybody for it." He pulled out his phone and started texting.

"Okay, fine!" Alana snapped.

"Look." Ed glanced back up and flashed what might be considered a smile. "I don't know exactly what she's doing—but it's good work. I do know that. So okay. That's all I can tell you."

Alana picked at her already raw cuticles, trolled her brain for questions Ed might agree to answer. She gave up. She'd already opened the door to leave when Ed suddenly added, "Except you could ask the Flower Lady, on the corner of Sixth and Second Ave."

Alana turned back around and smiled her thanks.

# Alana's Notebook

## Ten Questions for Messenger

1. *Who are you?*
2. *Why are you doing this?*
3. *Where do the messages come from?*
4. *What do you think they mean?*
5. *Is there any pattern to the kinds of people who receive messages?*
6. *How long have you been doing this? How did it start?*
7. *What did you do before messages started coming? A job?*
8. *Family?*
9. *Children?*
10. *Where are you from?*

*Alana created her own blog, reposted Marty's photo, and asked: HAVE YOU SEEN HER? She immediately received these posts.*

# Post: Brenda

Where should I start? I just want you to know up front that it makes me very uncomfortable to talk about anything like this. It's like, well, sex or money—or religion! Those topics you'll do anything to avoid. But this one's worse. (Okay. Shut up, Brenda. Just tell it).

I was leaving my apartment last April. There was a springtime smell in the air, even though it was cold, of course. I was just walking down the street, not paying attention, wishing I didn't have to go to work. A million thoughts drummed through my head, as always. A tree beside the fence had tiny green buds on it. A shoe lay in the street on its side—a red, high-top sneaker. Those were the only details I took in as I went on my usual path to work.

I checked my phone, and when I looked up, I saw this big, homeless woman wearing lots of coats and a red hat all squashed into this doorway. Her stuff was everywhere. She stuck out her arm and handed me a paper circle, which I could clearly see was the bottom peeled off an old, stained coffee cup.

"This is yours," she said.

Why would I ever take anything from a person like that? A reflex, I guess. Anyway, I took it and walked on. I headed across the street, and the whole time my head was screaming, *You idiot. It's dirty!* Another part wondered, *Can you get bedbugs from coffee cups?* Probably. I held it between my thumb and forefinger like something nasty—which it was.

I was about to drop it into the nearest trashcan—I won't litter—when I saw writing on the other side. It was like my eyeballs couldn't tear themselves away. The words were written in a hand I was just fascinated to look at. It was not printed; it was handwritten, each letter like a drawing or art. It was just a few words: **YOU'RE CLOSER THAN YOU THINK**.

I turned and ran back toward the woman as fast as I could go in heels, my coat and purse flying out in different directions. But when I got back, she was gone. The stoop was empty. I whipped my head up the street, scanned all the shoulders and the backs of heads, searched for that red cap of hers. Then down the other way. My heart was beating so fast it scared me. A sweat covered my whole body. I stared at the circle in my hand.

I didn't feel like myself anymore. I felt more, in every way. Up to now, the good news always seemed to be for someone else, while I watched, made myself smile. Empty-handed. But all that changed because of my message.

Forever.

# Post: Terri

Oh, I don't know how it started. I guess I just vaguely noticed her—you know, like a tree or bench. Even here in the city, you can see the exact same people every day, like landmarks among so many strangers. The lady with the fat Chihuahuas resting on a bench in front of the playground. The cops on the other side of the street, going in and out of the precinct. The blond gay guy who works in the Italian restaurant on the corner, who comes out by the back door for a smoke. His black shirt makes his face look so pale in the harsh light. Nobody says hello to a stranger here like we do back home, even if you see them every day.

And she was part of it too. I just noticed her slowly, realized I saw her almost every day—at the Rite Aid down from my apartment building. She had so much stuff gathered around her, I wondered how she managed it all. Did somebody carry it for her? Who? How do you find a friend like that here? Nobody seems to have time for friends. Yes—for dinner or drinks. But somebody to ask a favor of? Who would go out of their way to help you? I haven't found any friends like that.

One day I happened to walk down her side of the street on my way home. I thought she was sleeping because her head was bowed, her chin on her chest. When I got to her bench, she raised up her head and locked eyes with me, as if on cue. She reached out her dirty hand, chipped red fingernail polish, held an even dirtier piece of paper. "Take it," was all she said.

I did.

Why, I don't know. It was one of those situations where you don't think? You just do it.

The paper felt warm, as if she'd been holding it in her hand a long time before I showed up. Then I walked away as fast as I could. I mean, who knew what she might do? She gave off a good vibe, but I've learned you've got to be very careful with these people. Not make eye contact or smile, even if they do. It opens a door you want to keep closed. Her brashness, her connecting with me like that—it scared me. Guess everybody takes the paper notices people hand out for restaurants, clubs, shows, or knock-off handbags, just to get the people out of their face. But this woman was different.

I meant to throw the paper in the next trashcan I came to without looking at it. I itched to fish my hand sanitizer out of my purse. But I was in a hurry. I was late. I glanced down at the paper before dropping it in my pocket. The words took shape and sent a jolt through me. **IT WASN'T YOUR FAULT**. I stared at them and then back at her. But she was gone.

# THE FLOWER LADY

Alana turned onto Sixth Street and looked all the way up to Second Avenue. *Okay, there she is! Today's my lucky day.* She headed down the street. After Ed's one measly tip, Alana had looked for the Flower Lady there every day for three days straight. Walking down Sixth on this cold, clear morning, she'd caught sight of smidgens of pink, red, and white through all the people ahead of her. When Alana approached, she was surprised to see the lady in a wheelchair, surrounded by big, white paint buckets filled with carnations.

Alana waited in the short line of her customers. An old guy with a full, white beard who could have doubled for Santa Claus. Two middle-aged ladies grasping their designer bags across their middles like babies. A guy who rode up on his scooter, with plastic bags wrapped over both hands.

"Hello," Alana said, when she finally reached the front of the line.

"What can I do for you?" The Flower Lady had a rich, deep, woman's voice, despite being smaller than a ten-year-old. Alana felt her cheeks burn. She realized she'd expected her voice to be high-pitched. The lady's upper body was small yet normally proportioned, but her legs were so short they stuck straight out from the seat.

"I think you can help me. Ed told me you might know this woman who goes around the city giving messages to people."

The Flower Lady squinted and inspected Alana more closely. "Yeah. I know her. Why?"

"Well, I'm trying to find her. I want to write a story about ..." Alana paused. About what? She couldn't say yet, only that she had to write it. "All the good she's doing for people." Alana heard this pour out of her mouth unplanned. "I made this blog after I talked with Marty, this guy who got a message from her, and I asked anybody who'd received a message to post. I've already had some responses, but nobody knows where she is. Apparently, after she delivers the messages, she disappears into thin air. Crazy, right?" Alana laughed but the Flower Lady didn't. "Could you tell me where she lives or how I could find her?"

Alana watched the Flower Lady's face shut down.

The woman stared straight ahead. "I haven't seen her today."

*She's not a very good liar,* Alana thought. "Okay. But can you tell me where she might be?"

"Not really. She comes and goes."

"I know." Did she ever. "Well, thanks anyway. If you happen to see her, could you tell her I'm trying to find her?" Alana pulled her notebook out of her drab green backpack and jotted her name and cell number on a sheet of paper. She tore it out and handed it to the Flower Lady.

The Flower Lady looked Alana in the eye. "You sure it's just a story? You're not with the cops or one of those do-gooders or nothing, right?"

"No! I mean—yeah. Yes! Just a story."

"I shouldn't tell you this," the Flower Lady said into her bucket of red carnations. "Sometimes you can find her over on Fifth. Those benches along the school's parking lot fence. Check there."

Alana's heart lifted. "Thanks. Great! Oh, and I'd like three flowers."

"What color?"

"Red. I like red. Marty told me the woman always wears a red stocking cap."

The Flower Lady nodded and gave Alana a pinched smile. She plucked three droopy red carnations out of the plastic bucket and tied them with raffia. Alana watched in admiration as she maneuvered this whole process while seated in the wheelchair. She wondered if she could walk at all. It didn't look like it.

*Who helped her? How did she get the flowers out here in the first place?*

"One dollar each—that makes three dollars, please."

Alana dug into her jean pocket, fished out some ones, and handed them over. She longed to ask a million more questions, but it was obvious that this little tip and the flowers were all she would get today. At least it was something. She took her carnations from the Flower Lady's outstretched hand; the outer edges of the petals had turned a light brown.

Alana headed back down the street. For some reason, the smell of all those flowers in one space had reminded her of the one and only flower arrangement at her mom's funeral. It had been huge and overflowed with pink and white flowers, lots of those spiky ones. She was sure Mrs. Snyder, the mom of her best friend growing up who always gave Alana rides places since Alana's mom had to work, had paid at least $150 for it. The flowers were all in a big, flat-bottomed basket you were supposed to put in the cemetery after the funeral. Not even a storm or heavy wind could blow it over.

Mrs. Snyder hadn't known that Alana's mom had decided to be cremated, the cheapest and most practical option, and prepaid for it at the funeral home. There was plenty of time for Alana's mom to plan. Her ashes would be scattered in her family's area of the cemetery near her parents' and grandparents' graves, so the plot reserved for her could go to Alana when she died. Alana could still see her mom, writhing on her death bed, barking, wheezing, and gasping for breath to get these last orders out. She'd made Alana promise she'd follow the plans, that this was how things would go.

Alana wondered what her mother would say about this new trajectory she found herself on. No, she knew. Mom would call it a "wild goose chase." Thanks to her mother's money—every single penny hard-earned from a lifetime of nasty nursing duties, then squirreled away and left to Alana when she died—Alana was living every writer's dream. She'd been given a cushion to take the leap, quit her boring, soul-sucking day job and set out to find *the* story that would launch her career. She'd been looking for it for months now, but nothing had come. She'd questioned herself: Could she even do it? Meanwhile, money poured out of her account each month like water, no matter how hard Alana tried to save. But this time she had just enough, she hoped, to make it. To follow any and all leads. To do whatever she had to do to find the mysterious woman. This story had her name all over it.

# MARTY'S WARNING

After Alana bugged him every day, sometimes several times a day, Marty, the guy who had posted the photo and video, finally agreed to meet at Ed's coffee shop during his lunch break. Alana's spirits dipped when Ed turned away to concentrate on washing dishes and let the other guy wait on her.

Marty was middle-aged with wire-framed glasses. He wore a cardigan under a leather jacket and a stocking cap pulled down low over his ears. There was nothing remarkable about him. He could be anybody. Alana relaxed in her seat after talking with him for a few minutes. Marty seemed about as normal as you could get.

"I've got some questions," Alana began. They talked about his experience and then Alana said, "I have to admit something. I don't really get why your message was so important to you. I mean, 'Take a chance. Follow your dreams.'?"

Marty shook his head and looked at Alana with kind eyes. "Hard to explain. Sound corny?"

She shrugged. "Sort of."

"Listen, it was timing. Incredible *timing*. You see, I'd about given up. No more energy, no drive. Felt like everything I'd done with my life was wasted. I was out of time with nothing to show for it. So at the time, I was considering a big break. I mean, a break from everything I'd done or known. Starting over. And then, through no effort on my part, this message comes out of the blue." He shrugged and shook his head. "She was just—there. She gave me this. It's the greatest gift I've ever received. From that moment, my path has been clear. My brother and I went out on our own and started our own electrical contracting business. Now, don't get me wrong. I didn't say it's been easy. I've had to work my can off. But somehow, it was okay. I'm not afraid of hard work—no sir. Never have been. It was just the message and the timing together gave me the courage. And the fact that I was ... chosen. Is that the right word? Worthy to receive? I don't know. I don't understand it all either."

Alana jotted down *timing* in the notes she took. "I get it. Listen, I really want to write about her, the messages she's giving people and everything, but I'm having trouble finding her." She glanced over at Ed. "He's not much help."

Marty nodded and sipped the coffee Alana had bought him. "She's hard to find. I never did. Nope. Never saw her again."

"I noticed you took the photo and video down."

"Yeah." He looked away.

"But why? You were getting so many replies. That's what encouraged me to try and find her myself."

"Exactly. That's why I took it all down. I had second thoughts. You know how things can get out of hand, spin out of control before you know it? Nobody's fault. Just the way it goes."

"I guess, but this is such a great story!" Alana argued. "Something positive. Doesn't everybody need good news for a change?"

"I get what you're saying. I just decided to let her be. Leave her alone. That's why I wasn't too crazy to talk with you." He smiled. "But you wouldn't take no for an answer."

Alana laughed. "Ah yeah. I'm pretty stubborn. I just have a strong feeling I need to follow up on this."

"You'll have to decide for yourself. I'm not telling you what to do. Guess you could keep following the leads. Post something yourself."

"I already have," she told him.

# ALANA AND MESSENGER FINALLY MEET

One week later, Alana finally found her.

It was a bright, clear fall day. Messenger was sitting on the third stool from the left at the long table at Ed's on Third Street and First Avenue. Alana had just planned to go in for a coffee and see if Ed would tell her any more before she hit the streets to search. Ed wasn't busy, and since there was no line in front of her, she'd ordered before she'd even looked around the shop. Ed wouldn't make eye contact, but that was normal.

When she turned, Alana saw her for the first time. She sat with bags scattered around her, that red stocking cap pulled down over her ears. Her body poured over the sides of the short stool. Her heavy coat (or coats) couldn't hide the heft they held.

After weeks of playing hide-and-seek, following lead after lead, all leading up to this moment, Alana shivered all over, something she'd always done in intense moments. Trying to still her chattering teeth, she inched across the room very slowly, much like you'd approach a stray dog or a scared child you're afraid might bolt. On her way, Alana caught sight of Ed out of the corner of her eye. He did make eye contact with the woman, then nodded in Alana's direction.

"Hello? Excuse me, hello?" Alana sputtered. All the rehearsal she'd done in her head anticipating this moment left her. She waded through the woman's bags to stand beside her stool. Alana's heart pounded out of her chest. Surely everybody in the coffee shop must hear it too.

The woman turned slowly, and their eyes met. Her eyes were amber, like many had reported, but shone so bright with flecks of gold in them they dazzled. She held Alana's gaze for the longest time, like she could see things there Alana didn't even know about. It both scared her and made her feel safe at the same time. She didn't want her to stop looking. Finally, after so much waiting and searching, Alana had her full attention.

Then, she smiled at Alana. All her wrinkles fell into place as if that's where they belonged, and they opened her face wide. Something in her eyes, her smile, made Alana sense Messenger had been waiting for her too, had expected her to show up today. Was glad to see her even. Had Messenger planned to finally allow Alana to find her? Had Ed or the Flower Lady tipped her off? Or was it a deeper knowing? It really felt like they'd already met many times before. Like Messenger knew her. But that was impossible.

"Hello," Alana said again. "I've been looking for you."

"Uh-huh. That's what I hear."

"I'm Alana Peterson. I know you."

"Oh, you do, do you?"

"I mean, I know about what you've been doing for people. Aren't you the person giving out messages?"

She didn't answer.

"Could we talk a little? Can I buy you a coffee?"

"Ed gives me coffee for free."

"Oh, that's so nice of him. Listen, I'm really interested in you. In the messages, I mean. I made this blog. I've interviewed some of the people you gave messages to. It's all incredible. Could I ask you a few questions? Would that be okay?" Alana talked faster as she went.

"Why?"

"Well, you've been doing this for a long time, it seems, but nobody's reported about you, so I want to write a story about you and the messages. Would you agree to that?"

"About me? Why?"

Alana hadn't expected all these questions. "I just think what you're doing is fascinating and significant. You know—life-changing. For the people who get the messages, that is." *Lame, lame, lame!* Alana felt like she was failing a test. She chewed her cuticles and waited.

The lady smiled again, and Alana noticed she was missing some teeth in the back. "Sure, baby. We can talk. But not right now. I got to go." She stood up and gathered her bags.

"Wait!" Alana shrieked. *She couldn't leave now.* "Do you really have to?"

"I do."

"But how will I find you again? I've been looking for so long already."

The woman threw her head back and laughed as if Alana had told the funniest joke ever.

Alana tried again. "Please wait. Can I come along with you so we can talk?"

"Not today. Thanks, Ed," she called to him. He waved to her and nodded to Alana.

Alana couldn't believe this was happening. The woman was headed to the door—getting away. "Please wait," she called. "I don't even know your name."

"You don't happen to have any chocolates on you? Those ones wrapped in red foil? I dearly love them."

"No, but I can get some."

"You can find them at the Rite Aid." She turned and smiled. Paused a beat, as if deciding whether or not to say more. "You can call me Messenger," she added over her shoulder. "Bye-bye."

# MESSENGER STARTS SOMETHING

*I finally found her,* Messenger thought. She slowly walked down First Avenue a few blocks, then turned onto Fifth Street. She'd sensed the girl's presence for some time now, felt her energy draw closer. She had to smile when she watched her walk into Ed's. A smile of releasing. Her own plan to shake things up was set in motion. She would accomplish it through this girl, and nothing would ever be the same again. Her life task would be fulfilled.

Did she have the strength after all these years? The power to create her own swerve? Was the girl really the one? Yes. Those beautiful, bright eyes! They were the first thing she'd noticed. Those deep brown eyes that went on forever. Just like her daughter's eyes, she remembered. Now, that wasn't what this was about. That didn't enter in. But the fact she'd even register this synchronicity showed her it was time.

Messenger sat on her favorite bench by the fence along the black asphalt playground. The school building was run-down and the paintings on the asphalt, including a map of the US and a mysterious bull's-eye, faded and peeling. This girl was very young, Messenger had to admit. *But that's what we need. We can't keep doing things the old way. It's time now. Everything seems to say so*. Messenger could read the signs. *Clear as the nose on your face,* she thought. *No more secrets. What's the use with these young ones? Their brains are already different from ours. Evolved. More evolved ones coming in all the time. They can't remember not being connected in this new way. They know things on a level we had to work hard to come by.*

Granted, she felt some hard spots in this girl that needed releasing, but nothing she couldn't handle. *No,* Messenger thought. *I've seen worse. Well then, let 'er rip! It has to happen,* she thought, sorting through her stash of paper as a new message welled up inside her. *I'll just help things along a little.* She giggled. *What's the worst thing the Watchers can do to me for breaking the rules?* She wasn't sure. It would be bad, she knew. The Watchers were probably already on it—sensing what Messenger had in mind. They would know. She had to move quickly.

# TALE OF THE WHALE

That evening, Alana stood by the door at Tale of the Whale, where she hostessed a couple nights a week. She'd worked there ever since she moved to the city. Her best friend, Mary, had a roommate who was leaving New York City for a new job, so she'd connected Alana with Gus, the owner and manager of Tale of the Whale. Gus, desperate, had hired Alana on the spot. And Alana knew her money from her mom wouldn't last forever. Grueling as it was, her hostessing gig helped keep her afloat. Decorated with old fishing paraphernalia, crab pots, buoys, fishing nets, Tale of the Whale was supposed to look like a seafood shack you'd find in any beach town. It was okay food at an okay price and had been an okay side gig for Alana. Gus also gave her and the waitstaff a free meal, another plus.

Between waiting for new customers, Alana filled the water glasses of the few guests they had and planned her strategy. She had to admit—after all her struggles to find Messenger, when she'd finally met her earlier that day, she'd been a little disappointed. Messenger looked ... normal. Too normal. She could have been anybody.

*What did you expect?* she asked herself. *Light? A Halo? Something supernatural or woo-woo or weird? Come on, Alana. Be real.*

Messenger's clothes were worn, and it was impossible to tell how big she was with all the layers of coats. *She's short, at least compared to me,* Alana thought, and she wondered if Messenger had any hair beneath the red cap. One difference she did notice about Messenger—she didn't have that deer-in-the-headlights look.

"Excuse me, miss. Do you serve sea bass?" A short, plump couple who looked like twins interrupted her thoughts.

She assured the man they did, gave them menus, and seated them at a table in the back.

She filled a pitcher with water and worked her way around the guests' tables. Returning to her thoughts, Alana continued her assessment of Messenger. Alana realized that after she'd introduced herself and had been around Messenger for like, two seconds, she'd felt this feminine, maternal energy. That energy surrounded her like the mother she wished she had.

"Alana!" Gus called from behind the counter.

She glanced at the door and saw a group of four crowded there. "Sorry! May I show you to a table?"

They settled in, and Alana gave them each a paper menu. One had coffee stains on it, so she swapped it and handed the clean one to a man in the group. She pulled out a tray from under the counter and bussed a nearby table.

Messenger's eyes were definitely her defining feature, Alana decided. But she'd already been tipped off about that from everybody who'd included a description of her in their posts. Alana had never seen anything like those eyes. Her irises were this weird amber color with a milky white ring (cataracts?) around them. When she'd stared into Alana's eyes for just that short conversation, her gaze was laser intense. It felt like Messenger knew her better than she knew herself. Like you couldn't keep any secrets from her, even if you tried. But it was also a warm, encouraging gaze. The only word Alana could come up with was ... love. Love poured out of those strange eyes. Nobody had ever looked at her like that before.

"Excuse me. Do you have anything for dessert?" It was the chubby twin couple again.

"Sure." She brought their menus back, then returned to her post at the front door. *Thank God it is almost closing time.* She could get home, take a long, hot shower, and fall into bed, like she always did on work nights. The only problem with this job was getting that rank fried-food smell out of everything. Her thoughts returned to Messenger. *I can't believe I finally found her. I never thought I'd get this far. But now what? I hope things will get easier.* Messenger had agreed to help, to answer Alana's questions. But Alana had so many questions. Since she was still at work, Alana tried to count them and keep track of them on her fingers so she wouldn't forget any.

On her way to the train after closing time, energy bubbled up in Alana, and she almost ran to the station. *You have to stay professional,* she cautioned herself. She couldn't let her excitement or any warm feelings cloud her judgment. No doubt, all of this would take time. Messenger was a complex person, and there was a lot of information Alana needed about the messages—how it all worked, backstory about Messenger herself. After today, she felt more convinced than ever that this story could be a big one. But more than that, Alana felt drawn to Messenger in a way she couldn't understand or explain.

# ALANA ON THE HUNT

Every morning, Alana rode the train in from her apartment in Astoria. On the way, she scribbled questions for Messenger in the notebook she kept in her green backpack. After the long challenge of finally finding and meeting Messenger, she'd figured everything would go smoothly.

Wrong!

This is how it would go. Alana would start each morning walking up and down streets, scouring the neighborhood around Ed's. Finally, if she were lucky, she'd spot a dot of red weaving through the crowds and make a beeline to her. Messenger's warm smile, her open arms and the hug she always gave Alana, and her "Hey, baby," always made Alana feel she was happy to see her too. But she'd never stay long.

They would be talking together and suddenly, right in the middle of things, Messenger would touch Alana gently on the arm or cup her chin in her palm. "Time for me to go now, honey. Bye-bye!"

Gone. Alana wouldn't find her again for days.

"Could we please set a time to meet up?" she'd beg Messenger, trying her best not to sound desperate.

"No, baby. Sorry about that. My time's not my own." For Messenger, time as we know it did not exist. No cell phone, laptop, no real home, Alana suspected. Once, she came right out and asked Messenger where she lived. "Oh, here and there," she'd answered.

*What? Who says that?*

Ed was no help, either. The times Messenger would leave her in the coffee shop, Ed made a point of getting very busy cleaning up or helping customers. One afternoon, when Alana pressed him again with more questions about Messenger, he actually stopped wiping the counter and looked at her instead of multitasking. "I've told you everything I know. Nothing to add except a little advice. You're going to have to work on *her* time. Not yours." Ed's voice was soft, and he allowed himself that little crooked smile of his before turning back to work.

Alana knew Ed was right. That was the problem. Time. But as people like to say, time is money. She'd never dream of telling Ed this, but for Alana, both were running out.

# Alana's Notebook

## 10 Places to Find Messenger

1. *Ed's coffee shop.*
2. *Stoop on the middle of Fifth Street.*
3. *Benches along playground, across from police station. Look for lady with two fat Chihuahuas, resting on her walk.*
4. *On bench in park where you can listen to the fountain.*
5. *Church of the Transfiguration on Sixteenth Street. Left side near the red luminary candle rack.*
6. *Mary statue at same church. Lady with Yorkie in her bag. The dog barks at everyone who enters the church except for Messenger. Messenger loves their midday concerts.*
7. *With the Flower Lady on Sixth Street and Second Avenue.*
8. *In park near dog run. Talking to the dogs.*
9. *In the alleyway behind Three of Cups Italian Restaurant, where the guys sit on white plastic crates to smoke.*
10. *In the library, back in the stacks near the water fountain and restroom. The librarian lets Messenger have the key whenever she wants.*

# Messenger's Composition Book

## The Beat

*I usually leave Ed's—that sweet young man, he takes such good care of me—and go sit on the wooden benches on Fifth Street, beside the schoolyard fence. I close my eyes and go deep inside. Down, down, down, beyond all the words, the blabber, the stories I tell myself—have always told myself. After a while, I grow huge. I can feel my arms and legs grow until I am more than a giant. I am universe-size. I can feel myself on the inside and outside. Both.*

*This takes a long time to do. I sit and hold the earth, now a tight, small, blue, rubber ball, like you get with jacks. Balls that used to come in the same colors as pencil erasers. There it is—that beautiful, blue earth lying in my two hands. Everything stays put—I don't know how gravity works, but it does. It comforts us, holds us. I realize this earth ball pumps with life. Beats. It's like holding a heart in your hand—that must be a trip for surgeons. And the circles are everywhere! They connect more and more people—join them in a web of circles, all over Planet Earth.*

*So I bless the earth and everybody on it. Every single soul from the past, present, and future. Peace silently comes. Nothing matters—war, murder, violence. They don't matter one bit. Relax.*

*Things are better than they seem. Believe it! Because when you shrink the earth down like this, all that remains is the beat, the beat of life. It makes everything happen in the first place, keeps things going, and—wait for it—it's fixing things up!*

*Tiny, tiny movements—oh, so tiny. Same beat as everybody's heart, every creature's, even plants. No blood, but they're moving with the beat too. That fixing is at work at all times and in all places on my beautiful ball. The fire within the earth, the core that nobody can see? Going strong to the beat too.*

*You want to know the beat? How about trying to hear your own heart, for starters. Feel it beat inside you, without putting your hand on your chest. Your heart, the street drummers, the blood in your veins, the song of birds, the hawk's cry, drips of water. The space between your hands. Then feel the space between your cells. There's energy there. Did you know it? You can feel that first. Start with your own body. Then branch out to colors. Each has a different beat. Then music—so obvious. Hear the beat within the beat. Most of us don't even know this is happening unless we drop down to the beat too. When we do, we feel it in our bones—that healing's happening. Sit quiet and look around. Pay attention. You'll feel it.*

*I walk and pray and send light to every single person I pass. People don't understand the power they have and how easy it is to bless somebody. I see or feel the weather report for every single soul who passes by. Sunny, partly cloudy, stormy, drizzle, full-on hurricane. Even some earthquakes. Yes, tsunamis. Doesn't matter. I just send them my light. I don't have to speak a word—they feel it. It makes a difference.*

*Imagine a shaft of green light coming up through the center of your body from the earth. Green, grounding energy pulsing up. Then golden light pouring through the crown of your head, into your heart and meeting the green light there. A body of energies meeting like when you light a gas burner and poof! The flame mushrooms out, mixes the colors, surrounds you on all sides with lovely light and pulsing energy. That's how it feels to get a message.*

*Okay now. Here's how to bless. Open the top of your head. When the light comes in you, just dart your eyes at somebody and keep breathing. It comes out of your eyes to them. Believe it can do it—and it does. You add your own light to the Helpers who are already hard at work to protect you, those here on Planet Earth and those who have passed on joining them. They work on that healing I was talking about. So see, nobody should ever feel alone or on their own, no matter how rough things get. It's just not true. If only people could believe it. If they would just take a minute and listen to the beat. That's the big problem with all these phones and boxes and i-things. Everybody's so wired they can't receive. Those things close up all your receptors. There's nowhere for the light to come in. Blocked! No wonder every single person walking down the street looks like they're just about to cry.*

# ALANA AND MESSENGER

Alana prowled the streets, headed down Fifth in search of Messenger. She glanced at the neon mural, a woodland scene with bluebirds, cardinals, squirrels, and weirdly, a raccoon and a mallard duck, which spread the full height and length of the side of the Rite Aid building. The Ninth Precinct Police Station sat diagonally across the street from the drugstore. Two officers pulled a tough-looking guy in handcuffs out of the back of a squad car and escorted him through the door. A guy weaved ahead of her from trash can to trash can, picked out half-eaten food.

Alana found Messenger on a bench along the fence surrounding the school playground. After they talked awhile, Alana jotted notes in her notebook while Messenger fed dog biscuits to two obese Chihuahuas—one all white, one tan and white—they often saw on Fifth Street with their owner, an older lady who never spoke or cracked a smile. The three of them usually rested on the bench nearby. When the dogs finished crunching their biscuits, the lady pulled their leashes and headed down the street.

"She isn't too friendly, is she?" Alana commented after the lady had turned the corner with the dogs.

"Oh, she's all right. She lets me feed them whenever I want. Let's take a walk too."

"Okay." Alana slowed her usual pace, two steps short of a run, down to Messenger's. A crawl. Even though she moved slowly, Messenger strode. With every step, she planted her foot securely on the earth. Nothing could make her hurry.

Alana frowned. *Here we go again.* She sucked the side of her thumb she'd picked and made bleed. Today, she had a new idea. Alana put her own notes away and dug the fresh, new black-and-white composition book with ruled lines out of her backpack and tried not to get blood on it.

"Messenger, will you do me a favor? Will you write down anything you think of that would help me with this project? You know, maybe explain how all this started—you receiving the messages, how they come to you, what your process is. Or anything else you might think I need to know."

"Well ... I'm not sure."

"Listen, no pressure. Just stream of consciousness. Lists or bullet points are just fine. I would really appreciate it."

"Okay fine, honey. I will." Messenger took the book, opened it, and stuck her nose in the middle of it. "Mmmm. I just love that smell. Fresh paper."

Alana saw where Messenger was going. "I'll bring you lots of clean paper for your messages if you'll just use this for notes for me. Okay? Please?"

Messenger threw back her head and laughed so hard and so deep, as if Alana had said the most hilarious thing ever. Alana didn't know anybody who laughed like that. She waited patiently for the laughing fit to subside.

"Okey dokey, honey. Deal. I hear you."

"Good. Now, back to the messages."

"You hurt yourself." She took Alana's hand and studied her thumb. "Oh, my. Why do you pick at yourself like that?"

Alana pulled away and stuffed both hands into her pockets. "It's fine. Just a bad habit," she said. "I've always done it. My mom used to make me wear gloves at night, but that didn't help during the day. She once put this nasty-tasting polish on my nails. Yuck. Even that didn't work."

"Well, you've got to stop."

"I know. Look, can we get back to the messages?"

"Sure."

Determined to make progress (everything with Messenger seemed to take so much damn time), she phrased her question carefully. "Why are you doing it? What are the messages for?"

Messenger grew quiet as they walked. The pause continued, but Alana didn't dare break it. She felt lighter after Messenger had agreed to keep the composition book. It could be another way to gather information more quickly. They passed an older man so dirty he looked like he hadn't had a bath in years. Wearing only flip-flops, his feet were black, swollen. *Were they rotten?* Alana cringed. Then a big guy with long hair, a cowboy hat, and a furry orange coat pushed past them. Alana noticed Messenger watched everyone, and no one escaped her glance.

Messenger finally cleared her throat. "Some things psychology or drugs can't heal, no matter how hard you try, because they are spiritual in nature. Every hurt, every rejection, everybody just being plain mean to you for no reason, every disappointment, no matter how small. They all add up. And for some, it's too much."

She paused again. Alana held herself back to allow Messenger to talk at her own pace.

"You see, it breaks off part of your soul. The soul is brittle, like glass. It can break real easy. If people could only understand how very, very sensitive human beings are. But they don't, you see."

"But how do the messages ..." Alana prompted.

"That's what a message can do for you, if you'll let it. The message is exactly what the person needs to hear, so it can bring back that part of the soul that's broken. The soul wants to come back to the body. That's the natural state of affairs. So after you get your message, you need to do something to respond. Doesn't have to be a big deal—just change one little thing. Smile for no reason at the person you're fighting with. Or decide to wear something red today instead of gray. Walk around the block. Moving your body is key. That allows everything to shake back down. Hum! Hmmm—hmmm."

They turned onto Second Avenue and saw this skinny guy walking toward them. He wore supertight jeans, his arms like sticks, long, stringy blond hair. A huge, blond bird's-nest beard swallowed his face. "Hey, aren't you that lady? The one passing out those notes? Messages or something? I saw the guy's video and the photo. Wow, cool! It's you."

*Oh no!* Alana had important questions of her own for Messenger and didn't want this dude taking up her precious time.

But it was too late. Messenger stopped and looked right into his face. "Yes, honey. That's me, I guess. Even though I told those folks not to tell anybody."

"Well, wow! Cool! Listen, could you write one for me right now?" His nose dripped, and he didn't wipe it.

Alana linked arms with Messenger, tried to gently pull her away, but Messenger smiled at him, taking him all in for the longest time. "It's gonna to be okay, baby," she said, her voice low and rich. "It's gonna be okay."

"Well?" He held out his hand. "Give it to me."

"That's all. That is your message. You got what you need." Then she turned and started walking.

"Hey, no I didn't. Wait! Come back!"

But Messenger didn't even turn her head. "That's it for him," she murmured to Alana.

"Is that hard on you?" Alana asked, felt the weight of Messenger's body beside her, moving in her own time.

"Oh no, honey. I'm not responsible for the message or the way it's received. It's just up to me to deliver. That's what a messenger does. You've heard of messenger services?"

Alana laughed. "Sure."

"Well, that's what I do. I deliver. I hand over the message. Then I let it go. Flow and go. It's easy, really. Very clear cut."

Alana and Messenger didn't turn back although the guy called to them a few more times. They were midway down the street before he gave up yelling. Alana knew exactly how he felt. *We want every little detail,* she thought. *Somebody to tell us how things really are and how they're going to be. What we should do. Not just generalizations. "Give us the deets!" we say.* It didn't work like that with Messenger. That much she'd already learned.

Messenger turned to Alana. "He isn't the first person to tell me about some video. You saw it too, right?"

Alana nodded.

"You're not planning to do anything like that, are you?"

"Oh no."

"Okay, good. Listen. Let me tell you something about what just happened with that boy back there," Messenger continued. "If you let people stay on your mind, you send them your own energy. They will receive it, if you send it. Just bless them and shut the door. They'll be fine. We're all in good hands, whether we know it or not. My teacher used to always tell me, 'You are useful but not essential.' Nobody is. Just remember that, honey. We don't want to get too high on our horse, now do we?" Then she cut loose with a deep belly laugh until her eyes filled with tears and she wheezed. "No, Lord. Not too high on your horse and not too worn out either."

"I want to hear more about your teacher, but I've got to ask you—don't you ever get worn out?" Alana asked.

"Me? No! Energy is just pouring out, every which way, up through the earth. Down from the sky. Oh, our Mother is so wonderful and beautiful and *alive*. Tap into her energy; just let it come. You'll never lack a thing."

"But how? I don't get it."

Messenger stopped and rubbed Alana's back between her shoulder blades. "You are a body. You're in a body. So act like one."

"What?"

"Get in yours! I can feel your thoughts swarm around your head like a hive of bees. Get here. Now." She clapped her hands. "Wake up!"

Alana bugged her eyes open. "I'm awake."

"You think you're awake. But you're not." She shrugged. "Not many are."

Messenger's voice was so rich that Alana loved to hear her say anything, didn't matter what. It had a different vibration that just felt good to listen to.

"Oops. Gotta go now, honey. See you around."

"But I thought we were spending the day together. You promised to tell me more about your process, and I want to hear about that teacher you mentioned!" Alana listened to her own voice rise.

Messenger walked away. "Next time, bring me some of that chocolate I told you about, okay? I dearly love chocolate. Dark." She headed off down First Avenue without another word.

Posts Pour in on Alana's Blog

# Post: Jeff

I quit. I was sick and tired of giving. Of taking the blame for everything wrong in the world. Of taking the fall for a God I was positive did not exist—not as my parishioners saw him, anyway. And yes, I do mean Him. A black-and-white, easy-answer, glib-reply, clear-explanations-for-everything God. I was tired of taking responsibility for this monster people created in their need for answers, justifications, for order. Who punished evildoers with natural disasters of all kinds: infant death, cancer, plagues, AIDS, incest, any other trial or disappointment. You name it, and they call it His Will.

Gruesome.

I was also really tired of voicing doubts in the whole system and being met at best with blank faces at worst with whispers and dirty looks, passive aggression ("Don't you think you should dress a little more professionally? And that hair!"). Maybe I could have gone on, carried all these projections, all this grief, all these expectations for a while longer before I self-destructed. But the last straw was when this intolerance for doubt extended to the youth of the church, and I was asked to step in and do something. The problem was: I was on their side. The way it seemed to me, they acted a lot more grown-up than their parents or the elders of the church.

That was the problem—at least my diagnosis of it. Growing up. Nobody wanted to do it anymore. They wanted God to be Daddy—not like the daddy they'd got but a really good, nice daddy, perfectly attuned to them, who predicted their wants and needs before they did and granted all their wishes. He'd say, "Yes!" to everything. He would understand everything and never, ever let anything bad happen to them. It was okay if bad things happened to somebody else, but not them. Daddy would fix everything for them and punish anyone who dared do the least thing against them, and he would never hold them accountable for anything.

This would be just dandy, but it's so far from the truth as I've experienced it—with parents when a son comes out of the closet, or an aging parent is wasting away in pain, or a spouse just drops dead one morning over coffee. Or a house burns to the ground, leaving nothing behind. Where was Daddy when they needed Him? Off fishing or playing golf? Where?

So I finally stopped a minute. Well, to be completely honest, for a month. I took a leave of absence to "discern and prayerfully consider" what to do next because I was absolutely done.

Then, on my first week back, a young couple from the church who had tried forever to get pregnant—all sorts of tests and invasive procedures—finally got great news! She was pregnant and everything was going well. Or so we thought. I'm not a doctor and don't know who dropped the ball, but in the course of delivery, the umbilical cord wrapped itself around the baby's neck several times. She was a big baby, and she strangled before the doctors realized the trouble. She had to be delivered just as if she were still alive.

The couple—dark circles so deep around their eyes they both looked like they'd been punched, which they had—called me into the hospital.

"What do we do now?" the young dad asked me, his eyes wild like a spooked horse. The young mother was struck mute from shock and sorrow.

I embraced the dad—held him close as I would a son. But I had no words.

He pulled away, angry. "You're a priest, but you have no answers here? Nothing? You got nothing?"

I had no words for that lovely young man and his wife, no meaning, only silence in the face of a tragedy, the worst gift I could have given them.

The young mother found her voice. "Get out of here," she told me.

So I was walking down the street, heading to the Diocesan Office to quit. Yes, you can quit being a priest. They don't make it easy on you, but it can be done. I heard this weird humming behind me that sounded otherworldly or like some witch. A chill ran up my spine, and I turned to see a rough-looking old lady in a red stocking cap. My eyes met her amber ones. She didn't say a word, just handed me a slip of paper then walked off down the street. I didn't know what to make of her or of any of it until I looked down and read the message:

**WE NEED YOU TO HOLD YOUR POST.**

# Post: Elaine

Where to begin? Well, I guess I've always been a seeker—since day one. I don't know why. I was always trying to figure everything out, to make sense of this crazy planet we find ourselves on. My energy worker tells me I need to relax my third eye between my eyebrows—let it fall back and rest. But how, when we're in such a mess? Maybe being an Aries, too, has something to do with it. I'm always in my head. Anyway, I kept noticing this old lady in different places all over the neighborhood. A coffee shop. A park bench. The street. The bookstore. I didn't think much of it, just noticed. She could have been homeless, but she didn't seem out of it like most of them did.

Anyway, I smiled at her one day when our eyes met across the coffee shop. She winked at me, like she knew me, or we both knew something everybody else didn't. I glanced around the room to see if anyone else noticed, but no.

I looked back, and she stared at me—still smiling. I immediately cut my eyes away, then back down at my magazine. When I looked up again after an acceptable time, she was walking over. *Oh shoot!* I thought. *Here we go. She wants money. Should I jump up and leave? Pretend I don't see her?*

Before I decided, she put a hand on my shoulder. It felt so warm and substantial, steady, like it could hold me firmly on the earth in a way I hadn't been held before. I raised my head and looked into her face.

Her sparkling, deep eyes were clear amber but rimmed in white. "Here, baby," she whispered. "This is for you. It's what you've been looking for." She handed me a scrap of old notebook paper. The lines were blurry, like something had spilled on it. "Take it."

I stuffed it in my jacket pocket, jumped up and ran out, left my magazine and a half-drunk coffee. I even bumped into this guy checking his phone. I had to get out of there. Then my boss called with a question, and I listened to a voicemail from my niece, read a text from a friend I was supposed to meet later. I walked along the sidewalk, really felt the cement beneath my boots for a change, calming my pace, tried to breathe. I felt that paper in my pocket even though both hands hung by my sides. I wanted to reach in, grab it quickly, and drop it on the ground without another glance.

I thought about that lady, the way she hobbled over, as if that short journey cost her energy she didn't have. The last joint of her index finger twisted out at a right angle from the rest. Her nails were chipped and dirty, with traces of red polish. Why had she given the paper to me anyway? I was a stranger.

I didn't know what to do. I couldn't just drop the paper, but for some reason, I couldn't make myself read it either. I never read comments teachers wrote on my papers, whether good or bad. Something in me couldn't bear the scrutiny, as if my nerves would snap—like the string that flipped back and blinded my violin teacher in one eye. There's a breaking point for everything. This was the same. It took nerves I didn't have. What was the solution? Keep walking. Past stores and restaurants, churches and markets and florists and bars. Shuttered fronts of buildings and scaffolding. I imagined how I would explain not reading the message to another person. Me, a seeker. It didn't make any sense.

# Post: Anonymous

I leave my apartment to get some beer and Red Bull on a Wednesday afternoon around four. Just went down the street to the bodega. From out of nowhere this old lady in a red hat comes around the corner and grabs my elbow. She gets in my face and says, "Honey, what has broken your heart?" I hate being touched, so I pull away and yell, "What? What do you want?"

She waits, closes her eyes, then hands me this lousy, dirty piece of notebook paper. Why I took it I'll never know. Figured it was just some trash, like she was. Some lunatic. I just wanted to get my six-pack and get the hell out of there. Get back to *Call of Duty*.

But I read it. It was impossible not to. And it was a bunch of bullshit.

**YOU'RE WASTING YOUR LIFE.**

Man, it PISSED me OFF! Who was she to tell me anything? I tore it into a million pieces and threw it down on the sidewalk, right there outside the bodega. Went in, got my stuff. When I got back out, she was gone, so I headed back to my apartment.

The more I thought about that bitch, the madder I got. I kept seeing her weird-ass eyes. Those eyes were not right. Sinister. I went online to see if there were any posts about her. I found "Have You Seen Her?" and then your blog, asking for reports of encounters with this so-called Messenger. You're goddamn right I'm going to post. This Messenger shit is nothing but fraud.

Pastor Mike talks all the time in his online sermons about abominations that fester. He's very powerful, and the sermons have gotten me off *Call of Duty* and back into the real world. Anyway, the festering gets out of control. Control is a must. Order. The natural order of things. The way God planned it. These messages don't mean anything and are part of a larger conspiracy, something a whole lot bigger than you or her. I'd bet my life on it. God wants them to stop.

# Alana's Notebook

## Observations From Posts

*****She gives each person the message they seem to need at the time, sometimes at the exact moment they need it most.*

**One person at a time does make a difference.*

**It's not so much what the messages say but the timing that's important, creates a change in people's lives.*

**Oh—one really hostile post: some guy upset because he didn't like his message. Very different response than most others. Ask M. if she ever gets negative responses from people. Guess you can expect it. His message must have pushed this guy's button.*

# ALANA LEARNS MORE ABOUT THE MESSAGES

"How did the messages start?" Alana asked. She and Messenger had just made a loop, starting and ending at Fifth Street. It took Alana a few blocks to finally get in sync with Messenger's ancient pace. She'd brought Messenger a whole bag of her favorite chocolates wrapped in red foil.

"Yum! These are just wonderful!" Messenger exclaimed. She popped another one in her mouth. "You want one?"

"No thanks."

"Oh, come on, honey. It's never too early for chocolate. It always helps!" Messenger unwrapped one for her.

"Okay." Alana took the small square of dark chocolate and ate it quickly. "Now," she said. "Back to the messages? How did they start?"

Messenger nodded, her amber eyes focused on the sidewalk beyond them. "How can I describe it? Um, in the beginning was the beat. This constant beat! I was shocked when it just started inside me. Of course, it had been going on all the time, but that was the first I heard it in my head, my heart, my whole body. It was so strong, like a wave washing over me. It called to me. I had no choice but to answer. It's been very true to me and never lets me down. Later, words then messages came. Loud and clear—straight down through my arm, out my hand, and onto the page. For a long time, messages, messages, messages. Day in and day out. Liked to drive me crazy."

"So you just wrote them down? All day long?"

Messenger nodded. "I was shocked at first. I never was too good at writing—for starters. I did my best. Usually they were short. In the beginning, for the longest time, I thought the messages were for me! Oh my. Can you believe that, honey? Of course, that was before I realized what it all meant. What exactly was going on."

"Okay." Alana scribbled wildly. "What exactly *is* going on?"

Messenger stopped, nodded at the empty benches by the school where they often sat. The lady with the Chihuahuas must have already come and gone. They sat down together, and she continued.

"I can't tell you exactly how or from where the messages come. They usually come first thing in the morning, but they can come any time. I grab my pen and look for some paper, or maybe I get lucky and have some stashed. Usually I have to scrounge. The beat's insistent. It grows louder and won't let me be. My eyes start to water. I sit so very still and listen to the beat until words just pour out of me, and I obey. I let my hand go with the beat. My poor chapped hands sometimes bleed in the cracks (I try not to get it on the precious paper). I don't know what the message is going to be or what it says. I just let it all come out. I know when I'm done because the beat stops. Not entirely. Hah! I'd be dead! After the message is complete, the beat lets me go a little and falls back to the normal, calm beat in everything—in everyday life."

Alana jotted down Messenger's words, strained to keep up with her. *What beat?* She was dying to ask but didn't dare say a word or stop Messenger's flow. She'd never gotten on a roll like this, no matter how many questions Alana had pestered her with.

"So out the message comes without me doing anything, really. I just let my hand move. While it's happening, it's like time stops."

"That happens to me sometimes," Alana said. "When my writing's going well and just seems to flow."

Messenger's face brightened, and she smiled so widely, Alana could see all her teeth. "So honey." She paused, as if she was telling Alana something really important. "Remember that. You already know how it feels."

She wondered what Messenger was getting at. Alana rubbed her eyes and glanced down at her notes. "Oh, I know. Has anybody ever had a negative reaction to a message? Like it was something they didn't want to hear?"

"Sure," she answered. "But I can't help that. Have you happened to notice how some people don't like to hear the truth? But I do know for a fact that nobody receives a message she isn't ready for or more information than she can bear. People get what they need. That's just the way it works."

"Why?"

"Why?" She smiled at Alana. "Do you think I make all this up? I'm just telling you what I know, honey. Somebody way smarter than me is going to have to figure it out. I can't tell you."

"Or won't," Alana answered automatically.

Messenger unwrapped and ate another chocolate with slow-motion attentiveness then stared at Alana. "Oh honey. Those beautiful brown eyes of yours," she murmured. "Just like hers."

"Whose?" Alana's voice shook this time. "Whose eyes?"

# Messenger's Composition Book

## The Wave

*This job keeps me really busy. There's way too much to write down. So much richness—all around us—our universe pours it out 24/7. My messages come with the beat, like a friendly wave. The first thing a baby learns to do after smiling back at a face is to wave at everybody she sees. They get really excited and wave their feet at you. That's part of it—the part babies do and we all do the rest of our lives. Feel that beat—wave to the healing. Because Earth herself, she's doing it too.*

*Waves, I tell you. Keeping those waves and layers and currents of waves—pulsing, whirling—straightened out. Gentle waves, like ocean waves, can help move you where you want to go. But they can also overwhelm you. TV tangles them. Internet. Texting. Those damn tweets all the time. Are you crazy? Permanent knots. Takes days to sort it all out.*

*Used to be, I wasn't necessary. Way back when, people used to listen and could hear for themselves. No more. I can't say too much about this. They won't let me. The waves are too tangled up now. All these devices are not bad in and of themselves. They can help. They have a very good side to them. Connecting. Just like splitting that atom could have had a real good outcome instead. But death was on their minds. That's just how it goes.*

*Same with this internet. We shall see where that all leads. I'm working on that. The waves are speeding up. Everything is. Everything's faster, see? Moving to that one beautiful point when everything will change. But we don't have to fight about it or get all stressed out. Just relax, get in sync—it's the letting go that makes it happen.*

*Just picture everything falling into its place, being used and used well. Think of a rag rug, with all sorts of colors and textures woven together. Thrown-away threads, scraps of clothes and linens and tablecloths people think they don't need anymore. They've lost their usefulness in their present form. Refuse. All of it, the good and the bad, taken and woven together to make something new. A thing of beauty, complete and whole.*

*But it takes time—something people don't have much of anymore. What they don't know is—time is short but wide. Ride the wideness of time, and you'll have all the time in the world. There is time to pause. That's a way to find the beat too. And ride the wave.*

# ALANA GETS SOME ANSWERS

The day was cloudy and gray, and the cold settled in. It was one of those days that felt heavy, like it would never end. Alana had started out early morning and headed straight to Ed's from the train, not hoping for much. She'd looked for Messenger for several days with no luck. She opened the door to the coffee shop and as the little brass bell rang to announce her, felt her heart leap. Messenger sat there smiling, like she'd been waiting for her to show. She even agreed to answer some questions without Alana having to beg.

But first, Alana took Messenger's coffee up to the side counter and shook chocolate powder into the steaming brew the way Messenger liked it. She watched Ed ignore her. She poured a smidgen of half-and-half into her own cup, then headed back to their regular seats.

"That heavenly coffee!" Messenger said. "Thank you. My mother had a percolator. You don't know what that is, do you?"

Alana shook her head.

"It was a coffee pot that you sat on the burner, and it had a little glass globe on top. I'd watch it bubble, smell that rich, dark aroma. That was the sound and smell of early morning in my house. I just love watching people walk in here, see their faces relax as they wait for the brew Ed's making them." She smiled. "Same smell."

"I couldn't live without coffee," Alana said. She pulled out her notebook and pen and set her phone to record Messenger. "Ready?"

Messenger held up her coffee cup and clinked Alana's cup in a toast.

Alana pulled her shoulder-length brown hair into a ponytail. "Okay, would you please describe your process for me? You know—how it all works."

Messenger smiled. "If I knew that, honey, I'd be ... well, let's just say I don't understand most of it, either."

"But how do you do it, then?"

"Well, I walk. I walk for a while, get a coffee here at Ed's." She looked up and their eyes met. She raised her coffee cup as if to toast him, then flashed a big smile his way.

"Does the coffee help you focus?" Alana asked.

"Something like that I guess."

"And?"

Messenger paused. "I try and get myself out of the way so the message can come through. Some days, it's clearer than others. I can't control it, that's for sure."

"Then what happens?"

Messenger closed her eyes, suddenly looked very tired. She sipped her coffee. Alana was always amazed at how slowly Messenger did everything. Everybody in this city seemed on superspeed, herself included. Not Messenger.

"Don't worry. Just wait." She kept her eyes closed. "Just listen to the beat pound inside you. The words will surely come. Just unfocus your eyes, let your hand go and do what it wants across the page. Hold your pen loosely. Get it down."

"Is that it?"

She opened her eyes and took another sip of coffee. "Always say, 'thank you' when it's over. You'll know when that is. Your hand will just stop."

Alana jotted Messenger's words in her notebook.

"How 'bout giving me a few of those pages, honey? I already used all the paper you brought me last week."

"Okay, sure." Alana ripped out some pages and handed them over.

Messenger clapped her hands like a little girl. "Goodie! Thank you!"

Everybody in the coffee shop stared over at the ruckus.

Messenger folded the paper carefully in half and slid it into her coat pocket. "I'm always going through garbage cans. People think I'm looking for food. No sir! I need paper. You'd be amazed how many people put perfectly good paper, even books, into the trash. Can you believe it? All these beautiful, beautiful words. I love them so much. They are each and every one dear to me—to my heart. Then some fool goes and throws away a full cup of coffee, and it spills all over everything."

"Gross." Alana made a mental note to buy Messenger some more paper at the Rite Aid.

"Oh, I'm not picky. I'll write on anything I can find. Handbills, margins of pages torn out of books. Backsides of grocery lists, cardboards from pizzas—if they aren't too greasy. Sleeves from coffee cups. Last week I found a little spiral notebook with no writing in it. Perfect! It hadn't even gotten wet. Just a few coffee stains." She patted her pocket. "Thank you. These sheets of paper will do just fine."

"Messenger, you are keeping notes for me in that composition book I gave you, right?"

Messenger laughed. "I sure am. Lots and lots. And don't worry. I'm not using it for messages." She patted Alana's arm. "Okay, honey. Sorry. Gotta go now."

Alana sighed, watched her gather her things. She knew nothing she could say would stop Messenger.

"You going too?" Ed asked.

"Yep," she answered, turning her back on him for a change and shutting the door hard behind her.

Alana headed down the street, striding faster and faster, arms pumping, literally pounding the pavement so she wouldn't cry. Or explode! *This was all taking too long.* On the days she could even find Messenger, all she would dole out were bite-size bits of information. Alana stopped abruptly just before she almost knocked down this sad old guy who tottered along with the crowd, leaning on a strange, hand-carved wooden cane. She didn't even apologize.

*Focus, Alana,* she demanded.

She slowed her pace so she wouldn't run into another innocent bystander. Alana fought the panic rising up her body. She realized she was in way over her head. It had all seemed so promising at first. She wondered what people thought of her, tagging along after Messenger.

*What would my friends think?* she wondered. She had intentionally told no one about this project, had guarded her precious story so nobody would steal it.

*Who is Messenger?* Alana still didn't have a clue. Messenger wasn't in the same category as the people she saw on the street who talked as they paced, rummaged through trash cans, looked for something to eat, or picked up cigarette butts to smoke the remaining threads of tobacco. Or cursed the air, their invisible companions or tormentors. But where did she live? Where did she go? Alana had combed the internet every way she could think of, for hours, used every possible search combination to find some trace of her, some sliver of information about her past or present. Apparently, she'd accomplished something extremely difficult and rare—Messenger was off the grid.

*You've got to be calm. Patient*, Alana cautioned herself. *You've got to figure out how to write this story.*

She walked up First Avenue, shivered in the cold. Beyond the story, though, something else about Messenger kept her going. This was the first time she'd allowed herself to acknowledge it. Whenever Messenger touched her, even slightly, Alana swore she could feel something—electricity, energy, whatever you want to call it—pouring out of Messenger's hands.

# Messenger's Composition Book

*Drugs? Those poor folks are trying to drop into the beat too. I'm sorry to say that's cheating—it speeds things up in an unhealthy way. Blows their minds—sometimes literally. This body you got is your instrument, and your nervous system has its limits. Slow is good. If people understood the amazing power they already possess, any need or desire for drugs would fade away. They'd see with fresh eyes just how fascinating they are, how fascinating the world really is.*

*They'll say they're looking for permanent peace or Nirvana or something. Hell, no again! That's not it. That's not what life's about. There will always be sorrow, pain. Just the flip side of all the good stuff. Contrast. The trick is to wait it out. It'll flip. Guaranteed and in the same measure. That's what this swerve is all about, you see.*

*Listen. Everything's going to shift over as soon as enough people get it; that's the tipping point. Not a majority—oh no. Doesn't really take so many. That's what people don't get either. We don't know what in the world will bring the swerve, but we do know this. Once it starts, we have to work together. For all of our sakes.*

*I wonder sometimes how people can be so cruel to each other. The closer they are, the worse it is. Disrespect folks and not think one thing about it. What they don't understand is: The person they're harming? Themselves. It blocks their flow.*

*I want to be clear so I can receive the messages. That's what I work on all the time. Stay clear. Don't block it. There's nothing special about me. Everybody has the exact same wiring. The potential is there—put it that way.*

*Our children know. More and more are coming in with this new wiring—we don't understand or know how to handle it. These autistic children, Asperger's, whatever label you slap on them. It's not that they can't communicate with us. We just haven't caught up with them yet. They are what we will become. They just got here a little early. They're the pioneers, explorers. You could call them astronauts. They are sending. We just can't receive. That causes a lot of problems for them.*

*I'm like them. I speak to everybody, but I usually don't use my voice. Works better that way.*

# MESSENGER RECEIVES A MESSAGE

Alana was huddled with Messenger at Ed's one cold day the next week. They sat on their stools at the long table. Messenger loved her particular stool at Ed's. Whenever Alana suggested that a chair or booth would be much more comfortable (definitely for Alana with her long legs) Messenger shook her head. "No, baby. This is the exact right spot. The energy comes up here. Everything's just right for receiving."

Alana strained to feel something, anything through her seat. "Energy? From where?"

"From the earth. Right here." She picked both swollen feet up and put them back down. Holes covered her sad shoes. Alana decided no matter how poor she was, she had to spring for a new pair of sneakers for Messenger.

Messenger carefully folded the rough brown napkins somebody had grabbed and left on their table. "Oh goodie day! Won't these come in handy later?"

"To wipe your mouth?"

"No, child. For the messages. Napkins don't really work so good; they either tear or smear. But they'll do in a pinch since I'm out of paper again."

"I'll bring you some more tomorrow," Alana promised.

"Thank you!" Her face broke into a smile, practically shone.

Alana noticed she'd rubbed some lotion on her cheeks, and she looked more rested.

"Not so ashy today, huh?"

Alana just nodded. Messenger did that a lot. Read her mind. No, that was too out-there. She probably just observed where Alana's eyes rested, then used logic to figure it out.

Right?

Messenger pulled out the nub of a flat, red carpenter's pencil from one of her pockets and closed her eyes. "Give me just a minute," she murmured. She sat very still and her eyes watered.

*Is this a message?* Alana's heart leaped. She sensed that Messenger wanted privacy, so she turned away and let her eyes wander around the coffee shop. People stared at them, then dove back to their phones, tablets, laptops. Alana glanced over to the coffee bar and noticed a tall, blonde girl with checked bell-bottoms, very stylish, who ordered from Ed. Behind her stood this old guy they often saw on the street, his poor neck permanently bent forward at an excruciating angle.

Alana snuck a glance back at Messenger. She smiled with her eyes still closed, rocked back and forth to some gentle, silent rhythm. She scribbled with the pencil. Alana realized she'd never watched her write before. Messenger was left-handed. Her hand looked like a crab as it dragged across the napkin. She always had the shadow of ink or graphite along the side of her left pinkie finger and hand. Alana strained to make out the scribble. She thought she heard Messenger humming, but maybe it was the crowd or the espresso machine.

"Can I read it?" Alana asked when Messenger stopped writing, even though she knew what the answer would be.

Messenger kept her eyes closed and laid her hand over the napkin. "Sorry, honey. This one's not for you."

Alana felt like arguing. "But why not. What harm would it do?"

"Nope! You read it—you take some of its power." She did seem sympathetic when she said it. "Listen—I don't read them either. I just write them and whatever comes out, that's it. Bad penmanship and everything. No wonder I can't write so good. Teachers tried to change me to right-handed when I went to school, then fussed when I couldn't form my letters just right. Hope folks can read the messages and make out what they need to."

"Have you ever considered asking somebody to use a computer and print them for you?"

Messenger closed her eyes again. "Honey, those computers are all well and good. Yes, when they're about the business of connecting, they're very good. That net, you know."

"Wait—the internet?"

"Sure. You can call it that. Don't you see? More and more people are figuring out how everything's connected. But how come people still feel so alone?"

Alana thought about it. "I guess they miss real human contact. That's what people aren't getting."

Messenger's eyes flew open, and she took Alana's hand. "Listen to me; anything that means something to you, write it down by hand. Hand's directly connected to the heart—don't you know? Yes."

Alana later fact-checked and found Messenger was right—as usual.

"And I wouldn't get too dependent on those computers. Just in case."

Alana pushed because she didn't like the ominous tone to Messenger's advice. "What's going to happen to our computers? A disaster? Or a terrorist attack?"

Messenger smiled that you're-so-sweet smile of hers. "A disaster? No. But better safe than sorry. And don't you worry. No matter what happens, everything's going to be okay. From either extreme, it'll swing back. Always corrects to the middle."

"Seems like people are moving to the extremes these days."

Messenger laughed. "Yeah. It's about time to cue the aliens."

Alana's eyes popped. "Aliens?"

"If they arrived on the scene, we'd all cooperate like you wouldn't believe, right?"

"Probably."

"Uh-huh. It's about time. And it's about time for me too. Gotta go deliver this." She collected her bags and Alana helped her stick her arms into her outer coat.

"Can I tag along?" she asked.

"No, honey. Not this time."

That's what she always said. Alana fought her rising frustration.

Messenger put a hand on Alana's arm and kissed her cheek. She waved at Ed. "Take care."

Alana watched her walk slowly through all the people down First Avenue. "Where do you think she's going, Ed?"

Ed leaned on the counter. "No telling!"

Alana sighed and quickly finished her latte. Today, Ed had made a flower in the foam for her. She'd been shocked, then grinned at him to acknowledge it. She had to admit, Ed would be attractive if only he weren't so annoyingly aloof—especially about Messenger. She waved goodbye to him and headed out the door quickly because today, she'd decided not to obey Messenger.

Messenger already had a head start, though not a long one, judging by how slowly she always walked. Alana scanned up and down the block, past all the dead grass and trash in the tree medians, then walked around the neighborhood. She asked the Flower Lady, the lady with the Chihuahuas—who wouldn't even answer. Not even a simple question. She asked Ostap, the owner of So Hair, whom Messenger had introduced her to one day on their walk. He sat in his usual spot, straddled his orange plastic chair outside the barber shop. Nothing! Nobody had seen Messenger that morning, so they said.

*Are they lying?* Alana wondered. *Covering for her? Did she ask them to? Why when she's agreed to cooperate with me? What's she up to? Are they all just enjoying messing with me?* Alana was determined to find out. None of it made any sense. *Who can I trust here? Who will trust me?* And another burning question: *How does she disappear like that, when she always walks at a snail's pace?*

# MESSENGER'S DOUBT

Messenger headed down the street, pulled her red stocking hat down farther over her ears. Damn cold place! She wouldn't be surprised if snow came later. *Oh well*, she thought, *let it come.*

*How will I create this swerve?* She wasn't sure. She didn't know the whole picture. So far, so good. Nothing had happened to make her believe the Watchers suspected anything. Oh, she knew they would catch on soon, and she'd have hell to pay for all the rules she'd already broken. The rules she intended to break.

She just needed more time. Things were progressing with the girl. Two steps forward, one step back. Expected. What she hadn't expected, what she wasn't prepared for, was her heart. How the girl made her feel when they were together. *Her eyes are just like my daughter's!* Messenger stopped in her tracks and shook her head. *No!* she ordered herself. *Stop thinking about the other one. Focus.*

What Messenger was sure of, though, was her aim. *Follow that, no matter what it costs you. If your aim is clear, you can do anything.* That was her training. That was her way. It would not fail her now.

# MESSENGER AND ED

Later that day, Messenger sat on her usual stool, sipped the coffee Ed brought her, and allowed herself to think. *Used to be,* she mused, *doing what we're doing would get you killed in a New York minute.* She shook her head. *Now things have changed. Evolved.* She bet everything that the timing was right to let a little more light in, that there would be enough critical mass to hold the center. She sensed the girl was on her way. She closed her eyes and gathered energy in her heart. Of course, she had doubts. There was no way to know for sure what would happen. What she wanted to tell Jackie and all the rest of them was: The old way doesn't work anymore. We have to change it up. But she knew they wouldn't listen to her. *I'm going to have to do it myself. Risk it all. And that girl's just the one to help me.*

"Refill?" Ed called from the bar, interrupting her thoughts.

"Don't mind if I do." When he brought the coffee to her, she gave him her biggest, best smile.

Ed couldn't resist. He actually smiled so wide he showed some teeth. A first!

*Now, we are finally getting somewhere with him,* she thought.

A mom and her little girl, about five, walked over and sat across from Messenger at the long table. The mother placed a small to-go cup down in front of her daughter, then took the plastic cap off. Steam rose up.

"It's too hot," Messenger heard the mother warn. "Just wait a minute."

The little girl, her braids tied by bands with pink plastic balls, sat patiently and watched the steam. They all focused on that small cup until the mom tested the hot chocolate, then handed the cup back to her daughter. The little girl blew on it and took a sip. Whipped cream formed a foamy mustache all along her sweet upper lip. She giggled.

Messenger had tried to distract herself from the little girl, but she was tired. Too tired. *You're getting old,* she told herself. *That's all there is to it.* She couldn't hold the worn-out memory back today. She didn't have the strength.

Messenger saw, as if right in front of her, here, now, in Ed's, a glass storm door on the stoop of a row house, far away in Baltimore. Messenger's mother's house. She could see through the storm door glass a toddler, with four little baby teeth on the top, four on the bottom. Messenger knew that baby smelled so sweet, of baby powder and freshness. The baby had caught herself by laying her little palms flat on the glass to balance. She'd done it over and over again because, the way the light shone, many tiny fingerprint smudges danced across that glass. Her face glowed, her eyes impossibly bright. There was pure light in her smile, just for Messenger. Tears poured down Messenger's face as she smiled back at her. The baby waved, like it wasn't for the last time.

Messenger's arms filled with a terrible emptiness, knowing what she knew—that she would never hold that little girl again. Such a beautiful, horrible sight. She couldn't bear it. She had to turn away.

# PART TWO
# IT'S A BOOK

# WHO GETS THE MESSAGE?

The day was sunny but very cold. A few flimsy clouds spread out here and there, but mostly the sky shone clear blue. Alana and Messenger had agreed to meet in the park. Messenger liked the music and to walk around the fountain—very slowly, of course. The water was turned off since the temperature dropped below freezing most nights, so people liked to sit in it. On a sunny day, you could even take a sunbath. Alana's heart leapt as it always did when she spied a flash of red through all the people milling around. Messenger sat on a bench at the south gate. More and more, for Alana, a good day was one spent with Messenger. A bad one was when Alana couldn't find her anywhere, no matter how long she searched. Then doubts were her only company.

*Stay professional*, she constantly cautioned herself. *Don't get personally involved. You're a journalist. This is just a story.* But the just-a-story had grown legs. Every morning she checked her blog and found more views. More posts from people who'd received messages. Momentum was building. *Could this story become more than just an article?* Alana wondered. Could it grow into a book proposal that would snag her a nice advance she could live on while she investigated? A dream come true! A spark of excitement played across her gut each time she thought about it. Alana sensed there was much more about Messenger to be discovered, more than just the messages. She had to keep going. Alana sometimes felt guilty about how much fun she had hanging out with her and everybody in the neighborhood. She also had to admit how much lighter she always felt when she was with her. *What's happening to me?* she wondered.

"Hey there," Messenger said as she stood up and stretched out her arms. Messenger gave the best hugs in the world, warm and strong. She never let go until you did. Alana wrapped her own scarf tightly around her neck, breathed in the cold, crisp air.

"Don't you love that music?" Messenger asked.

Alana heard at least three melodies all playing at the same time—somebody crooned jazz on a sax, a little brass combo blasted a quicker number, and the piano guy who was always there played a show tune. People watching was excellent here in the park. Students. Street people. Tourists took photos, nurses pushed old folks in wheelchairs, and mothers or nannies pushed babies in fancy strollers.

"What's up for today?" Messenger giggled. "I know you have plenty you want to ask me!"

"Yes, I do! But aren't you cold? Want me to run and get us some coffee?"

"That's okay. We'll get some in a minute. Got any more of those chocolates?"

"No. Not today. Wait. I gave you a whole bag the last time we were together!"

Messenger chuckled. "Oh, honey. They're long gone. I gave them all out."

"To whom?"

"Oh, you know. My friends. Jackie and the Flower Lady. I think I gave one to Ed. Those kids begging around here."

"Who's Jackie?"

Messenger sighed. "Oh, you'll meet Jackie soon enough." She rolled her eyes.

"I'll buy you some more chocolate later today." She sat down beside Messenger and shivered at the cold wood beneath her seat. "You really aren't too cold?"

"Not a bit. It's a lovely day."

"It is. Okay. Ready for questions?"

Messenger met her eyes and smiled. "Sure, honey. Shoot."

"Well, I guess I get how you receive the messages. Sort of—"

"It's a mystery," Messenger interrupted. "That's all there is to it. Mystery. The mystery will always remain—no matter how clear things may seem. But listen. Don't ever fear mystery."

"Okay, if you say so. But I have more questions!"

Messenger laughed. "Of course."

"Okay. A message comes; you write it down. But how do you know who it's for? How do you find the right person to give it to? Aren't they all just random people?"

Messenger inhaled deeply, then blew the air out with a puff of steam; it was so cold. "Let me see. How can I tell you? Well, first I wait."

"Of course you do!" Alana smiled.

"Then, I hold the message in my hand, and I see myself—"

"You see yourself? How?"

"In my mind's eye. I see myself giving up the message to somebody. That's it. I get a very clear feeling—not a picture really of a face but a beat that's just theirs. Their vibe. When I find that person, I know it. I feel a ding right here." She pointed to a place just below her heart. "Where you cut a chicken breast in half—my wishbone!" Messenger laughed her head off.

Alana knew what wishbones were, though she'd never cut a chicken breast in half in her entire life. She only ate boneless.

Messenger wiped her eyes. "Why aren't you laughing? That was hilarious!"

Alana laughed too. "Okay—if you say so. Now you were saying ... ."

"Yes. Back to my wishbone, hee, hee, hee." She touched the same place. "It vibrates here, you see. So I know when I've seen the right person. BINGO! I give it to them. I recognize the person even though I've never laid eyes on them before. Oh—I get so excited. It's all I can do to hold back from throwing my arms around them, crying, 'Oh, goodie! It's you!'"

"You don't really do that."

"Are you crazy? They'd run for the hills! Oh, and let me tell you. It's real interesting the different reactions I get. Some people won't even take their message out of my hand because they don't want to touch anything I've touched. I scare them, I guess. Most people will take them, though. Some take the message to be nice, but I know for a fact they crumble it and drop it when they get a few blocks away. Doesn't matter. It's touched them. It still makes a difference."

"How do you know?" Alana couldn't believe how much Messenger was revealing. *Is she beginning to trust me?* Even though she recorded everything Messenger said, Alana also took notes, not wanting to lose a word. She struggled to keep up.

"It was a gift, you see. By taking it, they received. Each message carries energy with it beyond just the words."

Alana was distracted by a guy standing a few feet from their bench who preached aggressively at the top of his lungs about the end of the world. "There you have the four levels of heaven," he barked. "Listen to me, people! The four levels of heaven!" Alana braced as he approached them. Messenger looked him right in the eyes, and he stopped yelling abruptly.

"All right," he told her. "Have a nice day." Then he walked off.

Alana shook her head. "That was weird."

"He calmed right down, didn't he?"

The man made Alana think of the few negative posts she'd received. "Do people ever hassle you when you give them a message?" she asked.

Messenger frowned. "Sometimes I'll run up against a really dark one. He'll stare at me with dead eyes of pure hate. You've seen eyes like that in pictures—Hitler, Charles Manson, you name it. All humanity crossed out. All that's left—don't call it 'animal' and insult the species we share our home with—is darkness. But they chose it. Being the devil is a choice. That's what people tend to forget."

"Wow!"

"Yes. But there aren't that many baddies, really. Just forget all that. Don't give it energy."

To Alana, almost none of this made sense, but at the moment she just hoped to get a handle on the basics. "Back to people receiving their messages," Alana coaxed.

"Well, some people do read them. I love to watch when they do, but usually they won't in front of me. Once, I had a young man, skinny as a string bean, dirty as me, everything about him seen better days. He took his message, read it right on the spot, and I watched tears fill his eyes. He'd accepted it. Glorious to see! And this woman bent at the waist and bowed to me once. That was so nice! Every encounter, whether positive, negative, or neutral, changes things. It moves things forward."

As Messenger told these stories, Alana noticed she rocked gently back and forth on the park bench. Before she knew it, Alana was rocking in sync with her.

"Once there was this man in a fancy business suit, tan trench coat. Cufflinks! He grabbed the message from me and lowered his eyes to read it. The biggest teardrops I've ever seen poured out of his beady eyes—truly beautiful. He whispered thank you then hurried off. I knew he'd keep his message. No doubt about it. I know when every message is truly received. I feel that too."

"How?"

"Oh, I just feel it here." She pointed to the same wishbone spot. "I remember once, this little boy, big wire-framed glasses strapped around his head, bigger than he was, read his out loud, stumbled over the words. He read that message three times through before he got all the words right, then he smiled, looked up over those glasses with angel eyes. I dearly loved that."

A mother pushed a little dark-haired baby in a stroller toward their bench. When the baby caught sight of Messenger, she flailed her hands and kicked her feet. Cooed her head off. They all laughed, and Messenger talked to the baby. "Yes, yes! You are absolutely right! Couldn't have said it better myself! Bye-bye!"

Messenger turned back to Alana. "Have you ever watched a baby learn to walk?"

Alana shook her head.

"Oh, they go up, teeter, fall down, shake, get back up, fall again. Over and over. But the drive to move won't let them be, so they keep at it. Easy does it. Day after day. One day, you can't predict when, they get up, teeter. Just like they've done every single day. But instead of falling, they take right off and walk. It's done. They can walk, and they never go back. Simple as that."

Messenger rearranged the folds of her coat. She pulled her red hat down to cover one ear, then the other. Alana noticed she'd suddenly grown quiet, as if the whole subject was too much to bear.

"You okay?" Alana finally asked.

"What? Oh, yes. Just thinking about somebody far away. Yes—it's almost a miracle. Little children just rise up and go. They're gone. No warning. They just do it."

"That baby was so cute. Hey, do you have any kids?"

***

Alana was on the subway headed back home when she realized Messenger had immediately returned to other stories of people receiving their messages. She never answered Alana's question.

## Messenger's Composition Book

### Seven Altar Ideas

INCLUDE THE FOLLOWING:

1. *Photos—you don't need to know who the faces are; the eyes make them so powerful.*
2. *Anything that sparkles or catches light—glass, mirrors, marbles, chrome, or other metal.*
3. *Anything living—plants, flowers, leaves, rocks, dirt, moss, lichen, bark, feathers, seeds, sand, earth, wood—all bring different qualities. Food, water, drink of any kind. Alcohol has Spirit in it!*
4. *Holy items—relics, candles, and flames. Wax is excellent.*
5. *Art—drawings or prints or pottery or sculpture. Little figures of people or animals, fabric, old patches of clothing. String.*
6. *Animal items—fur, bones. Feathers. Human hair.*
7. *Pennies—don't worry about whether they're heads up or heads down. Finding them is the lucky part. Other coins, bills. They don't last long on any altar—magic!*

*Make your altar in a place of safety, as far away from electrical lines as possible because electromagnetism interferes. If it can be arranged on a known ley line, better yet. Outside in nature is best—fresh air, beneath the stars, sun, and moonlight, in line with wind or a breeze. Near running water is best yet, though still water is also good.*

*These altars are not only beneficial for the souls who come in contact with them but also for all beings, both physical and spiritual. The altars go deep. They send down roots of energy and connect all holy places on Earth and in other dimensions. Even if they are tampered with or—at worst—robbed or destroyed, doesn't matter! Don't worry about it! The act of making them brings power and positive energy to our planet and to other levels or dimensions. From there, the Helpers have witnessed your efforts and trials and hold you close with invisible arms. They work on your behalf at all times and in every way.*

# MESSENGER'S ALTAR

After getting a tip from the Flower Lady, Alana found Messenger on Fifth Street. It was an overcast day that felt colder than it really was. Damp and wintery, dull gray. The sun didn't stand a chance. It was lunchtime, so Alana left Messenger on their bench by the school yard and ran around the corner for sandwiches. Once they were made, Alana carried a big, white paper bag back and sat down beside Messenger.

Messenger clapped her hands. "Did you ask for extra mayo?"

"Of course! Ham and American cheese on white. EXTRA MAYO!" Alana handed Messenger her sandwich, neatly wrapped in white paper, along with a napkin.

"Wonderful! Thank you. What did you get, honey? Your usual?"

"Uh-huh. Turkey and Swiss on whole wheat. Hold the mayo."

"You don't know how to live," Messenger teased.

They sat quietly and enjoyed their lunch. Messenger devoured her sandwich, and Alana ate half of hers, then stowed the other half in her backpack for dinner. Messenger rolled the foil and sandwich paper into a tight ball, and they collected their trash in the big paper bag.

Messenger sat quietly for several minutes then abruptly stood up. "Come with me, honey. I want to show you something."

Alana's heart lifted. She was usually the one who begged Messenger to share—anything. A tip, a clarification, an explanation. They threw their trash in the basket, and Messenger led her to the opening of a narrow alley between the buildings where the guy from Three of Cups Sicilian Restaurant usually sat on a crate to take a smoke. Today it was empty, and they were alone.

As soon as they walked in, Alana noticed a strange buzz, a sort of echoing sound to the space. She wrapped her scarf more tightly around her neck. The smell of garbage, damp brick, and dirt filled her nose. The buildings blocked the sun, so it was dark, cold, and very damp. Messenger walked ahead until she came to a protected area behind one of the buildings and beside some trash cans.

"Here it is." She spread her arm as if showing Alana her greatest treasure.

Alana gasped.

Perched on two side-by-side plastic crates, which formed a sort of table, was an altar. Messenger had taken cardboard boxes to create different levels and surfaces for the treasures. On each, she'd burned candles and dripped wax—all colors—red, green, yellow, purple, and white. The wax dripped onto the boxes and down the sides. In the wax, she'd stuck pennies, marbles, bottle caps. Green Heineken beer bottles, cobalt blue wine bottles, and clear bottles all held white candles of their own. Live yellow, blue, and purple pansies dotted the surfaces, along with snips of pine. Several fresh carnations—from the Flower Lady, Alana suspected—added to the living parts there.

Alana saw the head of a doll, its eyes wide open. Sunglasses. Photos of people's faces—pulled from magazines or maybe missing-persons posters from the street—also stared out. Bits of red and silver foil from the chocolates she gave Messenger dotted it too. Shards of glass and mirror formed a mosaic in one section.

Alana pointed to the glass pieces. "Where did you get those?" she asked.

"Off the road after a wreck. They sweep up, but they always miss some. That's where I come in."

Alana continued to notice the buzz echoing through the alley. She could only stare at Messenger's incredible creation. She saw string—bright red and forest green, squares of red flannel fabric and a floral print. Rocks—some piled in neat little stacks. She wondered if they were held together by wax or just balanced there on their own. Smaller white church candles about as thick as your finger were stuck into the wax and formed the shape for infinity on one level. Messenger struck a match from a Three of Cups matchbook and lit the candles. It took her three matches to light them all. Meanwhile, Alana saw heads-up pennies stuck in the wax and what looked like black human hair. Maybe it was from a weave. There was also a tiny, delicate bird nest and some animal bones.

"Messenger," she finally exclaimed. "It's beautiful. I love it! Amazing! How long did it take you to make it?"

Messenger smiled so wide Alana could see all the blank spaces in the back of her mouth where teeth should have been. "A long time, let me tell you. I worked on it a little every day."

Messenger motioned to Alana to stand right in front of the altar then walked around behind her. She placed a hand on each of Alana's shoulders and gently moved and adjusted her. After a minute, she whispered. "Can you feel it?"

Alana turned around to face her. "What? Feel what?"

Messenger turned her back around and ran her hand up and down Alana's spine. She placed both hands on the back of her head, then rested them on Alana's shoulders. "Can you feel your feet?" she asked.

"Uh-huh."

"Anything else?"

"No. Nothing," Alana answered quickly. She pulled away from Messenger, turned and took her notebook out of her backpack to make some notes. "Do you use the altar to receive messages?"

Messenger sighed. "Sometimes. You mean you don't feel anything?"

Alana shook her head. "How does it help you with the messages?"

"It amplifies them. Also, it's quieter in here, off the street."

Footsteps echoed in the alley. Alana jumped. "Somebody's coming!" she whispered.

"It's okay," she told Alana. "Is that you, Professor?" she called.

"Madam? Can you come into my office please?"

"Okey dokey," Messenger said, and she headed on down the alley in the opposite direction from where they'd come.

Alana followed, noticed the alley curved slightly to the right. "Who is it?" she asked.

Beyond the curve, Alana saw an old man seated at a small desk. He was dressed in a ratty tweed jacket and wore frayed green wool gloves with all the fingers cut out. He stared intently at the blank screen of his old, boxy computer monitor.

"Hello, Professor," Messenger greeted him. "Meet Alana."

"Hello," Alana said.

"Madam, a message for you of the utmost importance." He handed Messenger a blank sheet of paper from the multiple stacks in front of him.

"Thank you very much, Professor."

"Not at all. Not at all!" He turned back to his desk and typed a hundred miles a minute on a keyboard that wasn't connected to anything. "Very busy today," he muttered.

"Don't work too hard," Messenger told him. Alana watched her fold the paper in half, then into quarters and slip it into her pocket. They turned back the way they came. As they got closer to the altar again on their way out, Alana noticed the echoing had grown stronger. They paused before the altar. Messenger turned and headed on down the alley, but Alana hung back.

Because she'd lied.

She had felt something—the moment she'd seen the altar, to be honest. No. Earlier. When they'd entered the threshold to the alley. What? A buzzy pressure with that weird sound. A tingling in her fingers and even her cold toes, down deep in her boots, even with her feet covered in thick socks. And when Messenger had stood behind her with her hands on her shoulders? She'd actually felt it through her whole body. The sight of the altar did something to her heart, made it leap or open up. She didn't know how to think about or describe it. She'd only felt that intense whole-body sensation a few times in her life.

But why hadn't she told Messenger the truth?

# ALANA'S QUESTIONS

Alana greeted Ed one dark, cloudy morning and ordered a drink. He had a short line for a change, so there was time to talk.

"Have you seen her? Has she been in yet?"

Ed shook his head, focused on the latte he was making for her. "Haven't seen her come down the street yet either."

"Good!" Alana said. She shivered, still cold from her walk from the train, then stared at Ed. "How can you stand that short-sleeved tee every day? Aren't you freezing?"

"Nope," he answered.

Watching Ed work soothed that tense clutching in Alana's gut. She noticed an intentionality to everything Ed did—steaming milk for a coffee, washing dishes, constantly cleaning the counter, mopping the floor—a studied grace. No matter how backed up the line got, Ed took one task at a time. Today, an iris tattoo on the inside of Ed's right wrist caught her eye. "Did you just get that?" she asked him.

"No. I've had it."

"Oh, okay. Sorry. Guess I just hadn't noticed before."

"It's a tribute to my mom and grandparents." He took a sip of his own coffee—black, drip—the endless cup he drank all day long.

"There's a Japanese card game that has flowers as suits. The iris is one of them."

"Nice! Were your mom and grandparents all from Japan?"

"My grandma was Japanese, grandpa American. They met when he was stationed in Japan after the war."

"Wow." Alana touched Ed's wrist and turned it to see the tattoo better. "Beautiful," she murmured. "The tattoo, I mean." When she touched him, she felt a charge go through her.

Their gazes met. Alana watched Ed's dark eyes soften for a moment, but then he pulled away.

"Did your mom like it?"

"Are you kidding? She hates tats."

They laughed.

"Is that why you make flowers in my lattes?" Alana blurted this out before she could stop herself.

Ed shrugged. "I guess."

The line behind Alana had grown, so she took her coffee and moved out to her usual stool.

"Bet she'll be here soon." Ed smiled, eyes still soft, then he turned back to work.

Alana settled in at a table and tried to distract herself from staring at Ed. She pulled out her notebook and flipped through the growing pages of notes. She wrote, *I want to pursue the book idea, feel the urgency to move forward with my investigation, yet everything with Messenger is so SLOW! I spend a lot of time with her, talk with her, listen to her. I want to trust her. But should I? How can I tell? Do I see in her only what I want to see? Can I stay objective? Logical? Rational? Is all this career suicide? Or should I just follow my gut, keep going, and see where it leads? RISK EVERYTHING? What would Messenger say if I asked her about turning our work together into a book? How could I convince her? I feel like she holds back so very much—like I've only touched the tip of the iceberg. Some of the things she tells me make sense or resonate. Some things make no sense at all. She seems to know things she can't know.*

*And that altar! What happened to me there? Why did she show it to me? Was it to watch my reaction and see if I felt anything? Like I did? Why didn't I tell her? Because it all scares the hell out of me. How to make logical sense of it? Journalists don't believe in magic, but they usually have a sense of wonder or the miraculous. It's our job to explain things. There must be a rational explanation to everything, right?*

*So how do you explain* Cathy's Birthday? a voice inside her asked pointedly.

She glanced up as Ed took her cup, then brought her a refill. "On the house," he said.

*He's sweet. Shy,* she thought. *He's trying to help.* Their earlier conversation was the most she'd ever heard Ed talk, to her or to anybody else. Why did that make her feel so happy? When she'd touched his wrist and their eyes met, she knew he felt it too.

She distracted herself from thoughts of Ed by remembering *Cathy's Birthday*, so long ago. Alana could mentally see, as if it were lying on the table right in front of her between her notebook and coffee cup, the old plastic ballerina from the top of the cake she'd won when she was seven. Sara Snyder's mom had taken the girls to a ballet called *Cathy's Birthday* and had bought them each a ticket for the cake the director would raffle off. After the ballet was over, the director had walked onto the stage with a clear goldfish bowl full of the orange stubs to everyone's tickets. Alana watched the woman stick her hand into the bowl, mix up the tickets, then pull one out. But something really weird had happened. Time had somehow slowed down. Alana could still feel it, sitting there in Ed's coffee shop. Within that time warp, Alana had known without a shadow of a doubt her ticket would be pulled.

She'd been right.

She'd held onto the plastic ballerina through all her moves and losses, one of the few keepsakes from her childhood. The ballerina always sat on her desk. She wore a sapphire-blue tutu painted over her too-pink plastic skin, and she had a painted-red bow mouth and a silver crown perched atop her brown bun.

Alana took a sip of the fresh, hot coffee Ed had just brought her and wrote: *What I felt that day in the dark auditorium, knowing the director was about to call my name, walking down the aisle and up onto the stage to get my cake and what I felt yesterday at Messenger's altar—same feeling.*

*Just add that to a growing list of unexplainables.*

# MESSENGER'S AIM

Several days later, Messenger sat on the bench by the playground. She panted, tried her best to catch her breath and slow it down. She didn't think they'd go that far. Not so soon. Totally destroyed. The Professor could have been hurt. Darkness was gathering.

But she set her resolve. *It's not right,* she thought, *to keep quiet about all that we know. Not when my babies are hurting so much. Hurting all the time. No let up. Just their hearts broken, ripped out of their chests. Huge chunks of their spirits broken off. Smashed. They're killing each other. Killing themselves! Everything's going wrong. Why? They don't know where to put their energy. Energy unexpressed for too long grows dangerous. Wants to destroy. Just look at the altar!*

She breathed. *Welcome Anger. Welcome Despair. Welcome Fear. Give the emotion a name and welcome it. Find it in your body. Hold it all until its energy shifts. Then surrender. Give up. Let go. Surrender to Love.*

She knew from hard experience that nothing could solve this except one thing. The energy of Love. You have to start from the heart, not the head. The heart was a powerful transmitter to send and receive, to change and transform. To come from any other angle is just a waste of time. So when emotions overtook her, she returned there. She'd been doing it for so long it was automatic. It never failed her.

# ALANA AND MESSENGER RETURN TO THE ALTAR

"Listen, can we go back to the altar today?" Alana asked Messenger when she found her at Ed's early one morning the next week. "I want to take of photo of it." Alana didn't tell Messenger she'd only just that morning gotten up the nerve to go back, to see if she felt the strange buzz in her body again, the echoing, or if it was just a fluke.

"Sorry, we can't," Messenger told her, no expression in her face. "It's gone."

"What! What do you mean?"

Messenger sighed. "Okay. I'll show you."

Alana picked up Messenger's bags and totes. Some days she had them with her, others she didn't. Alana didn't feel comfortable asking why. It felt too personal. Alana wondered what it was like to carry all your stuff around with you. She shrank from the thought but imagined it must be freeing too.

They turned down the alley, which felt even damper and reeked even more than the last time. They headed straight to the altar, but before they reached it, Alana spied the baby doll head flattened in a pile of mud on her left. The altar lay in shambles all over the gravel. Someone had completely trashed it, ripped it apart, kicked its parts up and down the alley. Candles here, rocks and bottles there. All that remained were the two crates, but they'd been stomped in too.

"Oh, Messenger! Who did this?" Alana asked. Her voice shook.

"Some of those baddies we were talking about. They also got the Professor's desk."

"I'm so sorry."

Messenger led her around the corner through a trail of dirty, soggy papers. The desk was turned over and all the legs broken. Alana figured they'd used those legs to demolish Messenger's altar.

"Did they get his monitor?"

Messenger shook her head. "He always takes the monitor and his keyboard home with him."

"Were you here when it happened?"

"No. We found it yesterday morning."

"I'm so sorry. I just don't understand why anybody—"

"Well, you know. They get off on destroying things. Feel like it gives them power."

"Ughhh! I'm so mad! Your beautiful altar." But part of her fury was anger at herself for being so afraid, for not taking a photo earlier when she'd had the chance. Now it was too late. "Want me to help you clean it up? Will you start over?"

"No. Not here. This place is done." Messenger stood still like a stone.

Alana bent down and picked up a candle. "Don't you want any of it?"

"Nope. It's ruined."

"Why aren't you mad?" Alana demanded, her voice rising. "You mean to tell me after all the work you put into the altar, you're just going to walk away?"

A tight smile spread across Messenger's face. She closed her eyes. "Oh my. What a fuss! Don't you know everything's okay?"

"How can you say that after what they did?" Alana was surprised to hear herself yelling. She frowned, searched Messenger's face for clues.

"Because I'm not surprised. Look, I don't play by their rules. What do you expect? Do you think they'll come up and give me a big old hug? Of course they're upset and want to destroy things. They sense the shift. Every action creates an equal and opposite reaction. That's why we have to carry it. Remember this always: Nobody likes change. Especially not the ones in charge."

"Who ... what are you talking about? What shift? What change?" Alana struggled to follow.

"Trust me. I know what's going on."

Then she did the most unexpected thing. She started giggling, slow and deep at first, then higher until her laughter sounded like a young girl's.

Alana, startled by Messenger's reaction, tried to resist, to hold onto her anger. "What in the hell is so funny?" she demanded. "How can you laugh like that? Are you crazy?" But then she felt her stomach release and giggled too.

"Crazy? Oh, whew!" Messenger gasped. "I sure am! Hee, hee, hee." Tears flowed down her cheeks, and her eyes disappeared into two slits. She gasped to catch her breath, then burst out again in another round. "Oh my. That feels so good, doesn't it? Come on. Let it loose like I did."

Alana was full-out laughing too, filled with an effervescent river of joy.

"Oh, they think they got me. All high and mighty. But hee, hee, hee." She wiped her eyes with a paper napkin she pulled from one of her folds. "Oh, honey. You're so sweet to be upset, but it's fine. They can't hurt me." And then she was rolling again, waves and waves of laughter.

Alana heard a woman's voice call "Messenger!" from around the corner, echoing down the alley. "I need to talk to you."

Messenger froze and put her finger to her lips.

"I know you're in there," the voice called again and echoed. "Come out this minute."

Messenger trudged toward the light at the opening to the alley on Fifth Street and Alana followed. A tall, thin woman wearing high-heeled cheetah-print booties and engulfed in a red, puffy down coat stood in the opening. A single, long dreadlock from the crown of her head trailed down her back.

"What happened in there?" she demanded. Her huge cat-eye glasses magnified her eyes and made them look enormous.

"Same old thing, Jackie. Same old thing."

"Oh!" The woman turned toward Alana without smiling. "I didn't know she was with you."

Alana didn't like the way this woman stared at her, like she was an insect in a collection. What's more, she didn't like how the woman seemed to already know who she was.

"Alana," Messenger said, "this is Jackie."

"Hello." Alana didn't smile either.

Jackie didn't answer. Alana wanted nothing more than to get Messenger out of that alley and away from Jackie. She looked down the street and saw Ostap outside the shop, straddling his chair and smoking. He stared down the street at the three of them.

Jackie turned back to Messenger. "Professor?"

"He's okay. Just the desk is all."

"That's good."

"Yeah."

She looked at Alana then back at Messenger. "Okay, then. I'll find you later." She shuffled down the sidewalk, clicking in her boots.

"So that's Jackie," Alana said. "A friend of yours? She sure doesn't act like it."

"Oh, Jackie's okay. She's mad at me—not you. Listen, honey. I've told you before—don't take anything on that's not yours to bear. Always better that way."

They headed back to the wooden bench by the playground. As soon as they sat down, Alana felt her anger well back up. "It's just not right! I can't believe somebody would destroy your altar when it's obvious you spent a ton of time creating it. It really was a work of art. Not to mention poor Professor's desk."

"Believe me. It was worse than that," Messenger said.

"Worse how?"

"Let's just say it was a message to me. A warning."

"Why don't you call the police?"

Messenger threw her head back and started in again with that wild laughter. "Hah, hah, hah," she cackled.

This time, Alana didn't join her. She jumped off the bench. "For God's sake, that was a simple question. Why can't you ever answer a simple question?"

"Oh dear. Mad again? Is that some kind of new dance?" she managed to blurt out between gales of laughter. She rummaged around in her pocket for another napkin and wiped her eyes.

Alana sighed and flopped back down, arms crossed. "Come on, Messenger. Be serious for a minute. You said you knew who did it. Well don't you hate him—or them—for it?"

Messenger looked at her like she'd just said the most ridiculous thing in the world. "Hate?" Then she laughed again.

Alana turned away. "To be honest, it feels like I'm always waiting for you to stop laughing at me!"

"Oh, dear. No. I don't mean to upset you. I know you don't get it. Look, he and his kind are just mopping up. It's all over but the shouting—like my mama used to say. And they know it."

"What? Who?"

"It's happening now. You know—the swerve. With change comes fear. The fight. Which is crazy because everybody knows in their hearts and in their cells, it's already happened. The earth knows—and rejoices. So what do you think all those folks who say no to it—who don't want things to change, who are on the wrong side of things—are going to do? When they feel backed into a corner, feel their world and everything in it, everything they were taught and thought and believed is threatened? What do people do when they're cornered?"

"Fight like hell?"

"You got it. As hard and as viciously as they can. That's all that's happened. They're scared out of their minds. They are not in their right minds with any of it."

Alana still didn't get it. "So you don't hold them responsible for what they did? You could justify anything using that rationale, you know."

Messenger shook her head. "No. They're responsible. I just see what's going on, that's all. And when you see what's underneath the surface and pull it apart, it's the damaged person you find, not the hate. Not the fear."

"Are you saying there's no real evil?"

"Oh, there's evil, all right. A whole lot of it. It's a force. But fighting evil with evil just makes a bigger mess. See how it infected you, just being around it in the alley today?"

"Me?"

"Yes, you. What did you feel in there?"

Alana thought a minute. "Anger. Hate."

"Uh-huh. I know. But that doesn't ever work. It just ratchets it up and creates a bigger mess. It's nothing compared to the love way."

Alana wanted to keep asking questions, but Messenger bolted up. "Walk with me," she said. "We need to keep our energy moving. It'll make you feel better."

They headed down Fifth Street, carrying Messenger's bags with them. They watched the cops across the street take a guy out of a squad car. Dozens of small, purple ribbons on small stakes in the ground—placed there in memory of fallen officers—waved in the breeze outside the station.

Messenger paused and pointed to them. "How lovely to remember them this way. Oh my, love is everywhere you look. Honey, there is no power on earth greater than love. That's the energy that bends the universe toward justice. Remember Dr. King? Well, he didn't come up with that idea, let me tell you."

"I've always loved that quote," Alana said, "but I'm not sure I really get it."

"Do you know how many times this world has been saved from complete disaster? Over and over, many, many times. Look at history. So often we hang by a thread, but love pulls us back from the edge. That and lots of energy from our Helpers."

"Okay, if you say so," Alana responded. "But aren't we supposed to fight?"

"No. Violence only makes things worse. Always. It feeds energy to it. You fight darkness with light—not more darkness. You need to change the consciousness of the opposing forces to focus on another level."

Alana's head spun. "What? I don't get it. Can you give me an example of what you're talking about?"

Messenger turned toward her. "Okay—sports. Whole countries that would give anything for a chance to kill all the people from another country, or sometimes even their own people, come together and compete. They might even become friends with their competitors. Or look at children. Oh my, our children are our greatest hope. You've heard of them bringing kids from warring nations or groups within countries to a camp together?"

"Uh-huh."

"They play together—have fun. Run around. Children live in that other consciousness. They're oblivious to hate. It doesn't occur to them unless somebody teaches them. They have to learn not to love. Love is our default, you know."

"I see what you're saying." Alana rearranged Messenger's packs and put straps over each shoulder. "It's all so overwhelming, though. And, it seems hopeless, as messed up as everything is right now."

Messenger smiled and nodded. "This is a very hard teaching, I know. But it's what I'm working on. That's my aim."

Alana stopped and turned. "What is your aim? Could you state it for me exactly?"

Messenger laughed and took one of the heavy bags off Alana's shoulder. "My aim is to go to Ed's for an afternoon coffee. Let's take a load off. I know he'd just love to see us." She winked.

Alana rolled her eyes and followed Messenger down the street toward First Avenue. *So close,* she fumed. *But Messenger will probably refuse to say any more about this. What would you call it? Cosmic?* Even though Alana didn't understand all of what

Messenger said, she sensed that the messages were part of this bigger picture Messenger alluded to.

At Ed's, they waited in line behind a woman with bright red lipstick, a cowl-neck sweater, and boots with studs all over them. She smelled really good—expensive perfume, no doubt. They chatted with Ed while he made their coffees. Their favorite spots were waiting for them. Messenger unbuttoned her topcoat, but she never took her red stocking hat off. She swigged her coffee.

"Messenger, please help me understand. I feel like I wasn't following what you said about evil."

"There is evil, of course." She held up a finger with chipped red fingernail polish. "Acknowledge it for what it is, then move on. Don't give it energy. Don't feed it. That's all I'm telling you. Attention gives energy, which gives power. It's all about the energy, as I've told you many times before." Her face softened, and she reached over and rubbed the space between Alana's eyebrows. "Relax right there. Feel better?"

Alana nodded. It felt wonderful.

"No, you'll never beat it by fighting. Be like water. Assertive, but yield to aggression. Bend but do not break. Don't fight terrorists with terror. Love, compassion. My advice is—keep moving. Keep the love flowing. Right, Ed?"

Alana looked up and realized Ed had been staring at them from the bar. Staring at her. He spun around, busied himself with cleaning the blender. But it was too late. At Messenger's words, they watched him blush beet red.

# COFFEE-SHOP LESSON

Messenger smiled at Alana. They sat on their usual stools at Ed's a few days later. "Did you get all that down?"

Alana held up a finger as she jotted the last of her notes. "Wow. Great. Thanks so much." She put her notebook back into her backpack and cleared her throat. This was it. She'd planned exactly what she would say, had even written it down, word for word in her notebook.

"Messenger, I wanted to talk to you today about a new idea I've had. A big idea. First, I really appreciate you spending all this time to help me with my story. But now I think this whole thing is bigger than that. Would you consider letting me expand it all into a book about you and the messages?"

Messenger was quiet for the longest time. Then she turned toward Alana. "Okay," she finally answered. "We can try that."

Alana jumped up and hugged Messenger so hard she almost knocked her off her stool.

"Whoa, honey!"

"Sorry! Just got excited." Alana steadied Messenger and sat back down on her own stool. A huge smile spread across her face, full of relief that she hadn't had to launch into the big sales job she'd planned. "That is so great! Thank you. Because I'm all in. I'm totally committed to this. And I'm going to work my hardest to make it happen. Okay now, can I put my notes and the posts on an expanded website? Would you agree to that? It would create more buzz and encourage people to keep posting experiences and spread the word about our project. Also, can you ask people to post on my blog when you give them their message?"

Messenger burst into the loudest, deepest laughter Alana had ever heard.

"Why is that so funny?" Alana demanded. "A book takes a lot of work and planning. I'm trying so hard here."

"I know. Cut it out! Don't try so hard, and you'll be surprised how much better things will go."

"You don't understand. We have to expand our online presence now that we're getting more engagement."

Messenger hooted. Everybody in the shop stared at them. "That's not how this works," she managed to say.

"It's not funny," Alana snapped.

"Oh yes, it is." Messenger collected herself and wiped away the tears running down her cheeks with a brown paper napkin. "Oh, honey—I'm sorry. It's just that—well—you crack me up!"

"But I wasn't kidding! These posts from people are deep and poignant. Why can't we give everybody a little encouragement, you know, like you say—energy. Hope. What's so wrong with that?"

Messenger, now serious, listened intently to each word Alana spoke. She nodded, then answered, "Baby, I know. Nobody knows more than I do. But you gotta wait."

"Why?"

"Timing's not right."

Alana felt anger rise in her throat. "Well, Messenger," steel filled each word, "when do you think the time *will* be right?"

Messenger sighed and wiped a lone tear that traveled down her cheek. "I'll be sure to let you know."

"Why not now?"

"Trust me." She touched Alana's arm. "You're going to have to trust me."

# Alana's Notebook

*Today, Messenger agreed to my request to turn our project into a book. And tonight, I'm having a panic attack. All my fears are drowning me. Do I really have anything here? Has all of this been a desperate fantasy? I've got to get a grip. Breathe. Breathe.*

*What's it all about, anyway? What would I tell Mary? Okay, there's this woman—I don't know how old. I don't know where she lives. I don't know anything about her past or her family, if she even has a family. I've only met a few people I suppose you'd call her friends. Okay, so no backstory, obviously. She won't really tell me much of anything about her daily life beyond the focus of the inquiry. And what is the focus of the inquiry? Well, every day, so she says, she receives a message. She writes it down. It's never very long—a few sentences at most. Then she starts to walk. She walks the streets slowly, until, through a physical sensation or a feeling she gets, she knows who the message is for. She finds them and gives it to them. That's it. Wow, writing it down like this really makes it sound like I've got one great big nothing on my hands. What a query! Pretty lame.*

*I just thought I'd have made more of a name for myself as a writer by now. After all, I wrote my head off for free, served my time at that click-bait blog—I did all of it. But what do I have? Nothing. Nada. Just this lame story about a sketchy old woman who tells me to call her Messenger. Sometimes I pray, "Is this all you got, God? Is this all you got for me?" Whenever I read about a new writer or even a favorite writer of mine, I'll figure out their age when they made it—I'll do the math and compare it to my age now, and then a voice inside me screams, "Hurry up, Alana. Hurry up! There's no time! You've fallen behind. You're running out of time." Some days the voice yells, "Too late! You blew it. Forget about it and take a good desk job. That's all you're good for anyway. What a fool to hope for more."*

*But I've got to keep going. Mom always said when I'd get discouraged, "In this family, we don't quit." Lots of journalists do get their start with just one story—not necessarily a big one—and go from there. First, they publish it as an article. But they can't stop investigating. They get obsessed with it and just keep going. The story morphs into a book. A big book! A best-selling book. Is that what's happening here? Is this my destiny? Is my future staring me in the face?*

*Or am I the crazy one—so desperate for what I want, like those loonies who see the face of Jesus in a pepperoni pizza? The Blessed Mother statue crying oily tears that can heal people? A callus on a tree that looks like the monkey god?*

*No. What holds all this together is a change. A real change in people's lives. Not everybody. Far from it. Some ignorant people don't even read their messages and throw them away. How stupid can you get? But some are truly changed—their lives turn. Even if the change is subtle. The point is—the messages carry weight. From the moment they're received, they have the power to change a life. One life at a time. One person at a time. That's how she works.*

# Messenger's Composition Book

## Think of a Play

*Think of a play. You sit in the audience with all these other people (souls), watch the action. Sometimes it's right in front of you on the stage, or sometimes the actors come from the sides or even from out in the audience. It's all still part of the play. So you have your own life, your reality laid over the reality of the play—the drama before you. But if it's a good play or a good night for the actors or both, you lose touch with your own reality—the big man wedged into the seat to your left, crowding your space or the middle-age woman on your right with the pungent perfume. Somehow, they disappear, and you become part of the world of the play.*

*But all the people who came to see the play with their hopes and their joys, their bills to pay—his mother who doesn't know him anymore dying in a nursing home, her kid strung out on drugs and in despair at seventeen, his grandchild sick with leukemia—are all still there. Even though you forgot all about them, they're in the dream of the play.*

*Okay—look! It's the same thing. The drama of your life and mine plays out each and every day. But there's a bigger drama going on too. People love drama—watching it on TV and creating it in their own lives. And there's an audience of Helpers watching us all, aware of our every move, every thought, every notion that crosses our minds, even if we're unaware of them.*

*Now think of New York or London, with dozens of plays, not to mention concerts, movies, ballets, lectures, any event. All presented at the same time, for different audiences. That, at a very basic, primitive level, is what's going on. How to cope? Divide your attention, honey. Become aware of the play and of yourself and of those with you in the audience, all at the same time. The unity. That's how it really is. It can get very complicated. No matter what seems to be going on, you must train yourself to look deeper.*

# THE FLOWER LADY WEIGHS IN

It was a clear, cold day after a snowfall the week before. Alana walked down Fifth Street and tried her best not to look into the nasty piles of snow, even though some of them were so big they were at her eye level. They stunk of garbage and urine.

Alana passed a guy who sat on one of the benches. He wore a black ski jacket, a stocking cap down over his eyes, sneakers worn into grotesque shapes. *How can he even walk on them?* she wondered. Crusty kids, eyes wild, strung out, strolled down the middle of the sidewalk. Alana cringed. A man lay on a thin sheet of cardboard flat out on the sidewalk against a building with his back to the crowds. Moms pushed their babies in strollers right past him, and kids scooted by on their skateboards, ignoring him.

So did Alana. She took a deep breath of cold air, pushed these images away, and mentally reviewed the questions she'd planned for today's interview with the Flower Lady. Alana had arranged it because she figured she should talk with Messenger's friends, get their take on her.

Alana found her at her usual spot on Second Avenue and was glad to see the Flower Lady bundled up in a purple down coat with a red plaid blanket covering her legs.

"Thanks for agreeing to talk."

"Okay, I guess. I don't usually talk to people. But given you're Messenger's friend … ."

*Am I?* Alana wondered. Just hearing the Flower Lady call her that gave her a lift.

"Ready? Okay. What's your name—your real name, I mean."

"Listen, girlie. My name's Esther—that's what my mama named me—but I hate it. Just call me the Flower Lady. Especially if you write something about me. Are you planning to do that? Will I be in the story too?"

"Probably."

"Okay, good. Call Messenger Messenger and call me the Flower Lady. It's better that way."

"Why?" Alana asked.

"Oh, we have our reasons." She leaned way over and fluffed some red carnations that had gotten twisted together. Alana wondered if the Flower Lady gave Messenger money—they were such good friends. But Alana really didn't understand how the Flower Lady sold much since her flowers usually looked really rough, with a slight brownish cast to them. Sometimes the water in the white plastic bucket smelled funky.

Alana waited while a guy wearing a fleece vest and short-sleeved polo shirt—guitar strapped to his back—bought one red carnation.

After he walked away, the Flower Lady turned back to Alana. "One thing I'll say about Messenger—she is doing good in this world. I haven't known her all that long. I just moved here myself a year or so ago. I've had trouble, but the good Lord has always seen me through. I really have a good life. In my line of work—flowers—people are almost always in a good mood. If they come to buy one flower, they'll usually buy two instead. Except for that guy who was just here." She chuckled. "Most folks double up. They're happy, smiling. They think about the magic moment when they'll hand these flowers over to their love." She gestured with her hands as she talked, like an orchestra director.

"Love comes through them to me. I can't explain it, but it does. I've never talked with another person about this or even tried to put it into words. I feel it—like an energy. Like everything good in the world. Like everything's going to be okay. Even though I have no money to speak of, and my legs are like this and I can't walk."

*Can't walk*, Alana noted.

"People help me. They smile at me. No, not everybody. There are some dipshits out there—we all know that's true. But overall, we're doing good." She laughed, and Alana was surprised how deep her laugh was. "Enough about me. I know your story's about Messenger. Don't worry—I'm getting there."

"Okay," Alana said. "Great."

"Since I started hanging out with Messenger ... I know that's not her real name but who cares? She must have a reason not to tell it to us. That's okay. Fine by me. What does it matter what you call yourself if you're a good person? She's the real deal."

Alana scribbled ferociously to keep up with this monologue. "So you know about the messages she gives people?"

"Uh-huh," she answered. "I watch a lot of stuff go on around here. I see a lot. I'm on this corner every day until my buckets are empty, and I'm sold out."

*Really?* Alana wondered.

"Well, I don't always sell out," she added.

Alana stared at her. *Is she reading my thoughts too?*

"But most days I make enough to eat and have enough to buy some more tomorrow. Even the cops in the neighborhood help me out. They look the other way when they see me here. That's why I left my old neighborhood. Cops said, 'Get a license or else.' So okay, I left there. I hated leaving my regulars, but what you going to do? I know I wouldn't do too good in jail. Outside is the place for me. I need lots of air and light."

"Me too," Alana said, nodded, maintained eye contact to encourage her to talk while she scribbled notes.

"That's what those doctors always told Mama. 'Your daughter needs fresh air and sunshine. Do her a world of good.'" She laughed again. "What they didn't tell us was that they wouldn't fix her legs. Wouldn't make them grow. That they couldn't do anything about that. Doctors always have a real hard time telling people the truth, I've found. I know they try their best. But believe me, they don't know everything."

"Uh-huh."

"So my dear mama always took me outside every single day. Didn't matter the weather. She'd tell me to hold my head up (I did the very best I could cause there's something wrong with my back too) and smile. Mama said, 'Sweetie pie, have the prettiest smile anybody's ever seen, and they won't notice your legs.'

"Well, that worked—sort of. Better than you might think. I always tried my best, and I still do, for Mama's sake. Mama felt real bad about my legs. But it's all I've ever known, so I wished she wouldn't worry and wished she didn't have to work so hard for us. Mama would bring back doughnuts from her job at the pastry shop. The sprinkles were my favorite, a whole sea of them floating on top of that chocolate glaze.

"Now let me tell you, Mama was rail thin, even though she worked around sweets all day. She'd eat them too. She just never gained weight. Guess she was on her feet so much."

Alana nodded. She knew skinny. Her mom had been tall, like Alana, but nobody was skinnier than Mom. That's what coffee, cigarettes, and working twelve-hour nursing shifts did for you.

The Flower Lady gulped air, then continued her story. "Oh, how I loved it when she came home with those doughnuts. Those were happy days—back when Mama was still with me. I miss her every day of my life. Is your mama still with us?" she asked Alana.

It took Alana a moment to realize the monologue had ended and the Flower Lady had asked her a question.

"No," Alana said. "She died four years ago."

"Okay then. You know exactly what I mean about missing your mama, don't you?"

Alana nodded, kept her eyes on her notes.

"To be honest, the only thing that really bothers me is I can't dance. I twirl around in my chair, but it's not the same. That's a real sorrow." She looked up as two men approached from Sixth Street.

"Hope that helps you with your story, dearie, if that's what makes you happy. You have definitely got a big story! A great one. Believe me! A lot is going on here. Excuse me now. I've got customers."

Alana walked down to the bench near the school playground and jotted more notes, trying to capture the Flower Lady's words. Even though the interview had ended up being more about the Flower Lady than Messenger, the Flower Lady's words of encouragement had reignited the spark that burned inside Alana whenever she thought about the project. *Yes!* She wasn't the only one who thought she had something here.

*Okay, you need to guard this story*, she thought. *You need to interview as many people as possible. You need to organize all notes and interviews into an expanded website, to continue to build momentum, ready to go when Messenger agrees. Then you need to write a killer query letter.* Before Alana could jot all these ideas down, raindrops wet the pages, and soon it started to pour. She wiped the notebook off with her hand and stuffed it into her backpack. Of course, she'd forgotten her umbrella. She covered her head with her scarf and ran. By the time she got to the train, she was completely soaked.

# Messenger's Composition Book

## ELEVEN THINGS EVERYBODY WANTS TO HEAR

1. *It's going to be all right.*
2. *You've got this.*
3. *You've done it before. You can do it again.*
4. *I love you.*
5. *I forgive you.*
6. *I'll help you.*
7. *My time is your time.*
8. *Tell me everything. Don't leave anything out.*
9. *It's going to get better.*
10. *I'm here.*
11. *You're not alone.*

# Post: Anthony

There ain't no way around this goddamn system. Makes no sense at all. Punishes people for doing right and rewards people for doing wrong. How can I get ahead?

Look at my mom. Knocked up again. Six kids in here already. Mouths to feed. Bodies to clothe. When I got old enough to know what it meant, I'd watch that damn belly of hers growing. Another and another. She wants a man to stay so bad she can't keep herself straight. I hate the word "baby" worse than anything. It means only one thing to me—less. Less food, less bed, less time my mom calls my name, sees me. Answers me. Notices my needs. I could just run. That's what most dudes my age do. I can't though. I want to, but I won't leave them. I've got to stick it out.

So when this dirty old woman sticks a piece of paper in my hand after we get off at the same stop, says, "Here, baby, this is for you." When I see it's not money, I drop it right there on the ground. Look her back in the face, like, what you going to do about it? She still smiles at me. Neither of us moves. We're frozen there. Then I run.

# Post: Steve

It's just plain weird how it happened. Recently, we were packing up all our stuff to move, and I was going through my desk drawer and found it again, after all this time. It happened twelve years ago, actually.

We were leaving the hospital after my daughter's birth. I was so relieved my wife was okay, the baby was okay, and I was totally happy. And exhausted. I walked to the hospital parking deck and then to my car.

You know that weird, otherworldly, underworldly atmosphere parking decks always have, especially at night? I also had no idea where I'd parked. I couldn't even remember parking, even though it had only been about ten hours before.

My wife had had a doctor's appointment that morning, and her water broke during the exam. She called me from the doctor's office, told me, "You're going to become a dad today!" I heard tears in her voice. That was before the pain really started. No contractions yet. That would all come later.

Anyway, after my daughter was born and everything was okay, the nurse had taken the baby to the nursery, so I headed home to get a shower and try to sleep a few hours myself. But I couldn't find the damn car. I walked back and forth down the long rows and up the ramp to the next level. I was so mad at myself and getting madder by the minute. I noticed this strange lady with all these bags just standing there. I hadn't noticed her on my last round, but she must have been there. I didn't remember hearing her footsteps, although mine had echoed the whole time in that two-note sound your steps make in a parking deck. I felt drunk, even though I was stone-cold sober. I passed the woman, looked up, and met her eyes. Nodded.

Something about her face made me stop. I don't know how to explain it. Her eyes, I guess. I recognized her, in a way, but couldn't remember how. She didn't speak but smiled at me.

"Do I know you?" I asked, suddenly so tired from all that had happened. It was all I could do not to lie down on the oil-stained, dirty, cold concrete and close my eyes.

"Nope. Here. This is for you."

Oh, no. One of those, I thought. But I was so tired, you see. Everything weighed down on me like a low-pressure system. I just took the slip of paper and stuffed it in my pocket, hoped that would satisfy her and she'd go away.

I looked over and right ahead of me was my car. It had been there all along. I didn't realize until I had almost gotten home that I hadn't seen the woman again as I drove out.

I didn't find the slip of paper until the next day when I was in the same parking deck, heading back to the hospital to take my wife and new baby daughter home. It was cold, and I stuffed my hands in my pockets and there it was. I'd totally forgotten about it—hadn't slept those few hours with everything and then some on my mind. I pulled it out and saw handwriting. I guessed it was the woman's. I stopped dead in my tracks even though I knew the nurse would be down with my wife in no time. **DON'T EVEN THINK ABOUT MESSING WITH THAT OTHER WOMAN.**

Something clenched inside me, and I didn't have enough air. Man, it freaked me out. It still does right now, holding it again after so long. I'd forgotten all about it. It was meant just for me, though, at that very moment. Nothing had happened, but it could have. I hate to admit that. It seems so long ago now. Like I was another person. That lady didn't know me from Adam. But she knew I was playing with fire. How?

# Post: Gloria

For me, the thing was: the message brought me the words I needed at that very moment. It also told me I wasn't alone. **UNSEEN HANDS GUIDE YOU. THE WORST IS OVER.**

I cannot tell you what that meant. I'd had to put my husband of fifty years into an assisted care unit for Alzheimer's patients. I'd just left him in the center for the first time, fighting back tears until I could get to the privacy of my own home. She stopped me on the street and handed me the paper with my message written on it.

To receive that message gave me courage I didn't have. Oh, yeah, I've got friends and my kids. But there's a hurt too deep to explain when your worst nightmare comes true, and you have no choice but to do this to your life partner. No other person can make it better. But to know there's a plan, that something or somebody's looking out for me, no matter how bad things seemed. I could believe everything would work out.

# MESSENGER IS A NO-SHOW

Alana shook. She'd chewed and picked her cuticles waiting for Messenger that morning, and she'd made both thumbs and her right forefinger bleed. *Ugh! Gross!* she thought. *Look what she's made me do. No, Alana,* she countered. *You did this all on your own.*

Messenger had agreed to meet her in the park near the pigeon guy because Messenger said she wanted to walk around the fountain. The pigeon guy had come, fed the pigeons. When all the breadcrumbs were gone, he let them perch all over him. Alana could hardly watch.

*Messenger's making me insane,* she thought. Alana had canceled coffee with Mary, whom she hadn't seen in weeks, to meet Messenger instead. Besides, she felt terrible. Her nose was running, and she wasn't so sure she didn't have a fever. Clouds had rolled back in, and it smelled like snow. Great! She walked around the park to calm herself down even though she'd already done two loops. Still no sign of Messenger. Alana knew it was her problem. She was blowing Messenger's no-show out of proportion, but she couldn't help it. Whenever people were even a minute late, Alana catapulted back to her childhood, when she was always the last one picked up. Oh, she'd understood why. Her mom explained it every time she was late. She was sorry, but her shift had run over. They were extra busy at the hospital or the relief nurse had been late.

In day-care days, Alana had known her mom was just next door, in the hospital. As a very little girl, the dreaded sound of toe tapping made tears jump into her eyes. Miss Carol, who waited by the curb with her, always smiled reassuringly. But she tapped her toe. Alana cringed at that sound. It got inside her and made her own fear grow that, after all her mom's promises, she really wasn't coming. No one was.

Alana shook her head, dismissed the memory, and began another loop through the park. When she returned to her own starting point again, she finally gave up. Messenger wasn't coming today. That was clear. Alana's thoughts flitted to the altar, now trashed in the alley. A stab of fear filled her. Had something happened to Messenger? Probably not. She'd been a no-show before. But now, to Alana, it felt like the stakes had been raised, that danger and violence lurked around them.

On a whim, Alana decided to head over to another coffee shop she liked, The Dove, on Fourth Street. She hadn't been there for a long time, not since her Messenger project had started. It had a chill vibe, and the bathroom was nice and clean. She could rest and regroup. *Another wasted day.* She sucked the side of her sore thumb. *Something's going to have to change,* she decided, *if this book is ever going to get written.*

# Post: Jake

I'm driving down the East Side Highway on a Tuesday, happy to be moving at a decent clip for a change. It's a clear, sunny day, and all is right with my world. That is, until this black aluminum bookshelf comes hurtling toward me from off the back of a blue Ford F-150 pickup truck. This isn't one of those experiences where time slows down. No. That happened to me before in a snowstorm when I did a 360 on I-95. This goes way, way fast. Hyperspeed! All I can do is swerve! Hard!

The bookshelf misses my windshield by a hair—scrapes the side of my car, bounces off and crashes to the road with the most sickening screech of metal on asphalt you've ever heard. I plow into a green Subaru hatchback and just about take out the whole passenger side of the car, which is empty—thank God! Anyway, we pull our cars over to the shoulder. The damn pickup guy just drives off like nothing ever happened, but I'm too shook up to catch his license plate number. He's long gone. I call the police and get out of the car, feel like I've been run over myself but am just happy to be alive.

This girl gets out of the other car, and despite everything that's happened in the last five minutes, I register that she's very good-looking. She's fighting back tears—I can tell by the way her chin shakes and she bites her bottom lip.

"Oh, wow," I begin. "I'm really sorry—"

She interrupts me. "How did you miss that bookshelf? What was that wack job thinking?"

"It was airborne, I tell you."

"I thought you were a goner."

"I know." I clear my throat, steady my own voice. "I called the cops. Sorry I mashed your car."

"Oh, no. I'm just so glad." She touches my arm, and we just stare at each other.

"It's going to be okay," I tell her. "They'll be here soon. Well—we're alive!"

She says, "If you hadn't swerved ... ." Her words hang in the air, something just between the two of us. That's when time does slow down. I hear the siren call in the distance but don't look away from her.

"Both of us could be dead right now," I finish her sentence.

"But we're not. You swerved just enough to save us."

My car's drivable, so after all this (she doesn't give me her number. Engaged!), even though it's the last thing I want to do, I head to my buddy's on the Lower East Side who's moving. That's the reason I was out in the first place, to give him a hand. I pull up to the curb by his apartment and notice this old woman on the street. I get out of the truck, make sure the door's locked, turn around. She's standing right there beside me on the sidewalk. Her hand's stretched out, and there's a piece of paper in it.

Our eyes meet, and that's when I feel like I've walked through a time warp. My knees buckle, like I'm going to pass out. She hands me the paper, and before I can get my head straight, she's gone. Where or how, I don't know. I look down at the paper, just a dirty scrap with something scribbled on it in smeary, blue ballpoint ink. I read it. I lean against the truck, know I'll crack my head on the sidewalk if I try to stand on my own. After everything that happened to me that day, then I get this message: **YOU JUST COLLIDED WITH YOUR DESTINY.**

It blows my mind! It still does today.

The girl breaks her engagement. We get married three months later.

# Alana's Notebook

## Transcript of Interview with Gloria

*ALANA: (Gloria handed her message to me.* **UNSEEN HANDS GUIDE YOU. THE WORST IS OVER.***) How has this one message changed you? No offense, but this message, at face value, seems … .*

*GLORIA: Vague? Trite, even? I know. It does, doesn't it? But what appears on the surface to be so random, isn't! At my point of despair, I received it. How would that woman know what I needed to hear when I needed to hear it? And she was right. The message was right. The worst was over. My husband passed away gently about a month later. How could she know that? She didn't know me at all.*

*The message told me everything I needed at the time. What are the odds against this probably homeless woman writing this important message down and then finding me outside the health-care center? I'm nobody special. Thinking back, it told me someone or something out there cared what happened to me, was working to help me. Somehow sent the message to me through her. It was such a huge relief.*

**NOTES:**

*I interview as many people in person as possible who've responded to my blog. After talking with many of them, it's clear Messenger has been at this for a very long time. Years. Decades. Nobody tried to connect the dots until Marty. Now me. Sometimes the person will pull a message out of a wallet, with fingerprints all over it, to show me. Were they Messenger's? Or the recipient's, who'd worn the message out from reading it over and over? Some people got messages and threw them away accidentally. Or lost them. One lady lost hers, and it still breaks her heart, but she'd memorized the message and copied it onto a card so she always has it. Others treasure them, consider their lives divided into before and after their message. Lives have been changed. One message did it.*

*Usually the message itself is simple and never that spectacular. "Continue on your path." "You are loved beyond measure." That's a recurring theme. "Unseen hands support you at every turn." Another favorite. "You are never alone." Then some of the messages are actually very specific. "Do this," or "don't do that."*

*Then there's the bigger thing Messenger keeps mentioning—the swerve or the change that the messages are a part of.*

*How?*

# THE CLINAMEN

Alana walked down First Avenue toward Ed's at about ten o'clock on a beautiful, bright Monday morning. Only a few low-hanging, fluffy white clouds broke the blue sky, and the temperature was in the fifties—warm for early November. Heaven. No wind for a change. But her thoughts didn't match the weather. She'd tried to shake off Messenger's no-show, but the sick, familiar feeling of being forgotten—that started in her gut and then spread all over—hadn't left her.

She sighed. *The way things are going, with Messenger so unpredictable, how are you ever going to get enough information for a book?* She passed tourists speaking German and French, rolling suitcases along the dirty sidewalks. She heard some British or Australian accents. A guy in a short-sleeved T-shirt that read DON'T TELL ME TO SMILE nudged past her.

Through Ed's window, Alana spied Messenger perched on her stool at the long table. She smiled and waved.

Alana forced herself to wave back, then went in and walked over to their table.

"You okay, honey? You look like you could use a hug." Messenger held out her arms.

Alana didn't answer but grudgingly allowed Messenger to embrace her. However, Messenger pulled away earlier than usual. Holding on to Alana's arms, she asked, "What's wrong?"

"Nothing."

Messenger patted the empty stool beside her.

"Did you save it for me?" Alana asked, her face neutral. She unzipped her coat and draped it over the stool.

"Just for you!" Messenger giggled. "Go get some coffee, then I've got some wonderful news!"

*She sure is in a good mood.* Alana frowned, as she left Messenger's side and shuffled up to the counter. *She doesn't care. She probably doesn't even remember.*

"Hey," Ed greeted her.

She managed to smile at him. "Hi, Ed. How's it going?"

"Great!"

"Super!" *Everybody's in a good mood but me,* Alana thought. "A cappuccino, please." An out-of-the-blue splurge she hoped would make her feel better. She took a deep breath, tried to shake off her mood.

"I'll bring it over in a minute."

"Thanks." She paid, then returned to Messenger, waded through Messenger's bags strewn around her stool, and sat down. "What's your news?" she forced herself to keep her voice light.

Messenger handed her a chocolate, then took a sip of her coffee. "Have you ever heard of a Clinamen?" she asked. Messenger's face shone.

Alana shook her head. She had to take advantage of Messenger's effervescent mood, so she decided not to mention the no-show. "A what?"

"C-l-i-n-a-m-e-n. I saw that word on a license plate this morning, on a green MINI Cooper. They are so cute!"

Alana dug out her notebook and jotted the word down. "Never heard of it. What does it mean?"

"Well, the license plate actually read CLINAMN. It stuck with me for some reason, like it was important. I was curious. Ed looked it up for me just now, right Ed?" she called to him.

Ed, busy with Alana's drink, nodded without looking up.

Alana stared at the word. A vague term from a poetry class in college tried to form, but she couldn't pull it back.

"Come to find out, there is actually a word—c-l-i-n-a-m-e-n."

"How do you say it again?"

"Who knows? We don't know for sure. Ed got lots of ideas from this definition/pronunciation site. Clean-a-men, Cline-a-men. Also, Clin-a-men. Potato, Potaa-to. Who cares! It's what it means that matters. It's the word I've been looking for, for so long. It means 'a change or a swerve.' It's exactly what I've been telling you about! Now we have a word for it."

Ed walked Alana's coffee over, set the cup down, and hurried back to the bar.

"Thanks, Ed," she said then noticed he'd made a heart in the foam. She felt her face flush hot. She looked up, but he was back waiting on customers. Wow! Messenger's bubbling over about her new word, Ed's heart, the warmth of the coffee shop—everything felt cozy and homey. Alana watched her anger melt away and turned her attention back to Messenger.

"So now your favorite word is 'Clinamen'?"

Messenger grew still, suddenly serious. "Yes. It's a very good word. Let's use it. I'm not afraid or nervous about it."

"Why would you be afraid?"

"Because it's big! Very big! Everything's going to shift with this Clinamen that's coming. I know you've heard of these Mayan, Native American, and other prophecies about end times. The Clinamen's what they were all talking about. Do you see?"

"I'm not sure," Alana answered. She tried to follow Messenger but couldn't help but wonder, *Is she just plain out-there? NUTS?* Alana pushed her fears aside and glanced over at Ed as Messenger talked on. *What does he think?* she wondered. "Do you mean the Clinamen will bring the end of the world? The Apocalypse?"

"Oh, no, honey. Not the end. A new beginning! Listen," Messenger continued. "Let me explain it another way. Everything's going to shift over, see?" She took a big swig of her coffee, and Alana noticed only a few red flecks of fingernail polish on her nails today. "It's just like that TV thing. Remember? When they switched over to another mode?"

"I don't have a TV." Alana streamed everything on her computer.

"That's okay. Me neither! I just watch it in stores myself until they kick me out. Look, I know I smell bad but give me a break!" She giggled. "What will make this switchover, this swerve happen? As soon as enough people get here or get up to speed, that's it. The tipping point. Let's just call it the Clinamen—like you said—my new favorite word."

"But what about your messages? How do they fit in?"

The coffee shop was crowded now and getting loud. Since they'd finished their drinks, people waiting in line for a table gave them dirty looks until Ed walked back over and set two brownies down in front of them.

"Chocolate helps everything," Messenger squeaked. "Have I already told you that?"

"You have. Thanks, Ed." Alana allowed herself to glance up at him, but Ed didn't make eye contact.

"No problem," he mumbled.

Messenger picked up her thread. "It won't take as many people as you might think, honey, to tip it. No-sir-ree! Not so many. That's what folks don't get either."

Alana prompted. "The messages?"

"Look, I'm just delivering these messages until the Clinamen. They come to me over, let's just say, the airwaves. Sometimes sweet. Sometimes bitter. I can't control it. I'll just use the words until I use them up. Talk about a revolution. This earth will no longer be a place for despots or dictators. They can't block this." Messenger pointed up at the sky with each sentence. Light shone out of her clear eyes and face as she got more wound up.

"So those places where they're still holding folks down—women especially? They're gonna get it," Messenger continued. "Everybody's going to get it. I mean everybody. Not just the rich man, bottom of his shoes cleaner than my whole body. They'll be no match for it. I shout hallelujah!" She popped up, stuck both fists out in front of her and rolled her hips around. "Oh, baby, yes! I got my groove back now. Feels so good!" Then she laughed when Ed clapped for her. She made a little bow.

Alana held on to the table because she felt the shivering begin and the vertigo that sometimes came with it. Excitement too. *Yes! This is it,* she thought. *The bigger story I've been trying to get her to tell me about. We're finally getting somewhere.* She glanced at Ed to read his face. He smiled back. Alana felt like they'd shared an adventure together today with Messenger. Alana finished the brownie and took the last tiny sip of the foam with Ed's heart.

*What a morning!* she thought. *Now, I've got to learn more about this Clinamen.*

# Alana's Notebook

## Clinamen Research

*Clinamen = singular*

*Clinamina = plural*

*Clinamen: very slight deviation, inclination or bias—the act of deliberately breaking a stylistic rule to enhance the beauty of an otherwise perfect whole*

*Clinamen: in poetry, a poetic misreading or a reading only accurate up to a point. A swerve.*

*Lucretius—century before Christ: He said a Clinamen described an unpredictable "swerve" of atoms so as to make change possible in the universe.*

*See Lucretius De Natura Rerum, Book II*

*"Again, if all movement is always interconnected, the new arising from the old in a determinant order—if the atoms never swerve so as to originate some new movement that will snap the bonds of fate, the everlasting sequence of cause and effect—what is the source of the free will possessed by living things throughout the world?"*

*Brought Out of the Dark Ages 1417 Poggius Florentinus—book hunter*

*Finnegan's Wake = James Joyce = MAJOR SWERVE*

*Harold Bloom—The Anxiety of Influence states that poets need to misread precursors (that's what I remembered from school).*

*Clinamen: contains concealed power—it is never what you expect—it never comes from where you expect it.*

*Yesterday at Ed's, everything seemed so clear, but today, I'm not sure. What's going on? First, the messages. Now the bigger story, this Clinamen thing. Are the messages just the tip of the iceberg? Messenger says the messages are part of the Clinamen, but she won't say how. At least I don't get it. Is Messenger in this all alone? Is Ed part of it? How about all the neighborhood characters? Jackie? The Flower Lady? The Professor? What about random people we see on the street? The Chihuahua Lady, too? And the destroyed altar—was that random or was there a purpose? Was it supposed to scare her? Or me? I need to find out more about her past. How did she become a Messenger? Maybe that'll help me figure some of this out. I've got to ask her about the composition book and the notes she said she'd been making.*

# Messenger's Composition Book

## THE CLINAMEN

*So you see, everything we think we know and understand is wrong. The Clinamen comes when we least expect it—yes, the thief in the night. We're completely unprepared and it comes. When you think everything is over, it comes. When you've given up any shred of hope, it comes. When you're ready to cash in your chips, it comes. When you think you've got it made, have it all, at least have it all figured out, it comes. When you feel so alone you wish you could die, it comes. That is the beginning.*

*A slight swerve that changes everything. A life. A city. The world. Nobody knows what it will be. Could be just a little, bitty thing. Maybe just a smile you give a sad-looking person. The words "thank you." Maybe you hold a door for an old lady. You let a hurried person go first in line or give somebody a hand up. That'll be it. Just one little push in the right direction.*

*Done!*

*We'll all be home.*

*Believe it.*

*It will happen. But understand it might be up to you. Even if you're worn out and don't feel like it today. You've got to take matters into your own hands. I'm just doing what I can do moment by moment. That's what my life, what the messages—that's what all this is about.*

# ED'S STORY

Alana sat with Messenger, watching Ed fill drink orders. Ed had been nice enough that morning but made no time to speak when Alana got to the front of the line. She could have been anybody. Alana and Messenger watched a beautiful young woman, gold bracelets up both arms, jewels clipped into her ebony hair, nose pierced with a gold stud. She had just walked by, arm in arm with an older woman. *Her mother,* Alana guessed.

Alana bristled when Ed paused to chat a minute with them; then, without thinking, she blurted out, "What's Ed's story?"

Messenger turned and glanced over at Ed, now waiting on an old guy with a full, gray beard and glasses, loads of keys on a huge keychain hooked on his belt. He wore a roll of blue painter's tape on one wrist like a bracelet. He came in often, and Alana had overheard Ed comp him coffee. Messenger sipped her coffee. "Oh, Ed and I go way back. Don't we, Ed?" she called out.

Ed bobbed his head and winked at Messenger. She gave him a huge smile. Alana sensed the magnetic energy between them and fought to ignore the stab of jealousy that pricked her heart. Alana steadied her voice. "So you just know him from the neighborhood?"

"Sort of. Ed's been my port in the storm for a long time. He's had a rough go of it, but he's doing much better."

"How? What happened to him?"

Messenger smiled. "That's Ed's story to tell you when he's ready."

*Well, that's not happening,* Alana mused. Even though Ed had opened up slightly, their conversations were still monosyllabic. The day she'd admired his iris tattoo and he'd pulled back? That was a perfect model for how they interacted. Ed was warm, cold, medium. Alana never knew what she'd get. *But what is Messenger hinting about him?* she wondered. *What happened to him?* "Ed doesn't share much with me."

"Really?" Messenger studied her face. "I thought you all were getting to be friendly."

As Alana noticed Ed was still talking with the old guy, *drunk* popped into her head. The word had flashed through her, like quicksilver. Not from her brain but a dawning within her. *Where did that come from? Why would I think that about Ed?*

Her face flushed when she realized Messenger was still staring at her. "Is that why he works all the time?" she asked, trying to cover.

"Maybe. All I'll say is this—and it's true of everybody. When something hurts you real bad, there's always two ways to go. Hard or soft."

"You mean life hardens or softens you?"

She nodded. "Which way would you say it's gone? For Ed, I mean."

"Hard," Alana blurted and crossed her arms. "Closed up. Tight-lipped. Doesn't give much."

"Look again, honey."

Alana glanced back. Ed was listening to a hipster boy who gestured wildly with both hands and sloshed his coffee on the counter, which Ed swabbed up.

"There it is," Messenger said. "Do you see it?"

"Soft?" Alana murmured.

"Uh-huh. You got it, baby. Good for you. Life makes hard places in people who need healing—childhood, things that happen along the way."

Alana turned her attention away from Ed and back to Messenger. "What about me?"

Messenger didn't answer. Instead, those amber eyes looked through her. At what, Alana didn't know.

Alana glanced back at Ed and frowned. "Have you ever given him a message? Was that how you met?" As nice as Ed tried to act, those flowers and that heart, Alana knew he was still withholding information from her. Messenger had just revealed there were secrets just the two of them shared. That's how Ed and Messenger wanted it to stay. Regardless of what was going on between Messenger and Ed, Alana wanted both of them to look at her in that loving way. Another stab of jealousy pricked her. *Get it together, Alana,* she scolded herself. *Don't get distracted.*

"No," Messenger's voice was quiet. "Just like you, Ed hasn't gotten a message. I've told you that's out of my hands."

Alana saw an opening. "Messenger, lots of people have posted about their messages and how they've changed their lives for the better. It's really amazing all the good you've been doing! But the Clinamen seems the bigger story here. Can't you tell me more about it?"

Messenger laughed.

"Okay. What's so funny?"

"Honey, you still have a lot to learn. We don't know how or when the Clinamen will come. We just need to keep moving forward. Working for the good until it happens."

Alana sipped the rest of her coffee. She'd been so excited about the Clinamen, had hoped it would be the key. But it had only left her with more questions. She had so many questions now, she didn't know where to start—the messages, the altar, now the Clinamen. Messenger's past. She had to get some backstory! Messenger seemed incapable of answering a simple question or staying on the subject. Ed could be helpful if he wanted to and provide another perspective on Messenger.

*What's this flirting about? Is he toying with me?*

Nobody was willing to talk to her or help her, which Alana felt was just plain wrong. Granted, Alana wanted to write a great story and make a name for herself. But was it right to keep something so wonderful—something that had definitely changed people's lives—a big secret like this? Didn't everyone deserve to know about the messages and what was behind them? Especially if some great change was about to happen?

She dove in. "Messenger, when are you going to let me launch? Everything you tell me makes me more anxious to get the word out. Interest is growing! Don't you want people to know more about what you're doing? Listen, it's rough out here. People feel alone. Hopeless. Desperate. Don't you want to let people know the good news about the Clinamen?"

"Mm-hmm, okay. You can't see the big picture, baby. I agreed to your book idea, remember? We'll do everything you want but only when the time is right. Not before. You just gotta trust. You've just got to be patient. Timing's everything, especially for the Clinamen. I'll let you know. Okay?"

"Okay. But could you at least let me read the notes you've made for me in the composition book?"

"Not yet. I'll give it to you when you're ready."

"You mean when it's ready?"

Messenger smiled. "Timing—remember?"

Alana slumped on her stool but had to agree and go along with her even if she wasn't happy about it. Messenger smiled again at Ed, then patted Alana's cheek. Alana was always surprised at how soft and warm Messenger's hands felt, even though she spent so much time outside. Messenger looked over the crowd of faces in Ed's and then through the window at the lines of people pouring back and forth outside.

"Listen, honey. Healing is what I'm about. I have a boiling energy to heal. Believe me, I know how bad things are for my babies." Messenger chuckled. "I call you all my babies, even folks older than me. This is about past, present, and future—all at the same time. Bringing hope for the next generation. But we can't get ahead of ourselves. Our aim is to work in the present moment. That's how it's done. That's the point of power. Sure, I'd like to gather you together once and for all so everybody will be safe and warm.

I want to make everything right for all of you. I'd put something gentle and nice on whatever ails you, make it feel better. Hold you awhile and just let the pain pour out. Listen to every word, every syllable, every moan, every cry. I'd collect every tear ever shed." She wiped her eyes, then turned back to Alana, spoke softly, just to her. "My messages are like that. I feel it when they hit their mark. They let folks know they're not alone. That's the biggest delusion there is. You *are not* on your own. No—even if you think you might want to be. That is not a choice. That's the one thing you can never be."

"Who are you?" Alana whispered. Each word shook as it spilled out of her mouth.

# Messenger's Composition Book

## Ten Elements

1. *Face of a baby*
2. *Calm of any animal or wild thing*
3. *Old person—as they go into themselves*
4. *Priest or monk or nun's laughter = real deal*
5. *Mother's gaze over sleeping head of child*
6. *Lovers' secret glances*
7. *Old man and his dog*
8. *Artist with paintbrush*
9. *Musician—eyes closed while playing*
10. *Every cell of a body hums with a new melody*

*Oh, Babies—don't you see? Don't you feel how very much you're loved? Feel it in your bones—your blood. Every part of you. You're beautiful. And you're powerful. Don't be afraid. Or better yet, let that fear get you moving. Get up off your butt and back into life.*

*It all started when you entered that torture chamber—school. They made you sit still and pay attention when you needed to move, to touch, to talk with your classmates. That's how we learn best.*

*They wanted you all to be just the same. But what you needed was love. What you needed was tenderness. Somebody to build you up, not knock you down. That's all. Just a little bit of kindness. Especially on those hard days when you came to school hungry or tired because you had to listen to your mom and her boyfriend fight all night long. Or you didn't know, when the school bus took you home in the afternoon, if you'd still have a home. Or if all your family's belongings would be sitting on the sidewalk. All your clothes dumped into a green garbage bag or blown into the street. You want people to treasure you, to see you, to hear your voice.*

*I want to tell the Baby Child who's twitching, who's about to:*

*Jump*<br>
*Cheat*<br>
*Cut*<br>
*Purge*<br>
*Binge*<br>
*Smoke*<br>
*Snort*<br>
*Shoot up*<br>
*Swallow the pills*<br>
*Down the fifth*<br>
*Beat*<br>
*Run*<br>
*Hide*<br>
*Kill*

*NO! Don't! It's not like that. It's not like that!*

*Loving is the direction you want to go in. Not fear. Don't go down that road. Love casts out fear. Learn the love way. You're safe here, baby. Believe it. We love you. Don't let anybody tell you different. The universe—every bit of it—loves you to distraction. An amazing, unstoppable force of love is behind you every step of the way. No matter how bad it seems or how mean or ornery people can be. All of creation is delighted you're here. We all worked hard to get you here in the first place, you know. And we're working every day to protect you.*

# YOU GO ON

One morning the next week, Alana found Messenger perched on one of the Flower Lady's upturned buckets huddled near her friend. Messenger's hand rested on the arm of the Flower Lady's wheelchair.

"Hi, there," Messenger greeted. "Give us one more minute."

Alana watched the Flower Lady put the finishing touches on painting Messenger's fingernails a deep, vibrant red.

When the last nail was painted, Messenger held up both hands and wiggled her fingers. "Va-va-voom! That's the name of this color!"

"Very nice!" Alana said.

"Oh, sugar," the Flower Lady croaked in her deep voice. "You look like a million bucks!"

Messenger smiled. "I thank you."

"Sure thing."

Some customers approached, and Alana saw her chance. "Messenger, can we take a walk? I've got some questions for you."

They said their goodbyes to the Flower Lady and walked up Fifth Street.

"Shane's back," Alana announced.

"Poor soul," Messenger clucked.

*Great*, Alana thought. *I get her away from the Flower Lady and now Shane.*

Shane sat on a small square of cardboard on the sidewalk on the corner of Third Avenue and Fifth Street. He had no coat, and the clothes he wore were full of holes. His face was red and chapped. Dirty, greasy blonde dreads, pulled back in a scarf, formed a halo around his head. The circumference of his vicinity smelled really bad, and it wasn't just the hamster in the cage on the sidewalk beside him. The hamster ran on his little metal wheel very fast. He could really make that thing go. Shane watched and absently picked at the sores on his arm.

"Hello, Shane," Alana called.

"You know, yeah—it's so cool," he answered, his voice high and breathy. "My hamster's name is Breakfast, so, hey, can you give me some money for breakfast?" His beady, unfocused eyes landed on the side of Alana, not on her face. Then he caught Messenger's eye and quickly looked away. He jumped up, puffed out his chest like a rooster, butted up against a guy in a flannel shirt and work boots who happened to walk by. Shane yelled, "I bet you fifty dollars I can arm wrestle you. Find a table! Find a table! Come on. I bet you fifty dollars you aren't that animal!"

Breakfast kept rolling on his wheel.

Messenger shook her head, pulled Alana along past him. A yellow cab drove down the street with its Flash Dance Gentlemen's Club sign lit up on the roof. Just down the block, on the steps of the Unitarian Church, a young couple slept intertwined, like the big pretzels the street vendors hawked. You couldn't tell whose arms or legs were whose. Messenger paused on the sidewalk in front of them.

"I want to brush the hair from their eyes," she spoke softly. "Spit on my hand and wipe the dirt from their faces. Tuck a blanket up around their ears to keep them warm tonight. Wind back the clock and fix whatever terrible thing happened that landed them here, asleep outside on cold concrete steps in the city with winter almost here."

Alana let her professional guard down. “I wish you had a message for them. To change things.”

“Me too,” she answered. “But—” A sob caught in her throat. She took a deep breath and sighed. “It doesn’t work that way.” She turned back to the knot of kids. “Angels guard you,” she whispered.

***

Later, they popped into Ed’s for coffee. Ed didn’t even say hi, just looked up at her and barked, “Order?”

“Two coffees,” she snapped.

He didn’t say a word. He only charged her for one. Hers. She grabbed them, turned without a thanks, and sat down.

“Thank you.” Messenger reached over and rubbed Alana’s forehead. “That better?”

“Uh-huh.”

Messenger chuckled. “You keep thinking so hard you’re going to get wrinkles bad as mine.”

“I know! Ed’s hard today.”

“Yes, he is. Don’t worry about it.” She paused, “Listen, your mom has passed, right?”

Alana was suddenly alert. “How did you know that?”

“Uh …” Messenger stared into her coffee. “The Flower Lady might have mentioned it.”

“Yeah,” Alana said. “Four years ago. Lung cancer. Well—breast, really. Spread to her lungs. Terrible.”

“Tell me about it.”

“She had breast cancer and beat it once. It was cigarettes too. She could never give them up. Even though she was a nurse. She didn’t last long after the breast cancer came back, and it spread to her lungs.”

“Were you close?”

Alana felt the air change, as if Messenger was holding her breath until Alana answered. Was this conversation about more than her just being nice?

"It was always just Mom and me, so sure, we were close. No family to speak of. Just my aunt in California and her daughter and kids. It was really just Mom and me. But she had to be gone a lot. All the time. She was a nurse. Once I was old enough to stay by myself, she'd take on extra shifts at the hospital. She had to work."

"She did it for you?"

"I guess. For us. When she died she left me a nice savings account."

"But that's not going so good, right?" she asked softly.

Alana stared into Messenger's eyes. *How did she know?* "No. it's going too fast. There's not much left." Alana shrugged. "That's what I've been living on, actually. That and a hostessing job I have at a restaurant a few nights a week. That's one reason I'm so eager to move our project forward."

Messenger nodded. "Do you miss her awful much?"

"I miss her. Of course, I miss her. She was my mother."

"She's still working on your behalf from the other side. But you never get over missing your mother."

Alana shrugged. "What can you do?"

"You go on," Messenger whispered.

# Messenger's Composition Book

## EIGHT SIGNS TO WATCH FOR IF SOMEONE YOU LOVE HAS PASSED (DON'T BE AFRAID—JUST WATCH)

1. *Coins turn up.*
2. *Electricity. This is their favorite because it doesn't take much energy for them to interfere. Lights flicker or bulbs blow.*
3. *Mirrors. Watch them at all times. You might catch somebody in there besides yourself.*
4. *Telephones, answering machines, and computers.*
5. *Radios. Songs always have significance and could be messages.*
6. *Butterflies, birds, and insects. Dragonflies and ladybugs.*
7. *Animals act funny. They whimper or refuse to go into a room or house. Cats stare.*
8. *Cool drafts or cold rooms.*

*Any or all of these could be a communication. They are close by and can help you if you ask. They will try and reach you SOMEHOW, but if you're hooked up to your boxes, you won't get the message.*

# Post: Nina

I'm trying to keep the faith without having any faith. Pray to a Swami, the Dalai Lama, The Buddha, Jesus, Mary, Muhammad, the Universe. I'll tell you where I see the Divine.

Recently, I noticed a monarch butterfly float way up there above me in the sky. I could hardly see it, just a flash of orange. So fragile! Headed to Mexico on an impossible trip, but it will get there.

I remembered that butterfly when I got the message from my eighty-four-year-old mother: after a childhood with an alcoholic father, an unhappy marriage endured for her children's sake, thyroid cancer, stage-four uterine cancer at seventy, massive amounts of chemo (which caused loss of hearing and any feeling in her toes and most of her short-term memory), atrial fibrillation, and several stents, now she had breast cancer and needed a lumpectomy.

That afternoon I walked to her apartment building to take her to the doctor. I really was dreading seeing my mother because I had no idea what to say. This dirty old woman snuck up behind me and stuffed a piece of paper into my hand. "For you," she said. I took a second to look at the paper. She'd written, **THERE IS NO DEATH. YOU ARE STRONGER THAN YOU THINK.** The second I read it, I was that butterfly. I knew I could face this whole thing with my mother. It was doable. Her message was for both my mom and me. Amazing.

# Messenger's Composition Book

*Goal of life = personal happiness*

*Sounds right?*

*We think happiness means money, fame, love of a man, love of a woman, love of a parent, love of a friend, love of a child, love of a pet. Security, prosperity, property, peace. We're all looking for answers. For a little help for ourselves. But we are every mother who puts her child to bed hungry, who doesn't have fresh water for her child to drink, who leaves her child along the road to die because she's a girl, who holds her daughter down for genital circumcision, who paints her lips and sends her into an old man's bed. Every mother who offers her sons to the mines, to the river, to the workhouse, who straps the bomb on his chest with one last kiss. We are all of them, and they are us. We all long to hear our mother call our name as only she can. Even after she's been gone thirty years, to hear that voice again, just once.*

# ALANA BREAKS THE RULES

After they'd shared a coffee at Ed's, Alana handed Messenger a whole fistful of chocolates, hugged her goodbye, felt those strong arms surround her, the buzzy energy in her hands and feet that came with any touch from Messenger. It was like holding a live wire, yet warm and soothing at the same time. Alana had researched it—all she could find to explain the buzz was *qi*—the Eastern life force, so strong and alive in Messenger. But when she'd asked for an explanation, Messenger always smiled as if Alana had mentioned something embarrassing. "We'll talk about that later." She always stalled.

It had been a perfectly normal day at Ed's, a perfectly normal conversation with Messenger. As usual, after a while, Messenger said she had to go. Alana watched her leave Ed's and head slowly down First Avenue. Alana pretended she was checking her emails in case Messenger happened to glance back. She'd just asked Messenger for the hundredth time if she could come with her to deliver a message. For the hundred-and-first time, she'd said no. This time, Alana wasn't taking no for an answer. It was time for her to witness this phenomenon. She needed a first-person account of her own to add to the website.

She gave Messenger a head start, then flew out onto the street, pulling the collar of her coat up against the damp and cold and seemingly imminent rain. Alana wove in and out of the crowds pouring along in both directions, kept her gaze down the street on the smudge of red already a block ahead. She could barely spot it through the crowds. She passed the Rite Aid, So Hair, and Karma Cafe. Three of Cups on the corner. The Professor's alley. When Alana got to the corner of Second Avenue and Fifth Street, suddenly she lost sight of Messenger's cap. She turned onto Second Avenue, ducked past the Flower Lady, headed down the street, run walking as fast as she could.

Up ahead, three blocks at least, that red smudge reappeared between the people. How did she get so far ahead at the pace she walked? It didn't make any sense. Time and space seemed to bend when Messenger was involved. Alana halted in her tracks, and a skinny, tatted boy in a white T-shirt and huge leather jacket ran into the back of her, almost knocked her down. She caught herself, and he walked on, earbuds still firmly in place, oblivious to the whole thing.

Alana stood close beside the hardware store and realized she was holding her breath. It was like watching a movie with no sound. She spied Messenger halfway down the block. Messenger pulled a slip of paper out of one of her many pockets. Just ahead of Messenger, Alana noticed a mother walking with her little girl, probably seven. The mom was dressed for the office, and the girl wore a deep purple coat, her long blonde hair spreading out across her back. *Why isn't the girl in school? What are they even doing down here?*

Messenger handed the girl the paper when the mom was distracted with her phone. Then, the mom put the phone in her pocket, noticed the paper the girl was holding, and glanced at Messenger standing a little bit away from them. The mother pulled the paper away from her daughter and threw it on the sidewalk. She wiped her hand and her daughter's hand with a tissue. Then, she turned and pointed her finger, like a knife, at Messenger and started yelling.

Messenger didn't flinch but turned and headed down the street away from them. The little girl bent down to pick the message back up, but her mother grabbed it and threw it down again, then yanked her daughter by the arm, stomped off. Alana's last glimpse of them before they turned the corner was the little girl pulling away to rub her arm and wipe her eyes.

Messenger was gone.

Alana hurried to the very spot where they'd been, bent down, and picked up the paper. **YOU ARE A TREASURE,** the message read.

# LUNCH WITH MARY

Alana sat on the bench beside the playground one bright morning, waiting for Messenger to show up. She checked her phone and realized she'd forgotten to call her best friend, Mary, back again to confirm their lunch date. Mary was an account analyst for a big firm—Alana could never remember the name. She made lots of money, lived alone in a great apartment on the West Side, the works.

Mary answered right away. "Finally! What's wrong? Why won't you answer my calls or texts? I was worried."

"Sorry! I've got a lot going on. I've been so busy."

"Everybody's busy, Alana."

"Okay, okay. I'll do better."

"It's just, you never were this flaky before."

"It's this story I'm working on."

"About?"

"I'll tell you more at lunch."

***

Alana was so happy they were meeting at "their place," Joe's, an old diner they used to always go to when they'd first become friends. The food was cheap but good. It was cozy and familiar, and Alana knew she could afford it. Alana found Mary staring at the menu when she breezed in, looking like the polished businesswoman as usual. Mary hugged her, and Alana settled on her side of the table, but even before the waiter left with their orders, Mary began her interrogation. "So," she said. "This big story?"

"Yeah. I'm actually thinking I might have a book on my hands." It was the first time Alana had said this out loud to anyone except Messenger.

"Oh, wow! That's great! Okay, what's it about?"

Alana told Mary just the basics of the Messenger project and watched Mary's face as she sketched, in broad brushstrokes, Messenger, the messages, the posts from recipients, the Clinamen. Mary kept her face open but focused. Alana could tell she was really listening.

"So," Alana added. "Do you think this whole thing is insane?"

"I get why you're intrigued by Messenger and everything," Mary commented. She raised an eyebrow. "No offense, but she sounds a little sketchy."

Alana laughed. "You are so right! Now really. Please. You can't breathe a word about this to anyone. Swear! I don't want any other writers to steal my story."

"Don't worry. I won't. But you can't let yourself get so obsessed about it. You know how you do. I haven't heard from you in weeks. Nobody has. It's like you've fallen off the planet. I'm worried about you." Mary brushed her perfectly colored and subtly highlighted hair away from her face.

Alana picked at her dry cuticles, avoided Mary's eyes. "I know, I know. I've been working really hard. I have to. I'm having money problems."

Mary paused as the waiter served their salads. When he turned, she added, more gently, "I thought your mom left you money … ."

"She did. But you know how fast money goes here."

Mary nodded and took a bite of her food. She looked back up at Alana and asked, "You're not living off credit cards, are you?"

Alana shook her head. "Not quite, but it won't be long now."

"Oh, Alana. I'm really sorry." She reached out and touched Alana's hand. "Do you think this book project is worth all the effort? I'm scared."

"Me too." Tears filled Alana's eyes. "But I can't stop now. I keep pushing Messenger to tell me more, to let me expand my website, keep the buzz going—all that. I get so damn frustrated with her! I'm putting as much pressure on her as I dare."

"I get it," Mary said. "But you better be careful how hard you push. I know you, Alana. When you get fixated on something, you're like a dog with a bone. You don't want to scare Messenger off. There's probably a whole lot more going on than you know about. What if she just disappeared one day, then where would you be?"

Alana felt like Mary had just punched her in the stomach. *Mary's right!* Another serious concern she hadn't thought to worry about yet.

Mary took a sip of water, and Alana noticed her beautiful manicure. "You need a diversion. Maybe a man in your life. Wait." Mary smiled broadly and turned her head to the side. "What's that look about?"

"Oh, nothing."

"Not nothing. Come on. Dish."

Alana sighed. "No, it's nothing, really. Just this guy who works at the coffee shop where I usually meet Messenger."

Mary rested her elbows on the table, crossed her fingers, and placed her chin there. "A barista? Is that his side gig?"

"No. He's the manager."

Mary laughed. "I know it's slim pickings out there in the men department."

"No! Ed's nice."

Mary's smile narrowed. "And? Describe him."

"Well, he has this amazing thick, black hair. Cut short. You have to study his face to realize he's part Japanese."

"Yum! Good-looking, then."

"Well, yeah. And he has just a few tats, no lame ones. This really pretty iris one came from a suit in a Japanese card game. Isn't that cool?"

"It is," Mary agreed, but her slight frown remained. "Has he asked you out?"

"No!" Alana cringed. She couldn't begin to imagine Ed ever getting up the nerve. "And really. There's nothing going on. He's super moody—makes flowers and a heart in my coffee one day, then the next won't even say hi. I don't have time for him or anybody, really. I've got to get this book written!"

***

As soon as she and Mary finished their lunches, Mary had to hurry back to the office. Alana promised to come to Mary's annual Thanksgiving potluck. "No excuses," Mary told her.

They hugged each other before Mary headed to the train. "Don't be a stranger," Mary said.

On her own walk back to the subway, Mary's warning about scaring Messenger off replayed over and over in Alana's head. She decided to ride back downtown and find Messenger, to reassure herself that everything was okay. As always, it had felt good to share her worries with Mary. She had acted supportive, but Alana could tell she had doubts about her project. *Why shouldn't she?* Alana admitted. *I have plenty of doubts myself.* She'd sacrificed so much. She was just plain tired of all the hide and seek. Of trying so hard to get Messenger to tell her what she needed to know. Messenger could be infuriating, and sometimes Alana wanted more than anything to just tell her off.

But there was another side to it all, too, she had to admit. *Who are you trying to fool? You love Messenger. When you're with her, you feel wonderful. Peaceful. Like you belong. You came to this city to follow your dream of becoming a writer. To find a story and serve it. Well, your story is Messenger.*

Alana thought back to the day before, when Messenger caught her off guard, had asked, "What are you serving?" That time,

Alana didn't reply. *But the answer is,* she suddenly realized, *this book I'm going to write. About you, Messenger.*

***

Alana headed down the street toward First Avenue, dodged an annoying guy dressed in green cotton pants and wearing round glasses and black ear gauges. *Great,* she thought. *Texting while he walks.* She streamed along the sidewalk with the crowd.

*Poor Mom would roll in her grave this very minute if she hadn't been cremated,* Alana mused. She hated to think of all the many ways her mom had scrimped and saved, had denied herself. Self-punishment. That's what her mom was all about. In a moment of clarity, Alana had realized long ago the self-punishment went back to when her mom got pregnant with Alana in college. Her mom spent the rest of her life punishing herself for that one mistake. She must not have thought she deserved to have fun, Alana figured, so she worked instead. She was really good at that. Alana remembered the ugly green plastic Tupperware cup with the clear cap her mom filled every morning with coffee to take to work, then refilled with water for the trip home. Alana would see it in the car's cup holder on the way to school and when her mom finally pulled over at the curb to pick her up in the evening.

A guy riding a skateboard down the middle of the sidewalk jostled Alana before she could jump out of the way so that Alana almost knocked an old lady down. "Watch out!" Alana yelled at him. She turned to the lady. "Are you okay?" The lady nodded and hurried away.

Walking along, Alana saw her whole project through Mary's eyes and felt the weight of her commitment to it like a bodysuit of lead. The stakes were very high. Alana remembered how, as a child, when the circus came to Fredericktown every year, she'd always looked forward to the high-wire acrobats in their tacky, worn-out sequined leotards and jackets. She held her breath during the entirety of their death-defying act, filled with anxiety at every move they made. That part made her sick to her stomach. What she loved was the moment when the agony of their performance was finally over, their act finished. Then, each performer, one by one, fell slowly, gracefully, effortlessly into the safety net below. It caught them like a soft, fluffy cloud. That's what she longed for—a permanent safety net. Alana knew that's what her mom had worked so hard to give her. *But once the money's really gone, my safety net's gone too.* Alana felt that harsh realization spread through every cell of her body, like water permeating a sponge. *That's what an orphan has to face,* she thought. *Well, not technically an orphan, but in fact true.*

She'd had no actual contact with her father since her parents' divorce when she was a baby, but she'd found her father, Marvin Peterson, through stalking his son, Marvin Jr.'s, Facebook page. It hadn't been that hard. Alana prided herself on her search abilities, one thing she'd learned from her previous click-bait job. Marvin Sr. wore glasses. Alana had been lucky. She'd gotten her mom's twenty-twenty vision. He had a cowlick at his part, the same cowlick Alana tamed by parting her hair on the other side.

When she'd first found him, four years ago right after her mom had died, Alana had stared at his face on the screen for a very long time. Then she'd searched her own face in the mirror for any of his features, besides the cowlick, but all she could see was her mom. Her mother's long, oval face, wide forehead (Alana still had a slight scar from a sledding accident), and deep-set brown eyes. Alana had gotten her mom's thick, brown hair, which Mom had never worn down, as Alana did, but always in a neat nurse bun. Marvin was fairer, though graying now. His three sons were blondes. They all looked like him. His daughter looked like his new wife. Whenever she allowed herself to go to Marvin Jr.'s page, which was seldom, she searched her father's face again, around his eyes or the corners of his mouth, for any hint of sadness or regret, any sign that losing her registered there. She saw nothing.

Alana focused on the faces of all the people who passed her on the street. *How many of them are operating without a safety net too?* Did she look as anxious as many of them did? She shook her head as if to shake off her fears. *Okay, Alana. That's it! Stop feeling sorry for yourself and do something! Take action! Honor Mom and all her hard work by pulling this off. Mom did it on her own, without any help from Marvin. You can too. You've just got to work more efficiently.*

Striding faster down the street, Alana decided she would go ahead and build her website, complete with her research, notes, lists, her own experiences of Messenger, posts from people who'd received messages, interviews. She'd be ready to go live the minute Messenger finally decided the time was right. She didn't need to tell Messenger about it. Why would she care, as long as Alana waited?

These plans occupied her thoughts until she stopped dead in her tracks and caused a mom to almost run over her with an umbrella stroller. Ice climbed up her back and scalp. She apologized to the mom, then walked the few steps to the curb, to be absolutely certain of what she thought she'd seen.

A green MINI Cooper was parked in front of her between a van and another car. She knew what the license plate would say, even before she looked. There it was, in black letters, all caps. CLINAMN.

Alana's shivering spread up and down until even her teeth chattered. She clenched her jaw tight, to stop it. *It's a sign,* she thought, and her heart soared.

# Alana's Notebook

*I saw the CLINAMN license plate! Right when I was thinking about Mom. Was it a sign to keep going?*

*What choice do I really have? I don't want to wonder the rest of my life if Messenger's story was my big break, the one I'd longed for and dreamed about, but then I blew it. I'd never forgive myself. I have to go on. Am I insane to think that Messenger's story should be a book? What about a movie? Or a TV show? Each person's message could be an episode, with an on-going narrative arc that follows the character, based loosely on me, who's struggling to uncover the bigger story arc. What about an expanded website? Worldwide readers? Are there other Messengers in other countries? Why not? Why wouldn't there be? All working together to shore us up? Could they be like a spiritual force field, like gravity, holding things in place on Planet Earth? Is that too uber science fiction?*

*Of course, I also want to work for something bigger than myself and help change the world for the better. To help move our planet forward positively, to break free from the same obnoxious, annoying rut we seem to find ourselves in. As I spend time with Messenger, I'm just so touched by this beautiful woman who's given her life to the messages. Her all. I can truly say I've never met anyone like her, so filled with love, with good intentions. To be in her presence, to hear her voice, to have her touch you—extraordinary. She's working so hard to do her part, to make the Clinamen happen. Something big is at work here. I still don't really understand, but hopefully Messenger will reveal more.*

*But the waiting, the frustrations, the disappointments, exhaustion, money worries mount. Just finding her is the first challenge of the day. She won't let me watch as she receives a message (just once, I happened to be there and witnessed it). While her secrecy really bums me out, it does make sense. She talks about vibrations. Would my vibration interfere with the delivery of the message or interfere with the exchange between her and the recipient? Is that how it works? Am I beginning to understand? To think like Messenger?*

*She won't take me along to deliver a message either. It's like that's something immensely private between her and the recipient. Vibrations again, I guess. I beg her, but she shakes her head. "No, baby. That's not for you to see."*

*Always when we're together, she reaches over and gently massages my forehead between my eyes, where wrinkles are etching themselves while I struggle to figure all this out. "Relax, honey," she says. It feels good. I know I'm always in a hurry, my shoulders up to my ears, my neck tight. I try to have good posture, but it's hard with all the writing. "Give yourself a break," she tells me. She's right. I'm making myself crazy. Something's got to give.*

*Messenger isn't going to change. That's clear. I'm the one who has to change, who has to accept her, this situation, and the way she does things. Stop fighting her. If I'm too aggressive or demanding, I might alienate her or scare her off like Mary said. I'll swallow my frustration and allow everything to evolve on her terms. Hopefully, she'll continue revealing morsels of information when we're together.*

*Meanwhile, I'll keep building my website, collecting posts and interviews, slow and steady. It will all work out. This is my story to write. I'll make a name for myself and promote all the good Messenger is doing in the world. Win-win. Create positive momentum. The money? I'll figure it out somehow. Maybe Gus can give me more shifts. Or a raise.*

*So yeah. I'll take Mary's advice. Easy does it. I'll accept Messenger as she is. I'll be more patient. I won't rush her or push her. We'll proceed on her time line. Maybe we'll even create our own Clinamen, Messenger and me, with this book.*

# CAT IN THE COFFEE SHOP

Alana and Messenger sat in Ed's coffee shop. Through the plate glass front window, Alana spied a guy she'd seen many times before but always near the other coffee shop around the corner from the park. This guy walked the streets of the city with his fat black-and-white tuxedo cat perched on his head. Really—the cat just sat on the guy's head. The guy was super tall, thin, and dark haired. His hair blended in with the cat's fur. The cat's tail would often wrap around his head right where his eyebrows were, forming a unibrow. He'd stand on a corner and people would give him money just to see it.

"Look, Messenger," Alana pointed. "Have you ever seen anything like that?"

At the same time, a woman opened the door to Ed's. The cat jumped down off his perch. This apparently shocked the guy so much he didn't react soon enough to grab the leash attached to the cat's red collar. The cat bolted through the door between the legs of a woman trying to come in.

"Whoa!" Ed cried.

The cat ran down the aisle, jumped right up onto Messenger's lap, and purred.

All these events happened within about thirty seconds.

"Oh my," Messenger said. "You are one good-looking cat!" She patted it between its ears.

The cat's owner stood beside them, fumed. He grabbed the leash from the floor and yanked the cat off Messenger's lap.

"Mrrrawr," the cat cried.

"For God's sake, lady. What did you do to my cat? People pay to see him stay on my head!" His face reddened, and he looked fierce.

"Hey, buddy." Alana had never heard Ed's quiet voice take a sharp tone before. "Outside. Leave her alone."

The tall guy looked around the coffee shop for allies. Finding none, he put the cat under his arm. Alana figured he didn't want to chance a repeat performance. He stomped out.

Alana laughed. "Way to go, Ed!"

Ed grinned at Messenger and Alana, then busied himself clearing dishes off tables. Today he'd made a fancy letter *A* in her coffee.

Everybody in the shop went back to what they were doing.

"Ed's all right," was all Messenger said.

"Yeah. But how'd you do that?" Alana asked her.

Messenger looked up from picking cat hairs off her lap. "Do what, honey?"

"You know."

"I had nothing to do with it."

"No?"

"Apparently that kitty doesn't like him as much as he thinks it does."

Alana just stared at her.

"Never know what a cat might do," Messenger added.

# Messenger's Composition Book

## Animals are in on the Clinamen

*The animals are coming closer because there's nowhere else for them to go now. We've cut down all the trees, taken all their homes to build things for ourselves. Taken it all. Soon they'll voice what we've done to them, to our planet. They will rise up, and the birds of the air and the fish of the sea, the animals near and far, ferocious and tame, will sing with one voice. And what will we humans tell them? If we're wise and courageous, we'll face the terrible truth—and join hands and paws with our four-legged brothers and sisters. And go forward—together. The moment the first monkey opens her mouth and speaks will be the tipping point. Soon all will follow, and that boundary between human and animal will fall forever. We'll see ourselves through their eyes. And be amazed but most of all—ashamed.*

# Alana's Notebook

*I'm struggling each day to stick with my new resolution about the Messenger project. But wild things just keep happening.*

1. *Messenger reading my mind*
2. *The car with the CLINAMN license plate at just the moment I was thinking about Mom*
3. *The cat*

*A new development: I wake up almost every morning and remember my dreams in great detail. They make no sense and go all over the place, but they stay with me all day. And that's not the craziest part. The dreams feel like déjà vus because people come into the coffee shop or stand beside me on the street who I know I've seen before. In my dreams! I'm sure of it. Did I actually see them or dream about them and then see them again? Some stand out, like the young woman dressed like a baby doll in a pink bustier and tight, accordion skirt with circles of pink rouge on her cheeks, anime-style. Some are just as ordinary and random as you could ever imagine—a guy in a navy blue T-shirt in Tale of the Whale. An overweight woman in black stretch pants, messenger bag draped across her body.*

*What's going on?*

# ALANA CONFIDES IN MESSENGER

Alana hurried through the crowds on her way to Tale of the Whale for her five o'clock extra shift. She happened to look up, and her stomach dropped like she'd fallen ten stories in an elevator in one second. She watched a drag queen in super high heels, breasts pushed up to a dizzying height, sway down the street toward her. A crown of peacock feathers stuck out from her head on all sides. She winked at Alana as she passed, as if they shared a secret. It wasn't the first time Alana had seen her. They'd met just last night in Alana's dreams. Alana clutched a nearby bike rack and held on for dear life. *What's happening to me?*

Alana hadn't told Messenger about any of these weird events—not even the CLINAMN license plate. Why? Her mom. Every time Alana thought about telling Messenger, a clammy dread filled her stomach as she remembered her mother's shocking reaction to the *Cathy's Birthday* incident. Alana had come home so happy. She'd won a cake! Even dearer was the magical experience of having known it would happen before it did. She hadn't told Mrs. Snyder or Sara, had saved it to share with her mother that night. She'd practically danced herself home, so eager to tell her mom everything that had happened.

"You will not tell anyone about this. Do you hear me?" her mom said when she mentioned her premonition. Having just come in from the hospital, her mom had stood at the door, her face fierce. "I swear," she muttered, slammed her plastic cup on the kitchen table, threw her lunch bag down beside it, and peeled out of her hospital sweater. "You know, your father used to talk like that. Believe me, weirdos ran in his family."

Alana started to cry at the mention of her father. She sank into the kitchen chair and watched her mom tromp around the kitchen, pull things out of the fridge to begin dinner. Then Mom added, "Your father was always fascinated by anything supernatural. He'd create preposterous claims meant to make him seem special. He just couldn't stay in the real world." She turned around and faced Alana. "No!" she demanded. "No fuss! No tears. I mean it. He's not worth it."

Alana shivered but nodded.

"Oh, Alana." Mom's voice softened. "Just forget all this foolishness. It was all in your head—just a coincidence. Say no more about it—to anyone."

Alana knew Messenger would never react like her mom had. It was getting too weird—she couldn't wait any longer. *I'll tell her tomorrow.*

The next day was cold and cloudy. Alana finally found Messenger after searching at least an hour, and the two of them headed down Fifth Street.

"Messenger, I need to tell you something."

Messenger was bagless today. She pulled her red cap down over one ear, then the other. "Okay, honey," she answered. "Wait. Got any of those chocolates?"

Alana laughed. After they'd settled on their bench, she pulled a big handful out of her backpack. Messenger stuffed them into her pockets and unwrapped the red foil on one. "One for you?" she asked.

"No, thanks."

"Are you sure? Chocolate always helps."

Alana shook her head.

Messenger popped the chocolate into her mouth, closed her eyes, and sucked. "Mmmm! That is so good," she gurgled.

"Great! Listen, you probably won't believe this, but I saw the car."

"The car?"

"The green MINI-Cooper with the C-L-I-N-A-M-N license plate."

"You did?" Messenger's voice rose, and a huge smile spread across her face. If Alana had told her she'd won the lottery, Messenger couldn't have look more pleased.

"Yes. A while ago."

"Well, why didn't you tell me?"

Alana ignored her question because she didn't really know the answer. "That's not all."

"It's not?"

"No. Another really weird thing. I'm remembering my dreams now." Alana sensed how excited Messenger grew, and it threw her off. She suddenly wished she hadn't said anything about any of it. "So ... yeah."

Messenger reached out and massaged her forehead. "It's okay, honey. What is it? Just tell me everything. Don't hold back."

"I've been seeing people from my dreams." Her voice shook. "On the street. While I'm awake. Last night during my shift at Tale of the Whale, this guy walked in and stood at the door waiting for a table. He was a totally average guy. He told me he was visiting from Harrisonburg, Virginia. 'I'm from Virginia too,' I said. Then I felt dizzy, like I was on a roller coaster, because I remembered I'd had the same conversation with him the night before in a dream!"

"Yes."

"You don't think that's weird?"

"No, not really."

Alana let out a huge sigh. She hadn't realized she'd held her breath this whole time. "It's happened a lot. I see people on the street and recognize them. What's going on?"

Messenger paused. "What do you think is going on?"

"I don't know. What does it mean? Am I going crazy?"

Messenger patted her shoulder. "I don't think it means anything except a door has opened for you."

"What does that mean?"

"Don't let it worry you. Just roll with it, honey." She patted her again. "You're not going crazy. I can guarantee that!"

Alana decided to take Messenger's word for it. She knew about these things, right? "Okay. That's good to know. But do you think these things just happen to some people? Or to everybody, and they just won't admit it?"

"They happen to everybody. But you have to be awake to notice."

"I guess they happen to you. A lot."

Messenger smiled one of her huge smiles where her eyes, her lips, everything about her face turned up and opened. "All the time, baby. All the time!"

# ALANA'S THANKSGIVING

"You *came*!" Mary exclaimed, too strongly, when Alana walked through the door.

"Of course! I said I would." Alana ignored the surprise on Mary's face. She handed Mary a pumpkin pie she'd picked up from the fancy bakery on First Avenue and a bottle of barely respectable pinot noir.

Mary always hosted potluck Thanksgiving for her friends because she had the biggest, nicest apartment, decorated in a slick minimalist style. It even opened onto a rooftop garden all the tenants shared. Since the sun was bright and clear, the air crisp but not too cold, her guests overflowed onto it. Everyone had brought great food to contribute. The vibe was cozy and festive.

Alana held her face in a smile that showed some teeth. Everything was going just fine, great, in fact. She was surprised how good it felt to be with people her own age for a change, even though she didn't know many of them well. She chatted with those she'd met before at Mary's, the usual suspects, with the addition of Stephen, a new guy from Mary's office. Stephen wore black slim jeans and a blazer with a white T-shirt under it that Alana bet cost a hundred bucks. Although attractive and friendly, his studied casual look segued into trying too hard. Stephen stayed by Alana's side after they were introduced. Inevitably, after the first few back-and-forths of polite conversation, he queried, "So what do you do?"

*Oh, no.* She cringed, knew exactly how this would go. "I'm a writer." She held that fake smile plastered on her face.

"Oh, wow. Blogger?"

"Yeah, sort of. Journalist."

"Awesome." She watched him straighten up. "With what publication?"

Yep. There it was. "Oh, none, at the moment. I'm working on an independent project."

"About what?"

She watched his eyes glaze. "I'm investigating this person who, well, actually, I really can't say."

"Why?" he asked, a little aggressively. "Is it someone we know?"

"Give it up, Stephen," Mary butted in. "This project's top secret. She can't talk about it."

Alana flashed a grateful smile Mary's way, then turned back to Stephen. "Sorry. It's complicated."

There was an awkward silence, which Stephen broke. "Well, guess we'll all be taking a break from work soon, with Christmas coming."

Mary sighed and stared at the floor.

Alana suddenly got it. Mary had invited Stephen here for her. She felt herself blush, and her first thought was, *I told Mary about Ed. What? He's not good enough?* Alana shook her head to clear it. "It'll be here before we know it," she heard herself reply.

"Time always goes too fast." Mary gave Alana the stink eye. "Actually, it's already Christmas, thanks to retail. Has been for a couple weeks."

Stephen's eyes roamed the room, but he added, "Yeah. The trees and lights and all."

*Come on, Alana. Make an effort for Mary's sake. She's trying to be sweet to you, not diss Ed.* "Oh, the lights are my favorite part. I love the tree, of course. Who doesn't? But I also love how they outline the buildings, cover everything with lights—trees, the bushes. Even the fences look soft and magical in the early twilight. Astoria has these wild retro bell lights strung across the power lines at every intersection. I can see them blinking all night out my apartment window."

Stephen finished his drink.

"I've got to check my turkey," Mary said.

"Heading to the bar," Stephen announced and walked away from her.

*So much for trying.*

Mary served the food buffet-style, and everyone soon settled their plates on their laps. The energy of the group built as people drank more wine, got more wound up. Voices and laughter grew louder. Alana sat between Mary and Stephen, both of whom talked at the same time but not to her. Alana watched as if outside herself and realized that, six months ago, she would have been very interested in Stephen, thrilled that Mary had invited him for her. But now, looking around at all of Mary's beautiful friends, so polished and smart and successful, Alana wanted nothing more than to be anywhere but here—at Ed's or on Fifth Street with Messenger and their friends.

But she couldn't leave yet, of course. Mary hadn't even served the desserts. At last Mary got up and headed in the direction of the kitchen. Meanwhile, Alana had to sit there, listen to Stephen drone on about his favorite subject—himself—for the rest of the evening, which would now plod along in super slow motion as everybody else grew drunker and louder. Alana knew from hard experience she was not a drinker and didn't want to be. Two glasses of wine were her limit.

"Alana." Mary was back and motioned her over. "Hey, girl. You okay? You're not looking so good."

"No, I'm fine."

"You were a million miles away." Mary put an arm around her shoulder and lowered her voice. "How's it going with the project?"

Alana shook her head. "Messenger's still not ready to go public. I took your advice, though. I'm not pushing her so much."

"Good." Mary took a big drink from her glass. "Mmmm. This wine is excellent. More?" She motioned with the bottle toward Alana's empty glass, but Alana put her hand over it. "No thanks."

"How's it going with Stephen?" Mary's eyes sparkled.

"Not great. Not really my type. Sorry."

"Not a barista?"

Alana heard the barb in Mary's voice. "Manager! And I told you nothing's going on with him. But if there was, Ed's great. You'd like him."

Mary drank again, paused, then changed the subject. "How much longer do you think you can keep going with the project with, you know—your problems."

Alana smiled. "Don't worry, Mary."

"Okay, fine." Mary picked up her glass and headed toward the kitchen. "Dessert, people!" she yelled over the din.

Alana set her wine glass down and crossed her arms. She had ages to wait before she could politely leave. *You can make it through this night somehow, Alana*, she told herself. She sighed. Thanksgiving meant only one thing. Soon she'd have Christmas to deal with.

# ALANA'S THREE CHRISTMASES

Alana sat on the bench by the playground fence on Fifth Street on the first day of December, hoping Messenger would show up. Her phone buzzed. She wasn't at all surprised to see who it was—Aunt Jane. Right on time.

"Hi, dear!" Aunt Jane trilled. "Just calling to see how you're doing in the big city. Staying safe?"

Alana laughed. "Sure am! Very safe."

"That's terrific, sweetheart! I'm so glad to hear it! Now—Christmas is right around the corner, and Kristen told me to call and invite you to come out and be with us. Remember the wonderful time we had a few years ago? Listen, Kristen's boys are getting so big. Matthew's in middle school now. You will not believe this, but he's exactly as tall as I am! When did it happen?"

Alana didn't hesitate in her answer. "You'll have to send me a photo. That's really nice, Aunt Jane, but I've already made plans to go with Sara Snyder and her family."

"Oh really? Back to Virginia?"

*Was that relief I heard in her voice?*

Aunt Jane didn't miss a beat. "Feels more like home, I guess, than here with us in sunny California."

"Yeah. I guess. Visiting the old neighborhood and everything. But listen, thanks so much. And you all have a great holiday too."

"Please stay in touch, Alana. I know Sue would want you to." Her voice caught. "She'd want us all to stay close."

"Of course. Thanks again. Talk with you soon."

Alana put her phone into her backpack and watched the lady with the Chihuahuas slowly walk past. She searched up and down the street. No Messenger. She decided to wait a little longer.

Alana leaned back against the wooden bench and slouched. *Well,* she thought. *Aunt Jane's taken care of.* But her throat felt thick and her body heavy. *Why are you feeling guilty?* The first year after her mom had died, Alana spent way too much money that she didn't have to fly out and spend Christmas with them. She hadn't felt at home. She felt like the odd one out, like she put a damper on Aunt Jane and her family's holiday. Alana had promised herself, if she could just get through the visit, she'd never do it again. That's how she'd come up with this strategy.

*Funny,* she thought. *Lying to Aunt Jane didn't feel so good this time.* Why had it never bothered her before?

When Messenger didn't show up on Fifth Street, Alana decided to head to Ed's to check there. On the way, Mary texted her.

What r u doing for xmas?

Alana stopped walking and studied the phone. She knew exactly where Mary was going with her question. She put the phone into her coat pocket and walked another block. Then she pulled it out again and typed:

*Going to my aunts.*

in Cali?

*Yeah.*

Lucky! Mom told me to invite u again.

Alana's stomach twisted. She paused again, considered finishing the text later. *NO. Just get it over with,* she told herself.

That's nice. Next year? When r u leaving?

*Xmas eve. Insane but no time off. Back the 26th.*

That sucks!

Let's get a drink before we both go. What might work?

Alana's stomach turned. She wasn't sure she could carry off her lies in person.

*Let me get back to you. Things kind of hectic.*

KK. Me too. Take care.

Alana walked into Ed's and didn't feel her spirits lift as she usually did. Lying to Mary felt terrible. And there was more lying to come.

That sick feeling in her stomach followed her to work that evening. On her break, Alana sat in Gus's office and called Mrs. Snyder back. She'd left a voice message for Alana earlier in the day.

"Hi, Mrs. Snyder! It's Alana!"

"Well, hello there! Calling all the way from New York City! How are you doing up there?"

"Fine."

"Are you keeping safe?" she asked.

*Mrs. Snyder's calm, soothing voice hasn't changed a bit since I used to sit at her kitchen table and eat brownies with Sara as a girl*, Alana thought. "Perfectly safe," she answered. "Everything's going just great."

"Good, good. Well, Sara and I were wondering if you'd like to come for a Christmas visit this year!"

Alana suspected it was more Mrs. Snyder than Sara, since she and Sara weren't in touch very often these days. She took a deep breath, but the smooth lie stuck in her throat. She had to force it out. "You're so nice to keep asking me, but I'm already going to my Aunt Jane's."

"California? My goodness!"

"Yes."

"That is just wonderful! Sun is what you need right now, I bet. It's darker up there, isn't it? Days are much shorter?"

"I guess you're right."

"And Christmas with your family. What could be better?"

"Uh-huh."

"Well, if you're ever in the area or just feel like visiting your old stomping grounds, you know you're always welcome here."

Alana's eyes filled with tears. "Thanks so much. I really do appreciate it."

"Honey, are you okay?"

"Yes, sure," she forced herself to reply, then held her breath.

"Okay, sweetie. You take good care of yourself. And Merry Christmas!"

Alana managed to duck out of the office and into the bathroom before Gus came in to call her back. She wiped mascara smears from beneath each eye and tried to breathe deeply. *Whew!* she thought. *What is wrong with me?* Before she'd always felt relief after she'd fended off her Christmas offers. Now, her stomach refused to unknot. *Come on, January*, she thought. She loved January, when all the holiday drama was over for another year.

# Alana's Notebook

*I just pulled up my blog, and there were even more new posts from all over the city. Likes and comments. I couldn't believe it. Other people have posted about how much just reading the posts meant to them. I'm so excited! I'm going to do some real good, help people and hopefully sell a lot of books. I've got to get going on the query and writing the book. I'm just not sure how to structure it. I want it to be dramatic and compelling—and I want the reader to understand it's real. All real. Some people have already questioned this on the blog, like I might be making up these stories or even making up Messenger herself. I've got to reassure people that, no, this is not some hoax or urban legend. Messenger is real.*

*I've got the expanded website all finished and set to go. It looks good. At least I did learn how to create a website from that last soul-sucking job. I named the site* The Messenger Files. *Provocative, right? I wrote an introduction to Messenger, an explanation of how I got interested in the project, created a section for the best of the posts—Marty's, of course, Brenda's, Elaine's, Scott's, and a few others. Also, transcripts of my interviews. Places to find Messenger. How she receives and delivers messages. Hopefully I've included just enough information to create interest in the book but leave people intrigued and wanting to learn more.*

*Now, I've just got to get Messenger to tell me more about herself and her past, how she started on this path to become a messenger. The farthest back in her story she'll go is when the messages first came to her, but she had to have a life before that. She ignores or refuses to answer any personal questions. She tells me she isn't important at all—just the messages. But she is important from the reader's standpoint. I mean, this isn't a normal life she's living. How did it happen?*

*I also need to focus on the Clinamen. Why would the Clinamen be dangerous when it will bring about wonderful changes? I need to learn more.*

*Just waiting for Messenger to give the go-ahead. Hope it's soon. Oh, Mom, you'd NEVER understand what I'm doing. You were always so practical, self-sufficient, organized, methodical. Frugal. Even Mary's doubting everything. I get it! My money problems are real. Mom's money's not going to last indefinitely. At least I have Tale of the Whale. Gus gave me one more shift a week, which helps, but I'm still dipping into Mom's money all the time to make it to the end of the month. It's getting bleak, and I don't want to end up on the streets myself. Hopefully it will all pay off.*

# Messenger's Composition Book

*Good news can be very dangerous. Just look at history. Anybody with a new idea or thought or healing ways. Good news always brings a power shift. People will do ANYTHING—lie, cheat, kill if they have to—to keep things just the way they are.*

*Problem is, all momentum is forward.*

*Never back.*

*There is no back.*

*Evolution.*

*Unfolding.*

*Motion.*

*Speeding up now.*

*Forward is the only direction.*

*Love is pulling us forward 24/7.*

*But there's always a price. A payment. That's the razor's edge—the more power, the more danger. The Clinamen—the swerve—is the most dangerous part. Chock full of dangers. Everything is at stake. Oh, me! I thought this book idea of hers would slow her down. Give us more time to work. No. Guess that was asking too much. Maybe it'll all turn out okay. I do know things are moving in the right direction. She's had openings and shows promise. She'll learn enough in the nick of time. At least to start. She'll know what she needs to know.*

# CHRISTMAS PRESENT

It was a cold December day—cloudy and blustery. Alana leaned on the bar and sipped her coffee, enjoying Ed's company. He'd comped her and made a holly leaf with berries in the foam. "Your Christmas present," he told her. Messenger hadn't been in yet, so she'd decided to hang around a while.

"So," he said. "Heading out soon?"

"Yeah. I'll go tomorrow to my ... aunt's." She needed a second to remember which Christmas she'd told Ed about earlier.

"California, right?"

Alana nodded. "Yep."

"Guess you'll be there a while." He looked up at her.

"Nope. Just a few days." *Alana, why didn't you tell him you were going to Virginia! You could have come back in sooner.* She sighed and bit her cuticle. All this lying was plucking her nerves.

"Not too long."

"No."

"A break from the project?"

Alana sighed. "Yeah."

"About that. Be careful. Do what she tells you."

Alana studied Ed's face, but he kept it neutral. "What are you saying?"

"Listen to Messenger."

"I've already decided to do that."

"Okay. Well." Ed smiled his crooked smile. "Hope you have a good visit."

Alana smiled back. "How about you, Ed?"

"Oh, I got a few things to do. This older buddy invited me over on Christmas. Quiet. Just him and his wife."

"Nice."

"Yeah."

***

Later, Messenger finally came in. Alana sat with her while her friend warmed up and sipped her coffee. "Ed told me you're going away for the holidays," Messenger said.

Alana looked down at the table and nodded. A charge of electricity surged up through her stomach.

"He didn't say where."

*Messenger knows. Is she trying to catch me? I should have known better than trying to lie to her.* "California," she blurted. "My aunt lives there with her daughter in a little town you've probably never heard of."

Messenger stared at her. Paused, then said, "How nice. Well, you have a nice trip."

"What are you doing for Christmas? Going anywhere? Spending it with family?" she fished.

Messenger kept staring. "I got plans," she said.

"Good for you! I'm glad to hear it." When Messenger didn't elaborate, Alana added, "Don't worry. I won't be gone long, just a few days. Then we can get back to work. We've got a lot of work to do. I guess your Christmas present is a little rest from me bugging you with all my questions," she joked, tried to lighten the mood.

Messenger squinted at her. "If you say so."

Alana's heart dropped. She looked away. She wanted to tell Messenger the truth. But she couldn't.

# MESSENGER AND THE WATCHERS

Messenger and Jackie shivered in the opening to the alley, speaking softly together. "A journalist? I don't have to tell you, Messenger, this is *not* our way. We work in secret. In safety. Our work is not for everyone to know about." Jackie was so agitated, her black, cat-eye glasses fogged up. "For our own safety!"

Messenger put her hands on her hips. "Why? Who says?"

"Look, you agreed to the rules when you signed up for this."

"It's easy for you to lecture me." She pulled in closer to Jackie's face. "You didn't have a family, did you?"

"No. But you knew the rules. You must walk away from your life to serve. Leave everything you have." She shook her head. "Doesn't matter for us anymore. We're old. What matters is this: I warned you a long time ago this girl is a terrible choice!"

"You don't know her."

Jackie sighed and steam poured out of her mouth. "She's a journalist! It's her job to uncover secrets and bring what's hidden out into the open. Public knowledge! How can she—"

"Yes. She's a journalist. She loves words as much as I do. She wants to write a book about the messages."

"And you said *yes*? Are you stone-cold crazy?" Jackie's voice echoed through the alley.

"Shush!" Messenger warned her. "Our old ways aren't working. They're falling apart. That's okay. It always happens like that. But we need something new in place to help bring about the Clinamen. 'Clinamen' is what I'm calling it now. Can't you feel it?"

"Call it whatever you want. Nobody knows when it's going to come! It could come today. Or—it could take a hundred more years! Nobody knows. We just have to keep doing what we're doing."

Messenger shook her head. "Come on, Jackie. You know it's coming soon. You feel it too."

"Let's stick with the present moment, why don't we? The Watchers know about the girl and what's been going on with you two," Jackie hissed through her teeth. "They know what you're planning ... ."

Messenger looked away, avoided Jackie's huge eyes. "And they're not happy. Okay, I get it. I know what I'm doing."

"I sincerely hope you do! Does the girl suspect anything?"

Messenger shook her head. "No. I don't think so. She's having openings, but she's not ready yet. We need more time."

"Okay, bottom line. The Watchers sent me to tell you to stop with this girl and regroup. Find somebody else. They sense danger."

Messenger chuckled. "Tell me something I don't already know."

"You're in deep. I can tell by the look on your face. What is it? Tell me."

Messenger looked straight at Jackie, her face calm and relaxed, like they were just discussing the weather. "Nothing."

"This plan you have is going to blow up in your face. Then where will you be? Why won't you tell me?"

"No, Jackie. Let's keep this on me, okay? I don't want you to take the heat for what I choose to do. The rules I choose to break. I'm willing to take my chances."

Jackie's voice softened. "Protecting you is my job, isn't it? I'm your Watcher. But I only have so much strength."

"You've got everything you need, and I thank you. I appreciate it." Messenger held out her arms, and Jackie embraced her. Then, Messenger gently took Jackie's glasses off her face. Holding them as if precious, she dug out a soft corner of her cotton shirt from under the folds of her coats and cleaned the lenses. As she rubbed, the tension between them slowly subsided. She checked each lens several times before handing the glasses back.

Jackie put them on. Nodded her thanks. "You know I'll do what I can," she said. "But I have to ask you. Are you ready to be found?"

## Messenger's Composition Book

### Fourteen Things People Rarely Say (But Should)

1. *Do less.*
2. *I have enough.*
3. *I can't afford it.*
4. *I'm wrong.*
5. *I made a mistake.*
6. *I'm sorry.*
7. *Let it go.*
8. *It's over.*
9. *Don't try so hard.*
10. *I'm satisfied.*
11. *Go first.*
12. *I don't need it.*
13. *You won.*
14. *It was my fault.*

# Post: Scott

I'm from South Carolina. My life started out rough. Mom died when I was eleven. My dad couldn't take it. He wanted to keep on partying. So I started going to this church with a girl from school. This older couple from the church, the Stickleys, actually took me in. Can you believe that? You hear about this kind of thing, but sometimes it really does happen.

So everything was great. They fed me and bought me clothes and did everything for me. They never made me feel like I wasn't their real son. They took me to church Wednesdays and Sundays every single week. We prayed over every bite of food we ever put in our mouths, even at Burger King.

A few years passed like this, and I started to grow up and my voice started to change and crack, and I knew things were going on down there—you know—my junk. I slowly realized I wasn't so much interested in the girls in our youth group as I was in the boys. Yeah. It took a while for this to sink in. I fought it.

One night, I was getting ready for bed. I looked out the window and saw these two guys walking down the street. They didn't know anybody was looking. I saw the one guy take the other's hand. The way it made me feel to watch them look at each other, then drop hands when somebody else came down the street told me everything I needed to know. That "Oh shit!" moment is one I'll never forget.

So even as young as I was, I knew there would be no talking about this. No gently breaking it to Mom and Dad. They would take it real hard—to say the least. Their God, their church, their friends didn't have room for the likes of me. So I kept it secret for a long time.

I knew it would be bad when I finally got around to telling them; they'd be heartbroken, but nothing prepared me for what did happen. It was the end of summer, and I was about to go off to college in a few weeks. I'd won a football scholarship to the University of South Carolina. I just couldn't take it anymore—was feeling really rotten about myself and my secret—like a major part of me wasn't even home. They'd been so good to me. I owed them the truth.

So I told them. I sat them down one night after supper and basically said, "Mom, Dad, I'm gay."

First, my mom fell out of her chair, sobbing on the kitchen floor, cried, "No, no, no!" Rocked back and forth. My dad just sat there without moving a muscle. My only hope was him. He was always such an easygoing guy, like nothing could knock him off base. He stared at me, and his face grew darker by the minute. Finally, after what seemed like hours, he spoke. "Go pack your things." He didn't add "son" like he always had before. "We don't abide filth in this house. We're done."

It was my turn to stare. Frozen. Until he yelled, "Now! Go!" I jumped a mile. That was the first time I'd ever heard him raise his voice.

I went to a friend's house. We told his mom my parents and I had been fighting. She wasn't home much herself—she stayed over with her boyfriend a lot, so it was perfect. My buddy and I basically lived on our own. I had enough money saved to take a bus to USC and a little extra to spare. I just went with my clothes. Jason gave me a blanket from his mom's closet.

It didn't totally hit me until late one night. I was up studying. Something crossed my mind—nothing important, but I thought, I'll give Mom and Dad a call and tell them about it. I'd even picked up my phone before everything tumbled down on my head. The whole thing was real. I went into the bathroom and ran the shower so nobody in the suite could hear. I sat on the toilet seat and bawled.

That feeling of aloneness when I was there at that school, not knowing anybody else very well—it filled everything up, every cell of my body. I felt like I wasn't me anymore, and I was worried people could tell by looking at me. I'd told a few friends at high school, two girls and one guy, about being gay. They were pretty cool with it. But after Mom and Dad's reaction, I went inside myself big time. I wasn't sure if I was more worried about people finding out I was gay or finding out my parents had kicked me out. I was not only gay but also homeless.

So there I was. I couldn't stay at school for long with no money coming in. You still need spending money, even with a full ride. And I didn't have time for a job, what with football and school. When the money ran out, I left and came here. Figured I'd get a job, find a place to live. Hoped people might think differently about me. Yeah, right. It seemed like a good idea at the time. I ended up on the street here in the city. One day, this old lady handed me a piece of paper as she passed me on the street. She looked scary, all except her eyes. Those eyes! I could have fallen into them. There was a kindness I hadn't seen in a long time. She wrote on that paper, **SUICIDE IS NOT AN OPTION.**

How did she know?

# MERRY CHRISTMAS, ALANA

On Christmas Eve, Gus decided to close early, so Alana left Tale of the Whale at about eight o'clock. She maneuvered through the huge crowds and headed straight to the train. She couldn't wait to get to her apartment, strip out of her work clothes, and relax. She'd told Messenger and Ed goodbye right before she had to go to work, but she still couldn't shake the haunting feeling about the lies she'd told. It ate away at her usual sense of power and freedom to do exactly what she wanted on Christmas Eve and Christmas Day—to escape the whims and obligations of others, not to be the charity case everybody felt sorry for.

Christmas had never been a big deal when her mom was alive. Mom worked at least some of the holiday shifts because the pay was so good. "We can celebrate whenever we want," she'd assured Alana. But this year, Alana felt different. She might have considered going home with Mary or to the Snyders' in Virginia, even. The reason she didn't was simple. She didn't have money to go anywhere. But she felt a longing in her heart not to be alone this time. Mom would tell her, "Alana, that's silly. Buck up! It's just two days out of the whole year. Big deal!"

Alana climbed the front stairs to her apartment in Astoria, a four-story brick building on a residential block. She unlocked the two outer door locks and walked into the vestibule, cringed at the usual broccoli and mystery-meat smell that poured out of Apartment 1. She climbed one flight to her apartment, unlocked her three locks, and opened the door.

Alana's heart always sank the moment she walked in. The space included a tiny sitting area to the left, occupied mostly by her roommate's dingy love seat. They were not friends but had matched on a housing website. A kitchenette with old, apartment-size appliances was to the right. The door faced into their bathroom, hardly big enough to turn around in. She couldn't get the floor or the grout around the bathtub clean, no matter how much bleach she used, so it always looked dirty and gross. Her mother would have been disgusted. Beyond the kitchenette/sitting area room were the two bedrooms, Alana's to the right. She walked in and threw her backpack down on her mattress and box spring that sat on her bedroom floor.

Alana had gone for a minimalist look for her room, or so she told herself. The comforter on her bed was gray. She had a few candles, dishes, and a green vase she'd never put a flower in, all from her favorite store, Aubergine. Her desk was always piled high and disorganized, papers overflowed onto the floor. There was never enough room. She always bumped into things, bruised her hip or her shin.

The apartment felt empty, in a good way. Jessica had left to go home to Michigan for the holidays. *Where did I tell Jessica I was going for Christmas?* Alana couldn't remember. She'd remind herself to be vague when Jessica got back in a few days.

Later, Alana sat on the dirty love seat and streamed *White Christmas*, the movie with Bing Crosby and Rosemary Clooney in it, Danny Kaye, too, that she and her cousins had watched every Christmas growing up. She and her mom had always gone to Aunt Jane's house, that is, until Uncle Jack died, and Aunt Jane moved to California to live near her daughter, Kristen. Kristen, her brother Tad, and Alana would go downstairs to their playroom to watch TV while the grown-ups lingered at the table.

Watching the movie now, Alana stood up to dance, like she and her cousins used to do, along with Danny Kaye in "Choreography" and of course for the finale, "White Christmas," when Bing Crosby and Rosemary Clooney get together.

After the movie was over, she ordered Chinese. She'd already decided to get Indian for Christmas Day. She spread her food on the small, square coffee table in front of the love seat and opened a bottle of a red cab blend Mary had been nice enough to give her. She poured herself a drink, then held up the glass. "To you, Mom!" she said.

Alana got her jasmine candle from her bedroom, lit it with a wooden match, and set it on the crate beside the sofa, just as if it were any other day. She settled back down on the love seat, wiggled into its cheap cushion. It was still too early to go to bed. She clicked on her social media account then surfed some more. She watched herself, pretended she didn't know what she was about to do. Like she'd never done it before. She hadn't for ages, truly, but after all, it was Christmas Eve.

She scrolled through and studied the latest posted photo of Marvin Peterson Sr. with his three sons—one with a wife, his daughter, and of course, that blonde wife of his, all gathered around their Thanksgiving dinner table. Alana studied the photo. She thought the new wife looked nice; she was prettier than Alana's mom. They were all dressed up and smiling. A nice-looking family.

"Thankful for our blessings," he'd written. Alana had read that Marvin and his wife lived in Charlotte, North Carolina (she knew he'd left Virginia right after the divorce), and he worked for a bank down there. She couldn't tell from his page exactly what he did, only that he obviously worked with money. *Cool. She could sure use some of that right now.* He played golf.

Alana pulled her hair up around the crown of her head and twisted it into the hair tie from her wrist. She poured another glass of wine, took a swig.

Her mom rarely talked about her dad, but every once in a while, she'd slip and drop a tantalizing detail. "Get your nose out of that book and go out and play," her mom had fussed at her. Then she added before she stopped herself, "Just like your father. Always had his nose in some goddamn book." Mom never understood that if Alana had a book, she had company. She never felt alone. And she had a safe new place to be.

Alana sipped her wine. "Do you still like to read?" she asked her dad's photo. *I wonder if we've read the same books. Did you read books to your sons and your daughter when they were growing up? At night, to help them fall asleep?*

Maybe it was the wine or the MSG, but tonight Alana pictured Marvin Peterson walking past the bookstore in his part of town. Charlotte was a pretty big city, she knew, even though she'd never been there. Charlotte would have at least one bookstore. Or maybe Marvin would be surfing the web. Would he prefer an e-book or print, as most older people did? Didn't matter. He'd just happen to see her book. He'd realize who Alana Peterson was. It was his last name after all.

And he would come looking for her. Maybe he would rethink some decisions he'd made. He and her mom had been in their senior year of college when they got the awful surprise her mom was pregnant. Alana knew Marvin was turning fifty this year. At fifty, you take stock. You read about that all the time. People evaluate their lives. Sometimes, they connect with people they've wronged to ask forgiveness. She imagined, when he first put it all together in front of that bookstore window, he'd be shocked. Then feel ashamed for what he'd done. But then pride would bloom like a flower. And also wonder. *I wonder where she is*, he'd think. *Where is my little girl now*?

She would never admit this to anyone, but she'd decided to forgive him. Now that Mom was gone, there was nothing to hold her back. All he'd have to do would be to write: "Dear Alana, It's Dad. I'm sorry." Just those few words were all it would take.

Alana felt suddenly exhausted. Must have been the wine. And stuffed from the cheap Chinese food. She shouldn't have eaten that last half of egg roll, but it had tasted so good going down. She looked around the apartment and sighed. *You won't be able to afford this much longer,* she told herself. She clicked off her dad's page, closed her computer. She'd launch the Messenger project soon, she hoped. The very second Messenger told her she could. That's how it was going to happen—how she was going to make a name for herself.

*Merry Christmas, Alana. You can go to bed now,* she told herself. Tomorrow was Christmas Day, and then it would all be over for another year. Only Messenger had suspected. Otherwise, it seemed she'd pulled it off again. *Great,* she thought, half-heartedly. Alana settled down in her bed for the night and allowed the one present she'd given herself every year since her mother had died to fill her. Her gift was hope (*Don't ask me how,* she mused) that next year, next Christmas, everything would be different.

# Alana's Notebook

## Transcript of interview with Scott

*Notes: Scott's message was probably the most dramatic of all the people who've posted so far. When he agreed to an interview, it was like a late Christmas present.*

*Alana: Thanks so much for your time.*

*Scott: Even though it all happened a few years back, it still sends chills through my body to remember her handing me that message out of the blue like that. I mean, I'm not sure (he paused and his eyes filled with tears) if I'd be here today if it hadn't been for her. It was an amazing gift.*

*Alana: How has it changed your life?*

*Scott: Well, as I just said, I'm still here. Still in the city, obviously. Still trying to make it day to day.*

*(long silence)*

*Alana: I have to ask, have you had any contact with your foster parents?*

*Scott: No.*

*Alana: I wondered, since gay marriage is legal, attitudes have changed.*

*Scott: No. Nothing's changed. Listen, can I ask you a favor? You say you're in touch with the woman? She calls herself Messenger, right?*

*Alana: Uh-huh.*

*Scott: Will you tell her I'm okay? Will you tell her thanks for me? And tell her I haven't thought about, you know, ending things, ever again. Not since I got my message.*

# SNOW DAY

S*now in the city is magical,* Alana thought. Somehow it buffers the noise into echoes, and all the nastiness is covered in white. Messenger and the Flower Lady had their spots, thresholds they could stand in, covered doorways they could huddle under, spaces between buildings, eaves where they could stay dry. That afternoon, Alana found them huddled together under the awning of an apartment building on Fifth Street. Alana had found them jammed in there, the Flower Lady's wheelchair against the wall, some of Messenger's bags in front of her wheels. They crumbled stale bread and coffee cake onto the sidewalk. A few dozen sparrows—chocolate with fawn markings—had gathered, ate, and hopped around as if tame. They looked almost pretty against all the white-covered sidewalks, their little footprints the only marks dotting the fallen snow. Alana shook herself off, startled them all away. Messenger and the Flower Lady looked up.

"Why don't you two go to Ed's and get out of this weather?"

"Oh no! It's wonderful!" Messenger held her hand out beyond the awning to catch snowflakes.

The Flower Lady giggled. "Don't you know it's good luck to be outside in the snow?" She raised her chin and took a deep breath. "Just smell it."

Messenger hummed. "I love it! Honey, today's a snow day. No school today!"

The Flower Lady squealed, "Wheeee! Snow day!"

They were having such a good time—like silly schoolgirls themselves. *That's one thing you can say about Messenger*, Alana thought. *Wherever she goes, she has fun.*

"Whose apartment is this?" she asked them.

"We don't know," the Flower Lady said. "Ostap manages the building, and he lets us sit here when the weather gets rough."

As if on cue, Ostap came around the corner, bundled up in a navy stocking cap. He carried two coffee cups and handed one to each. "Ladies," he said. "Compliments of Ed. Sorry," he muttered to Alana.

"Oh, I can get my own. No worries!"

"We're snug as a bug in a rug," Messenger said. "That's what my mama used to say when she tucked me into bed at night."

"Your mother?" Alana saw an opening and jumped right in. "And where was that exactly? Where did you live as a child?"

"Okay!" Messenger licked her chapped lips. "Want to know about my home raising? I'll tell you everything you need to know. Well, there was this nice young guy, had a real sweet, clear face. He walked down the street and carried this great big cardboard box, maybe to make a playhouse for his kids. I stopped him, and he jumped a mile! Scared! Of me!" She laughed. "Oh, I didn't mind. I felt sorry for him. Anyway, I held up my hands so he could see I wasn't packing. 'Where you going with that box?' I asked. The cardboard was so clean and smelled like a fresh sheet of paper.

"He looked stunned, caught in a split-second decision whether to speak or to just push past me. I knew he'd answer. He had that kind of face. 'Here! Take it. It's yours!' he said. Now, I wasn't expecting to hear that. He handed it over, then ran off."

Alana interrupted. "So how does this relate to your home raising?"

"Hold your horses, I'm getting to that. So, Shane, you met him and the hamster."

Alana sighed. "Breakfast."

"Yes, Breakfast. Shane came along and looked that box up and down. 'Where'd you get that? Are there any more? Can I have one?'" Messenger shook her head. "I let his eyes hold me a second too long, and I just handed it over. Can't help it. That's just the way I was raised. You share what you've got. It's that simple. Oh, honey, speaking of sharing, want some of this coffee? I got an extra cup here somewhere you could use."

"Yes! I'll give you some of mine too," the Flower Lady chimed in. She opened the coffee top and offered some to Alana. "It's real hot and real good."

"No. That's okay. You two drink yours. I'll go over to Ed's and get one."

"You sure?"

"Uh-huh. Thanks." Alana turned to head around the corner. She'd try to turn the conversation back to Messenger's past when she returned. "You will still be here when I get back, right?"

"I guess so," Messenger said.

"Because I do have some questions for you today."

Messenger and the Flower Lady burst into raucous laughter. "Why am I not surprised? Questions is your middle name! Okay, okay. We'll wait here for a while."

Alana walked back toward First Avenue, but there was a long line at Ed's. She waited, got coffee, and added some pastries for them, then hurried back around the corner and down the street.

"You have got to be kidding me!" she said out loud. The threshold was empty. The sparrows had returned, had made footprints all over, and there were fresh crumbs in the snow for them. But Messenger and the Flower Lady were gone. Why were there no wheelchair tire tracks in the snow, either way, on the sidewalks? Alana checked both sides of the street.

She stood in the doorway under the awning, furious with herself. *Why didn't you take their coffee and stay put? The snow was making Messenger sentimental, and she was talking about her childhood. Does snow do that to everyone?*

Alana thought back to her own snow days spent with her best friend, Sara Snyder, and Sara's older brothers. They'd pull their sleds down the street to a small park where all the kids in the neighborhood went. The steepest hill felt like an enormous mountain and stole your breath on the way down. They'd sled from early morning to lunch, when they'd go inside to eat grilled cheese sandwiches and drink hot chocolate Mrs. Snyder had made them. Then, they'd head back out.

Alana's mom would have to work, of course. Alana was that girl who always went to her friend's house, never the other way around. The only time she ever saw her mom on a snow day was when Alana collided with Tommy Rodchester midrun. Tommy's old-fashioned, wooden sled ran straight into her forehead and split it wide open. She still remembered how her shockingly bright red blood (it seemed like so much) soaked the white, clean snow. Tommy, usually a big bully, started to cry. Alana didn't know if it was because he'd hurt her, the sight of blood, or both.

"You're fine, Alana. You're just fine," her mom repeated in the emergency room. She'd come down from her job on Fourth East. She held Alana's hand while her daughter lay on the table under the light, and the doctor sewed her up. "Come on now. No fuss. Hold still. Just a few more stitches. You're fine."

But she wasn't fine. Blood wasn't fine. The emergency room wasn't fine. Stitches weren't fine. That was the first time she could remember getting the shakes.

Alana stomped the snow off her boots, and the little birds scattered again. She crossed the street, looking everywhere for Messenger. *I'd give anything to get one measly childhood anecdote like that from Messenger,* she thought. At least today she'd learned that Messenger had a mother she knew and could remember. Alana had trouble imagining Messenger as a child. The best she could manage was a smaller version of Messenger who walked the streets as she did now, a little adult who let nothing bother her or stand in her way. As usual, Alana's questions piled up. That Flower Lady was a trickster. It never failed. Whenever Alana found Messenger with her, she'd always distract her or steal her away.

Okay—a mother. Messenger didn't have to have a mother. Alana didn't have a dad, really. She took off her gloves and typed the following questions into her phone:

1. *Have you always lived in the city?*
2. *Where did you live as a child?*
3. *Did you ever go sledding? (*Alana knew many city kids who never had. Imagine!*)*
4. *When did the messages start? At what age? Were you scared?*
5. *Did you tell your mother about them or just hold it inside?*
6. *How long did it take you to act or to deliver your first message?*
7. *How old are you?*

Messenger could be really, really old. Or not. Once Alana came right out and asked her, but she'd dodged the question. Alana's guess was minimum of fifty. Maximum of seventy? Seventy-five? But Messenger got around so well—no cane for her. She didn't move fast, that's for sure, but Alana had found evidence that she'd delivered messages in all parts of the city. Of course, she could take the subway or buses to different places. Still, she walked a lot and was outside almost all the time. In fact, Alana had spent significantly more time outside since she'd met Messenger than in all the other years she'd been in the city combined.

She walked up and down half a dozen streets then headed back to Ed's to see if maybe they'd returned. No. Alana went into the bathroom, peed, and checked herself in the mirror. Snow was everywhere—her hair, scarf, shoulders—all over her coat. She thought she'd shaken most of it off before she'd come in. She frowned at herself in the mirror, then pulled all her hair back into a ponytail.

Ed looked up from brewing coffee.

"Have you seen her?" she asked him.

"You look cold," Ed said. "I thought they were waiting for you on Fifth."

"Yeah. So did I. They left while I was in here. I've been looking ever since."

"Want to stay?"

Alana's head popped up from brushing off more snow.

Ed actually made eye contact. "To warm up," he added, then looked away.

"I'd like to." She smiled. "But I can't. I've got to get to work by five. Guess I'll just search until then."

"Good luck." Ed shrugged. "You know, she doesn't mean anything by it. It's just the way Messenger is."

"I know. Thanks, Ed." She put her gloves back on, left the warmth of the coffee shop, and trudged back out into the snow.

# Messenger's Composition Book

## ELEVEN PORTALS

1. *Mind is a portal.*
2. *Heart is a portal.*
3. *Body is a portal.*
4. *Silence is a portal.*
5. *Wonder is a portal.*
6. *Sound is a portal.*
7. *Pain is a portal.*
8. *Fear is a portal.*
9. *Gratitude is a portal.*
10. *Love is a portal.*
11. *Death is a portal.*

# Post: Carmen

"No," the minister told me. "I'm sorry, I can't marry you. I want to, but the bishop won't let me."

Okay. What now? I mean, tears were streaming down my cheeks, and I wanted to full-on sob but had to hold it together. I slammed the door to the church as I left, but it didn't help. You know, Shere and I were trying to do the right thing, and where did that get us? Shit out of luck, as always. I wandered down the street; this tirade against all of them fumed and seethed inside me.

The worst part was, I didn't know how I was going to break it to Shere. We'd already had so many disappointments in this department. This was the tenth minister we'd asked! I hated to disappoint her. Being married in a church by a minister of her own denomination was so important to her.

I was still fuming. When I got to the front of the coffee line, I ordered, but something made me turn around. There she stood, right behind me. I was so lost in my own rage I hadn't paid attention. She looked ancient. My eyes flew down to her poor, swollen feet overflowing her shoes. I gazed into her light brown eyes. She reached out and handed me a coffee sleeve with writing on it.

"Better take it," the guy behind the bar advised. I noticed we were suddenly the only ones in there. Anger drained out, and I was spooked. Was this a setup? Were they working together? For what?

"Don't be afraid," she told me.

The writing on the sleeve said **YOU GOT THIS**.

I ran out of that coffee shop and down the street. I needed time to just stop a minute, an hour, a day, so I could figure it out. Time to ponder this crazy coincidence. Because believe it or not, my mother used to tell me, "You got this," all the time. All my life. I miss her so much. Mom always had my back, the way I try to have Shere's. Mom had been so wonderful when Shere and I told her we wanted to get married. When I read those words on the coffee sleeve, I could hear Mom's voice, telling me, "You got this," loud and clear. Even though she's been dead for three years.

# Messenger's Composition Book

*PLACES: Incorporate as many of these elements into your life as possible:*
*sun*
*moon*
*water—moving is best*
*churches—usually best when no one else is there but you*
*campfires or bonfires*
*mountains*
*the ground beneath trees*
*wooden docks*
*sunlight shining on water, making diamonds*
*breezes through trees, leaves*
*sand*
*stones*
*waterfalls*
*crunch of crisp leaves*
*snow*

*Like each season, change usually happens in a very insignificant way. A tiny wave, a twitch, an impulse, a shift. Sooner than later, everything changes because of the immense and intricate ways we're connected. Connection is everything. That tiny impulse or thought creates a ripple, a wave that washes over everyone on the planet and beyond to the universe. All connected. The connection is what makes it real. And baby, that's what true magic really is.*

# ALANA HEADS TO AUBERGINE

Alana tried her best to follow her resolution: let Messenger take the lead. “Relax. Do less. Let it flow. Wait until the timing is right,” Messenger had told her. But following Messenger’s advice was easier said than done. Doubts crept in, overpowering Alana’s good intentions. She knew she had nobody to depend on but herself to pull this off. Could she? She wasn’t so sure anymore. The surge of adrenaline wasn’t pumping like it had at the beginning. Yes, she was getting new posts every day, testimonies to Messenger and the changes her messages had made. Fifty or so views a day wasn’t bad. But Alana knew you had to stay ahead of your story, keep the buzz going, and create more. She knew time was running out just as fast as her money. Plus, something felt wrong. She couldn’t put her finger on it, but she sensed in her body the need for alertness at all times, a knowing that something was about to happen. No doubt all the strange coincidences—the vivid dreams and then the sightings of people from them, the CLINAMN license turning up—all put her on edge.

Riding the train in on a clear, raw morning, Alana felt all her worries clutch her gut and refuse to let go. But then she realized, *Wait—I know what to do! Aubergine! Here I come!* Her heart lifted the minute she’d made up her mind. She would listen to Messenger and take a break. She’d go somewhere beautiful and peaceful, the one place where she could always catch her breath, forget about everything, and feed her senses. Alana had always loved the woods behind her house growing up. She and Sara Snyder had spent many hours there exploring, building forts, climbing trees. Aubergine had somehow created that same natural vibe, even though it was a store. There, Alana always experienced the connection Messenger talked about, the flow.

So instead of heading downtown as usual to search for Messenger, Alana took the W train uptown, then walked a few blocks past dirty snow piles. She entered through the double doors. Immediately, her gut let go, and all her stress evaporated. Because here, it was spring! At Aubergine, they were always one season ahead. Heaven! Alana stood still and breathed, took in the sights, all the natural elements—wood, plants, the beautiful light pouring down from everywhere. She noted every wonderful smell—patchouli, lemon, orange, vanilla, jasmine, rose. Felt the energy of beauty and light. Creativity.

She immediately discovered their new spring theme—the sea! She took her time, wound her way through the different vignettes the designers had created. Crystalline barnacles, white-tinged with peach and pink, grew unexpectedly from most of the flat surfaces—a table, a trunk, the tops of shelves of crockery. Specimens of starfish, sand dollars, and anemones stood at attention under glass cloches on the apothecary table. A huge mast with tie-dyed sails rose up out of the dining table and reached for the ceiling. Alana could almost feel the soft sea breezes flutter in and out of them. Sea-salt crystals filled bowls and glasses and added the smell of the ocean to the scene before her. She looked up, couldn't believe they'd actually hung a huge stuffed whale created from sailcloth painted every imaginable shade of blue from the high ceiling.

The staff allowed you to linger as long as you wanted. No pressure. Alana never bought much. A mug from the home department or a tin of Red Rose Salve for her chapped lips and sore cuticles was all she could ever afford with her sad budget. But that was fine. It was enough to remind her of this magical place and brought a little color to her apartment. Any little touch made a big difference to Alana. Her mother had never done much with their house back home. How could she have? She was always working.

Alana sat down in one of the dining chairs and breathed in, relaxed her shoulders and back. *What am I really looking for from The Messenger Project?* she asked herself. Her eyes rested on the aqua wine stems before her, each filled with sea salt. When she grew quiet like this, she sometimes did get an answer. *Meaning.* As corny and millennial as that sounded, it was true. That's what had reeled her into getting involved with Messenger. Alana had recognized that Messenger's work meant something. It made a difference.

Alana noticed one of the young merchandizers she'd seen there before scurrying around, trying to push a table obviously too heavy for her across the floor. She was small, wore an oversize turquoise T-shirt tucked into just the front of her black jeans. Alana envied her gorgeous, curly dark hair. The young woman surveyed the shelf she was filling, her head tilted slightly to the right, as an artist would gaze at her canvas. She arranged new products, organized them by color, size, texture. All the same ones lined up and in neat rows. That's what Alana loved so much about this place. Artistry but order. Patterns. Patterns everywhere. Everything connected to something else.

Alana got up from the chair and wandered around some more. She slowed down enough to look at every single item and touch many of them. About a half-hour later, she finally turned to go. There was nothing, no matter how small, that she could afford. But it didn't matter. She had drunk it all in, felt refreshed, like she'd taken a vacation. Alana headed down the long flight of marble stairs to the lower level, breathed it all in one last time.

She walked out the door and down the street, down some more stairs to the Rockefeller Center concourse to get a coffee. Something made her glance over at the crowds of people sitting at tables, crammed into small spaces near the entrance to the skating rink. Alana froze, then felt the dizzy vertigo that was becoming familiar, when two worlds collided. She couldn't trust the ground beneath her feet. Jackie? Here?

Jackie, Messenger's friend, the one who didn't like her, sat alone at one of the square tables. She wore both her cat-eye glasses on her face and a pair of brown plastic sunglasses perched on her head. Newspapers were piled high on the table, and her plastic gloves were black from the newsprint. In one hand, Jackie held a big pair of pointed scissors that could double as a knife, in the other, a large, round magnifying glass. She stared at what she was reading, her eyes wide, eyebrows raised.

Alana watched, deciding whether to speak.

Jackie took a swig of the two-liter plastic bottle of cola beside her, anchoring one of the newspaper piles neatly in place, then looked up in Alana's direction, her eyes magnified by the glasses. She laid the scissors down. "Hey, sugar!" She waved. "Come on over here! Is Messenger with you?"

Alana slowly inched over to her table. *She's in a good mood,* Alana thought. "No—I'm alone. What are you doing here?"

"I come here a lot to get my work done. It's a good place to spread out and think. How 'bout you?"

"Oh, I just love this store nearby."

"Sit down a minute, take a load off." Jackie gracefully motioned to the chair beside her, twisted her wrist as if doing an arabesque.

Alana paused. *Maybe Jackie will tell me something.* She slowly sat.

"How's your work coming? I know you and Messenger have been working mighty hard. You're writing about her, right?"

"Yeah! I think it's going to be a book."

Jackie leaned forward. "Messenger might have mentioned something about that."

*Maybe Messenger told her to be nice to me,* Alana reasoned. *Hopefully she didn't warn Jackie not to talk.*

"Everything still a go? You and Messenger still working on it together?"

"Oh yes. Today I'm just taking a little break. I find her downtown just about every day. It's slow going, but I'm learning much more about her and her process. And you won't believe how many posts I've gotten from people who've received messages."

Jackie smiled broadly, but it looked more like a grimace. "That's wonderful! How many people have written you so far?"

"Right now, one hundred and four."

"A hundred!" Jackie held onto the table with both gloved hands.

"And four." Blood rushed to Alana's face, and all her doubts raced back. "Maybe that doesn't sound like a whole lot, but it's a start."

"No. You two have been working mighty hard. A hundred is quite a few. A hundred is plenty. The word is spreading, thanks to you."

Alana nodded. "Some posts are really amazing, some not so much. But they're varied, and they keep coming in. Seems like Messenger's been delivering messages for a long time."

"Tell me more, sugar!"

This new Jackie seemed interested and enthusiastic about the project. Messenger had obviously talked with her about it. *Maybe Jackie can help me convince Messenger*, Alana thought. What did she have to lose? "Things are going well, and I really think this project has a lot of potential. But my problem is this: Messenger keeps telling me to wait. I've built a really good website, with just enough of my research, interviews, and posts to create interest in the book. It's totally ready to go, but she tells me to hold off launching it, even though I know I'm losing valuable momentum. I'm trying to be patient, but it's hard. If I could only post it, I could continue to build on this growing interest in her and later launch the book."

"So you're just waiting for Messenger to give the go-ahead?"

"Yes, that's right. Except I still have major holes in my research about her. I've got to include some of her backstory, but Messenger won't reveal anything about her past. Where she's from, her family—nothing. Some people question whether she's even a real person, so I have to get some more concrete information for the book. So ..." She paused and noticed how quiet Jackie had grown. But she'd gone this far—might as well go for it. "How long have you two been friends? Can you tell me anything about her past? Any little fact or detail would really help."

Jackie pushed her glasses up her nose. "There's something you need to know about Messenger."

Alana's heart soared. Was she meant to run into Jackie today?

Jackie scanned the concourse, then drew herself up to her full height. "Messenger's playing with fire. A very dangerous game, indeed!" Her voice was low but fierce, and her eyes darted here and there.

"What do you mean?" Alana asked, confused by her sudden mood change.

"Somebody's gonna get burned. A lot of somebodies."

A chill ran through Alana, a stab of danger. She knew she'd said too much and shouldn't say any more. What danger was Jackie talking about? Danger to whom? *Is this danger what I've been sensing?*

Jackie picked up her magnifying glass and furiously flipped through the newspaper pages.

*What was she looking for?* Alana didn't dare ask any more questions.

## MESSENGER'S QUESTION

The next day was steely gray and bone-chillingly cold. Alana hurried into Ed's and waved to him but skipped the long drink line. She found Messenger perched on her stool at the table.

"Whew! I about froze getting here." Alana pulled off her hat and gloves and stuffed them into her coat pocket.

"Tell me about it!" Messenger gave Alana a big hug. "No coffee?"

"I'll get some later. Line's too long."

Messenger's eyes sparkled. "Oh, I bet Ed would let you cut." She winked.

"Messenger! Ed and I are just friends."

"Well, Ed's a good friend for you to have. But don't think I don't see the flowers and hearts and things he makes for you in your coffee."

Alana couldn't keep a smile from spreading across her face. "Yeah. It's sweet. But listen, I have something to tell you," she said. "You won't believe who I saw yesterday!"

"Who?"

"Jackie!"

Messenger carefully set her coffee down on the table. "You did?"

"Yep! I was uptown shopping and found Jackie at a table in the concourse, with her scissors and all her newspapers piled around her. She has to read with this huge magnifying glass. Listen, is she blind?"

"Hardly."

Alana noticed Messenger looked tired around her eyes. "We had a nice conversation."

Messenger sat very still and stared straight ahead. "About what?" she asked.

"Oh, this and that. She wanted to know how my work is going, you know, with the story. She is so sweet. She seemed so interested in our project." Alana knew she was baiting Messenger, but she didn't care. Maybe she could use this.

"She's sweet, all right." Messenger settled herself on the stool, both feet planted firmly on the floor. She picked up her cup and sipped even more slowly than usual. She put the coffee down, turned, and locked eyes with Alana.

Even though it made her uncomfortable, Alana found, try as she might, she couldn't look away.

"What did you tell her, honey?"

# LAY LOW

Bright and early the next morning, Messenger spread herself and her things out on the bench beside the asphalt playground on Fifth Street. She closed her eyes, happy that the air wasn't so cold today. She hadn't even seen her breath walking over. She calmed her heart, felt it balanced on her diaphragm, with each breath in and out, a little massage, a pat to her sweet heart.

She was not surprised to hear someone clip, clip, clipping down the sidewalk toward her. Messenger didn't open her eyes. "I've been expecting you. Had no doubt you'd turn up. Like a bad penny."

"You better believe it!" Jackie plopped down and Messenger scooted over to give her more room. "Well, I hope you're happy. What a mess! You've really gone and done it now."

Messenger slowly opened her eyes but stared straight ahead. "Done what?"

"You know what!" She shoved her glasses back up her nose. "But I'll be happy to remind you how you've made one mistake after another. Uh-huh. One after another. You got too involved with this girl. Too close. You know that's not allowed. The first rule is—"

Messenger turned to face Jackie. "I'm tired of rules."

"Not only does that girl intend to write a book about the messages—it's worse! Do you know what she's planning to do at any minute? Go public with this website she's made *all about you*! Everything's going to blow up in your face. And you know what'll happen then."

"Oh yes." Messenger was so tired. One-hundred-years tired. "I know."

"Well, stop it all right now before it's too late."

"Shhhh."

They both watched the lady with her Chihuahuas amble up, frown at them, then walk by.

Messenger shivered. "Is she a Watcher?"

"You know I'm not supposed to tell you who they are!"

"Calm down. We all know who they are, even if we're not supposed to."

Jackie chuckled but immediately straightened her face. "Don't try and get me off subject. This is serious."

"I know it's serious," Messenger said, her voice sad. "It's almost time."

"Thanks to you! You could have stopped it all when I told you to. You could have let this girl go and found another one. But no. You're just so stubborn." She narrowed her eyes at Messenger.

Messenger stuck out her tongue.

They laughed.

"Never could follow rules," Messenger said quietly. "Humph. One rule I did follow—I wish to God I hadn't."

"You mean leaving your daughter?"

Messenger nodded.

"Leaving her and your family was for your—and for their—protection. It's the same reason you're not supposed to know who your Watchers are—except for me. Our work has always been dangerous. Besides, we've all made sacrifices."

"No. Not like that." Each word shot from her mouth like a bullet.

Jackie touched her arm. They sat in silence while a couple pushed a stroller with a dark-eyed baby in it. The baby smiled up at them, waved with her hands and feet. They talked baby talk to her until the mother moved on.

"My daughter's her age now," Messenger said, watched the mother's back.

Jackie paused. "Oh—you mean that Alana? And you've had no contact with your own daughter … ."

Messenger turned. "No. That's one rule I did obey."

"And that's been a terrible burden to bear. But why are you doing this now? Breaking all our rules? Trying to upend everything? Why do you insist on your own way? You know the danger you've put yourself and the girl in."

"Oh, Jackie, it's all part of it. Can't you feel it? The change is coming quick now. The swerve. The Clinamen. It's too late for the old ways. We can't keep doing like we've been doing. We need everybody working on this together. Not just us. We've got to come out in the open. We've got to let folks know they're not alone."

Jackie snorted. "Your memory must be failing you, old woman! You know what folks do to us the second they get an inkling of our aim? Or whenever too much light gets released too fast? Do I need to remind you what they've always done before?"

"No. I haven't forgotten."

"They'll do it to you. Sure as I'm sitting here!" She drew herself up to her full height, the same way she had with Alana in the concourse, but her voice was sad. "That dark energy is building."

"I know. I'm ready for it."

"You sure about that?"

"Uh-huh. Just give me some time, okay? Will you do that for me?"

"Too late. The Guardian Watchers sent me to tell you this: they've ordered all Watchers to withdraw your protection because your actions have put us and our work in danger. They order you to stop seeing the girl. Stop delivering messages. Leave the city."

"Oh," was all Messenger could say. She leaned back against the bench, as if all the air had been punched out of her.

Jackie shook her head and chuckled.

Messenger turned.

"I have to hand it to you, though, Messenger. You did it! You've created a swerve, all right." She wrapped her coat tighter around her and dropped her voice to a whisper. "You're not the only one tired of following the rules! What the Guardian Watchers don't know is—I'm not obeying them! Neither are any of your neighborhood Watchers. We're all staying the course. Holding our posts for you. We'll do everything we can to keep you safe."

Messenger's face shone. She took Jackie's outstretched hands. "Thanks. I thank you."

"Why would we stop protecting you after all this time? Humph." She crossed her arms and pumped them against her chest. "Those Guardians keep making more and more rules for us because they're afraid of losing their control. Well, that's just too bad. Listen, here's my idea. For now, we need to slow things down for everyone's sake. You need to lay low. Make yourself scarce. Make the Guardian Watchers think you're obeying them. Stop seeing the girl and stop delivering messages. Just for a while. Then we can figure out our next step."

"This might actually work for the good," Messenger said. "Alana's not ready yet. She still needs to build her confidence and learn to trust more."

Jackie snorted. "That's the least of your worries. Forget about the girl and focus on what I'm telling you! You've started something here with all of us. A revolt! None of us wants to stand by and watch anything bad happen to you. We've been at this together for way too long."

"We have, haven't we? But," she stared into Jackie's eyes, "the end's coming for me. I know what my next step will be. I'll miss you. Miss all this. I'm going to miss her too. There—I said it. Broke another rule."

"You broke lots and lots with her. Let's just hope she doesn't do something stupid and post that website. That could really ruin my plan. No telling what might happen then. Besides, the Guardians would go ballistic!"

"She promised me she wouldn't. Guess we'll just have to wait and see how it all unfolds."

Jackie grabbed both of Messenger's arms. "So will you please do what I say, for once? Lay low for a while—and we'll all work with your swerve. What do you call it again?"

"Clinamen."

"Yeah. Whatever. Ostap's already found a place for you. Come on." Jackie stood up and grabbed two of Messenger's bags. "We're going there right now."

## Messenger's Composition Book

### Let Go

*Let me tell you something. When the time comes, let go. A life needs air to burn brightly and well. That's what feeds it—space. Air. Pile too much on, jam too much in—you'll smother it. You can smother a life—like you smother a child or a fire. It's tempting for all of us. Instead, let it be. Only add something once in a blue moon. Just feed the spark of life. That's all it takes. Taking away is better. Want somebody to look at you like you're flat-out insane? Tell them, "I have enough." That'll blow them away. To another planet, even. Try it and just watch. Yes! Know when to let go. That's what it's time for me to do.*

# MESSENGER IS MISSING

The next three days in a row, Alana searched but couldn't find Messenger anywhere. The weather matched her mood—day after day of cloudy low pressure, a constant threat of rain. Winter would not let go.

Alana tried to remain calm. *You're going with the flow, letting Messenger be Messenger, remember?* This wasn't the first time a few days had passed without her finding Messenger. Messenger would probably turn up when Alana least expected it and laugh at her for being worried. But just in case, she checked back in with Ed every day for reassurance.

On day four, after making her rounds and looking through the neighborhood, Alana smiled when she got to Ed's and saw that business was light. He'd have time to talk.

"No Messenger?" Ed asked.

"Nope."

"She hasn't been here either."

Alana sighed. "Coffee, please." She unbuttoned her coat and sat on the stool at the end of the counter. "What's the longest you remember she's ever gone missing?"

"Oh, probably a week, I guess." Ed handed Alana a coffee then turned to fill the grinder with beans. "Must be hard to keep moving forward with your project the way she comes and goes."

Alana narrowed her eyes. "This isn't about the project. Should I be worried?"

"I don't think so. I just know she always comes back. Did you ask the Flower Lady today?"

Alana tried to focus on the wonderful smell of brewing coffee. "Yes! I've talked with everybody every single day she's been gone. The Flower Lady, Ostap, the Professor, Shane—even the lady with the Chihuahuas."

"Did she answer you?" Ed asked.

"Are you kidding?"

Ed laughed. "What about Jackie?" he asked.

"Nope. Haven't seen her."

"Maybe they're together."

"Maybe." Alana sipped her coffee, paused, then added, "I'm probably overreacting, but I haven't told you about something weird that happened last week. I saw Jackie in the Rockefeller Center concourse."

Ed looked up from wiping down the counter. "All the way up there?"

"Yeah. She was being unusually nice to me about the project, asked me a lot of questions, but then she turned dark."

"Jackie's like that. Hot and cold. She can turn on a dime."

"No, it's more than that. She warned me that Messenger was playing with fire. That's how she put it. Messenger was in danger, 'was going to get burned.' What do you think she meant?"

"Beats me. Jackie is ... Jackie." He shrugged.

Alana finished her coffee and slid off the stool. "You think I'm worrying about nothing?"

"Give it more time. I bet she's back here tomorrow."

Alana sighed. "I hope so! It's just, if something happened to Messenger, I don't know what I'd do!" She buttoned her coat and headed back out the door to keep looking for Messenger.

By day seven, a whole week of combing the streets, searching in all their usual spots, asking and asking if anybody had seen Messenger, Alana had chewed her cuticles to shreds.

"Listen, Ed. I'm getting worried, aren't you?"

"Not yet. She'll turn up."

Today, Ed's words did not reassure her. She suspected Ed was the kind of person who even if he were worried would be slow to admit it. Alana took a breath before answering, so she wouldn't snap. "It's weird that she and Jackie are both suddenly missing. Something may have happened to them. Don't you think we should call the police?"

"What exactly would you tell them?" Ed asked.

Alana bristled at Ed's always calm voice. "That Messenger's missing, of course. Jackie too."

"Messenger? Do you know her real name?"

Alana's heart dropped. "No. I don't."

"Me neither."

"I see what you mean. But maybe we could give them a detailed description. They could at least keep an eye out."

Ed stopped washing dishes and focused on their conversation. "Don't go to the police yet. Tell you what … when I get off later, I'll go out and help you look, okay?"

Alana relaxed slightly. "That would be great, but I have to be at work early today."

"Okay. I'll go out myself."

"Will you text me if you find her?"

"Sure."

"Okay. Great. Well, I guess I better give you my number."

Ed fished his phone out of his back pocket.

They exchanged numbers as if it were the most natural thing in the world, but it felt intimate, somehow, having Ed's cell phone number in her phone. It also felt good to worry with somebody else, even if Ed wouldn't admit he was worried. Alana most definitely considered calling in sick so she could stay with Ed, wait for him to get off so they could search for Messenger together. She would have done it, too, if she'd had any cash to spare.

# Alana's Notebook

*I don't know what to do. It's day nine, and Messenger's still missing. I never heard back from Ed, so I assume he didn't find her either. He was sweet to go looking. He tells me not to worry, not to go to the police, to wait, but I sense even Ed is getting worried. Jackie's strange warning and the fact that she's missing, too, haunts me. What did she mean? That's the first thing on my list to ask Messenger when she comes back. Is Jackie's warning a part of this cloud that follows me around all the time, this sense of dread I don't understand but can't shake? I wake up exhausted every morning from nights full of dreams, mostly bad ones. Every nerve in my body feels like something bad's about to happen. Has it already happened? To Messenger? Please, no!*

*Of course, the project is on hold until we find her. I was going to ask if she'd agree to let me post, not the whole website but just a few paragraphs and a photo of us together—to prove she's real and I'm not just making all this up. That'll have to wait. But waiting's getting harder and harder. I know I promised Messenger I'd wait until she gives me the go-ahead, but I can only take so much. When she agreed to work with me on this project, I thought that meant I could count on her—that she'd stick around. And she has, up to now. But since she's disappeared, I'm out here twisting on a limb. I can't trust someone who just leaves.*

*I'm so close! All I need is just a little more information and Messenger's go-ahead. It would be so easy. If I could post the website, then write a query, I know I could land an agent who'd sell the book. Not to mention get me at least a little advance to live on. Because my financial disaster is definitely not on hold. If only. The only things keeping me off the streets are my credit limit, a little bit of Mom's money I've held back for rent, and my job at Tale of the Whale. I never thought I'd be that person. How long am I going to have the luxury to wait on Messenger?*

# MESSENGER'S GONE

Day ten. Messenger was still gone. Alana had passed from concern to worry to cold panic—not only about Messenger's safety but also about the project. On day eleven, Alana had gone to the police station on Fifth Street, tried to fill out a missing person report but ended up leaving most of it blank. She didn't know the answers to most of the questions (Name? Address? Next of Kin?). That experience only added to Alana's realization of how little she knew about the details of Messenger's life. The officer was nice, listened to everything she told him about Messenger and Jackie. "How can two women just disappear?" she'd asked him. He smiled and told her, "I'm sorry to say, ma'am, it happens all the time. And I have to ask you, have you considered this? Maybe they don't want to be found."

On day twelve, Ed agreed to help Alana go door-to-door on First Avenue, Fifth Street, and all around the neighborhood to ask the store owners to post flyers in their windows. When Ed's shift was over, they left together. Alana suddenly realized how seldom she'd seen Ed anywhere but his coffee shop. She couldn't help glancing at him, over and over, as they walked. It was the same feeling she remembered having whenever she'd see one of her elementary school teachers outside of school.

They headed down First Avenue. Alana held her flyers that asked anybody seeing Messenger to text or call. She'd included the terrible photo Marty took of Messenger, though she really didn't think it would help. She regretted she'd never talked Messenger into letting her take a better one.

"Thanks for helping me with these," Alana said to Ed. "Do you think it'll make a difference?"

"Hopefully," Ed answered.

"I also posted a similar one on my blog. At least it's something we can do."

Despite her worry, Alana fell into a comfortable pace walking with Ed. People poured past them on both sides. Alana kept her eyes peeled for that telltale smudge of red—Messenger's cap. But it was nowhere to be seen. As silly as it sounded, Alana had felt they'd crossed some threshold just having Ed's cell phone number in her phone. But she also realized how little she knew about him. "Do you live around here, Ed?"

"Yeah. Over on Fifth Street. One of the buildings Ostap manages. He gives me a really good deal because I help him out with repairs and some of his super duties."

"Wow! Nice."

"Makes it easy for work. It's amazingly small, but I don't have much. You?"

"Astoria. It's cheap! That's about all I can say."

"Yeah. Guess we should get started handing out the flyers," he said.

"Okay. Do you think they'll post them?"

Ed nodded. "Most of the owners around here are nice about that kind of thing."

"Good. Ed, I'm really worried."

"Well, Messenger's nothing if not mysterious, with the messages and everything. Unpredictable. Remember when she found that word 'Clinamen' and got so excited?"

"Yeah, I know. Right?" Alana actually considered telling Ed she'd seen the CLINAMN license plate too. She wanted to but didn't. Ed might think she was out-there, too, like Messenger.

They decided to walk up First Avenue all the way to Houston and then work their way back. When they got to Houston, Ed said, "I guess it's more efficient if we split up."

Alana's heart sank. "Yeah. Sure. You're right." She actually needed to hurry in order to get to Tale of the Whale in time for her shift. But there was a moment when she was handing Ed a stack of flyers. Ed took the stack in his right hand, but when she went to hand him the tape, he tried to take it with the same hand and fumbled. The tape fell to the street, and he grabbed her hand instead.

"Oops, sorry," she said, but she didn't let go until he did.

Ed picked up the tape and dropped it into his jacket pocket. He put the flyers under his arm. "Good luck," he said. He hesitated; he didn't seem to want to split up either. "If I have any news, I'll text you."

"Okay. Thanks again, Ed. Let's stay in touch." Then she added, "About Messenger, I mean."

"Okay. Will do. And try not to worry."

"You too."

He raised his hand in a wave and headed down the street.

***

The morning of day fourteen, Alana trudged down First Avenue. Rain poured in torrents, wind blew up underneath her umbrella, turning it inside out, so by the time she burst through Ed's door, she was soaked.

But things were only going to get worse. The moment she'd dreaded but knew would come finally arrived. Alana ordered a coffee and noticed Ed paused after he'd swiped her card.

Ed handed her card back and blushed. "Uh, on me today."

"Ed?" Her throat tightened.

Ed turned and poured her coffee. "Here," he said.

"Really, Ed. You don't have to ... ."

He shook his head. "No. It's fine. Uh—sorry, but you need to know. Your card was declined." He told her with the perfect combination of firmness and gentleness.

"Thanks. Must be a mistake," she sputtered. Sweat formed on the back of her neck. "I'll have to call the bank."

"Hey, I understand." Ed sighed. "Believe me! Don't worry about it."

"Ed—this is embarrassing to ask, but has it ever happened before?"

Ed turned toward the next customer in line. "Third time," he murmured.

Anxiety about Messenger's disappearance mixed with her embarrassment and dread. What was she going to do—about all of it? Alana took the coffee and ducked out of the shop as fast as she could.

***

The next day, day fifteen, still no Messenger. No news about her from the flyers or the blog. Alana had dug some ones and change out of her desk drawer and paid for her coffee in cash. She was grateful to know she could eat at Gus's before her evening shift. When she got to the coffee shop to check in, Ed wasn't too busy and had time to talk.

"But Ed, what if Messenger can't get back to us because she's hurt. Or worse? Maybe we should call all the hospitals. Do you think they'd give me information about her if I'm not a family member? All I can figure is something terrible has happened. What if she's gone for good? What if she doesn't come back?"

"I don't think she's gone for good." Ed paused, then added, "I think there must be a reason. Look, back when I first quit drinking ..."

Alana's face flushed at this revelation. *Her knowing about Ed had been right!*

"I worked as a barista here for the former manager. You might have seen him here before. Older guy. He comes in sometimes."

Alana thought she knew exactly whom Ed was talking about.

"I'd see Messenger on the street, and I told her to come in for coffee."

"Did she give you a message?" Alana interrupted.

"Nope. No message. But as we got to know each other, there was something different about her I came to recognize. Like a force field or something. Know what I mean?"

Alana stared at Ed as if she were seeing him for the first time. She nodded. She knew exactly. "Oh, Ed."

"Anyway, I got to believe she's okay, wherever she is. And if she's gone away, she has a good reason."

"Like what?"

"Beats me." He smiled and turned back to his dishes. "Besides, if she was leaving, really leaving, she'd tell us goodbye."

On her way to work, Alana called Mary. She knew, unless Mary was in a meeting, she'd immediately pick up. "Hey, can you talk?" Alana asked.

"Sure. What's up?"

"It's Messenger. She's gone."

"Gone? You mean … ."

"No! Not dead. At least I hope not." Alana shivered. The wind blasted her between buildings. "She's disappeared, and we can't find her anywhere." Tears filled Alana's eyes.

"How long has she been gone?"

"Fifteen days!"

"Oh no!"

"Yeah. We've done everything we can to find her. I even put up flyers."

"Well, hopefully she'll come back. Alana, did you listen to me and go easier on her?"

"Yes, I did. I really did. I've never been so patient in my life. And look where it's gotten me. Are you saying I scared her off?"

"Chill. No. I know you're upset. What about your project?"

"I don't know."

"Didn't you tell me you had a website ready to go? Couldn't you go ahead and launch it? Maybe that would bring you some clues about where she's gone. If she's still delivering messages and all."

"She said not to. To wait."

"But she's gone, right?"

Alana's mind sprang into action at Mary's suggestion, playing out different scenarios if she were to post.

"Think about it," Mary continued. "At least you could get something out of all this work. Just an idea. Listen. I've been meaning to check back with you. How's it going with your ... you know, your money situation."

"It's just fine," Alana lied. "I took on some more shifts at the restaurant."

"If you need a little help ... ." Mary's voice was soft and gentle.

"I know. No. Thanks."

"Think about it. Sorry, but I've got to go."

***

On day sixteen, Alana sat at the end of the counter at Ed's, waiting for him to finish serving the line. As far as she could tell, Messenger was gone, and she wasn't coming back. Period. But where was she? She had to be somewhere. They'd heard nothing from the police, the hospitals, the flyers, nobody in the neighborhood. Nobody. Alana just couldn't believe Messenger would choose not to be in touch with them, as Ed had suggested the day before, for any reason. What reason could justify that? A tightness gripped her chest. *Oh well, Alana. What did you expect?* a voice inside her scolded. *Everybody leaves you in the end.*

After Ed tried once again to reassure her, Alana snapped, "But what if you're wrong, Ed? And why are you defending her? You don't know anything about her. None of us do, really." Alana looked harder at him. "Unless you do, and you're not telling me. Is that what this is about?" Frustration and anger rose up and choked her. "Was all this part of the plan? Did she tell you to let me down easy? She couldn't break it to me herself, so she got you to do it?"

"No!" Ed interrupted. "That's not it at all."

Alana wouldn't give Ed the satisfaction of looking at him.

"Listen to me," he continued. "I'm worried, okay? She's like a mother to me too. I'm used to her checking in with me every day."

"What do you mean?"

Now Ed stared down at the counter. "She's been working with me on ... a project too."

"What kind of project?" Her voice was sharp.

"There are things you don't understand."

"Then tell me, Ed."

He looked up. "Ugh! You sound just like my wife!"

"Your what?" Alana's unbelieving eyes searched Ed's.

"Ex! Ex-wife. A long time ago. I'm sorry, but I can't tell you any more about Messenger."

Alana stared. *I know nothing about him.* "Why can't you?"

"I promised Messenger."

*Why does it feel like I'm fighting with my boyfriend?* "That's not good enough," she snapped. "I'm done!"

"Wait! Alana!"

Even angry and storming out of the coffee shop, a part of Alana registered Ed had called her by her name for the first time. She ignored it, slammed the door, and stomped down First Avenue, headed to the train. *What a fool you are! They've all been working against you from the start.* She never lifted her broken umbrella, just let the downpour soak her to the skin.

*A wife? A wife! Who drops something like that, just out of the blue? What other secrets has Ed been hiding?* She fumed. Alana had no idea, really, what was going on between Ed and her. Was it just a love of Messenger that they shared? Or more? But Alana knew one thing. She needed to find out a whole lot more about him, about his ex-wife, for starters, before they went any further.

Alana looked up ahead on First Avenue and spied Jackie's cheetah-print booties. She flew, dodging people as best she could.

"Jackie!" she called over the street noise. "Jackie." Jackie must not have heard her because she continued clomping down the street. But Alana was faster. Jackie jumped when Alana tapped her shoulder, spun around. Alana recognized from her closed face she hadn't meant to be found.

"Hey there, sugar. Sorry, but I'm in a big hurry today! Gotta go!" She turned.

Alana grabbed her arm. "No, wait. Where have you been? Where's Messenger?"

Jackie pulled away from Alana but didn't run. "She's gone."

"I know she's gone! We've been worried sick! Ed and I have been looking for her for over two whole weeks. Do you know where she is?"

Jackie held her face completely still. Unreadable.

Alana wasn't having it. "Answer me!" People passing stared at Alana's raised voice, but Alana didn't care.

"Messenger is fine. You don't have to worry."

Fury rose in Alana like a flame. "So you do know where she is. Why won't you tell me?"

"I can't."

"You won't!"

"You're just going to have to let her go. For now. It's for the best."

"When is she coming back? Tell me!"

"I can't really say."

"She's not coming back. That's it, isn't it? She's left me."

"No, not exactly. Settle down—"

"No! I know it." Alana gasped. A sob like jagged glass cut her throat. "That's what you're saying. Messenger's gone."

Alana didn't really remember getting on the train, riding back to Astoria, climbing the steps to her apartment. Her heart raced, sweat covered her back, even in the raw cold. She couldn't catch her breath. *Messenger's gone. She's really gone.* Messenger's betrayal, abandonment, her own desperate money problems, her jealousy of Ed and Messenger's close relationship, her insecurities about her talent, that she'd just wasted all this time on Messenger to be left with nothing, her credit card bouncing, embarrassing her in front of Ed, her hurt that Messenger would leave her alone—all these thoughts chased her around her apartment. Ed and Messenger were against her. Jackie and Messenger were against her. Alana was mad at all of them, everybody, but mostly furious with herself. She sat down at her desk, picked up the plastic ballerina, and held it in her hand. *I really thought I could find a way to pull this off. I just knew it! In my body, in my heart. In my gut. Like I was born to do it. Born to write this book, to let the world know about Messenger.*

Alana thought back to the conversation with Jackie. She'd tried to hedge, but Alana understood what the message really was. Messenger had left her. She was gone. She wasn't coming back. Ever! This was it. The end.

All of Alana's good intentions evaporated. They were built on the assumption that Messenger would help her. That she was an active part in the project. That she had more to give. All that had changed now that Messenger was gone. *Do something! Fish or cut bait.* As Alana saw it, she had only one option. It was probably lame, probably wouldn't end up amounting to anything. But at least it was something.

She didn't hesitate. She opened her computer. Pushed a few buttons.

She posted *The Messenger Files* website.

Afterwards, Alana sat very still at her desk. She noticed one of the flyers in her trash can; it stared up at her with Marty's photo of Messenger printed on it. That photo had started everything. Memories of Messenger—the times they'd spent together—filled her. Then something very strange happened. First, she felt a fullness, then a sharp stab in her heart. It shocked her. *I'm too young for a heart attack, aren't I?* Then, a buzzy flow of energy surged through her body. Electric. Then words, all these words flooded her brain. A sea of words. The few of them she could make out—"love," "trust," "protection," "peace"—mixed with many others she couldn't quite catch. It was like she was listening to snippets of conversations running in and out but couldn't make sense of the patterns or find a connection she could grasp.

Words, words, words.

Then it stopped as abruptly as it had begun. She shook. She had never felt so out of control, feared she was having a stroke. Alana held her head between her hands, managed to stand and walk the few steps to the bathroom, splashed water on her face.

Even though it was still raining, Alana decided to take a walk around the block to clear her head, to hopefully get her bearings, before she had to go to work. She had never wished more to call in sick, but that wasn't an option. Still shaky, Alana stepped out onto her apartment stoop, opened her broken umbrella, one side sagging, and headed slowly down the stairs. On the sidewalk, Alana turned, noticed a car parked along the curb. Its forest green color caught her eye first. Bright, even in the gray day. Strong shivering vibrations ran through her entire body. Her old trick of clamping her jaw shut tight couldn't stop her chattering teeth. The MINI Cooper. License plate, CLINAMN. What was happening? Another sign? Of what? Alana had no idea.

# PART THREE
# CLINAMEN

# MESSENGER RETURNS

On day seventeen, Alana strode into Ed's with two aims: she wanted to make up with him after their fight, and she wanted to tell him what she'd done. Alana waited at the end of the bar until Ed finished with the coffee line and walked down to where she stood. She stared at the counter, unsure how to begin. "Look, Ed. I'm really sorry about—"

"Me too," Ed interrupted. "I shouldn't have laid all that on you—all my personal stuff." He hung his head.

"No. I'm glad you did," she said. "And we can talk about it more, if you want to. But for now, I have to tell you something. I hope you're going to understand."

He nodded, focused on her.

"Well, I was really upset yesterday," she began. "As you know!"

They laughed.

"After I left here, believe it or not, I spotted Jackie on the street!"

"What?"

"Yeah. I should have texted you. Sorry, but I was still mad. All she'd tell me was: Messenger's safe, and Jackie knows where she is. But hearing that Messenger abandoned me like that made me madder and more frustrated and feeling so helpless and betrayed. So last night, I did it. I launched the website I've been building all this time, *The Messenger Files*. It's live."

Ed stared at her. "Why?"

Alana weighed her words. "It doesn't seem like Messenger's coming back. Or wants to help me anymore. I thought it was the only way to salvage something from all my work."

"But I thought she told you to wait."

Alana felt the blood rush to her face, but she met his eyes. "Yes, she did."

"What if she does come back?" Ed asked softly.

"Well, that doesn't seem likely. But if by some chance she does, then I guess I'll have to tell her the truth."

"Good." Ed poured and handed her a coffee. He'd automatically comped her ever since her card had been rejected. "That's good."

"Why do you think she wouldn't let me post?" Alana asked. "I could never get a straight answer."

Ed shrugged. "I don't know. But I guess it must have been, you know, important."

"That's what worries me," Alana confessed.

***

On day eighteen, Alana went into Ed's as usual. The line was long, but she was fine with waiting—she didn't have anywhere to go.

Ed soon caught her eye. "Look who's here!" He pointed toward the back. Alana turned. There was Messenger, sitting on her stool, just like she'd never left!

Alana's body shivered from head to toe. *I'm dreaming*, she thought. But no. Messenger was here. Now. Tears filled Alana's throat, and she lurched toward her.

"Messenger! Where have you been? We've been so worried something terrible happened to you!"

"Oh, I'm just fine! Nothing's wrong with me. Just needed to lay low for a while. Nothing to worry about." Messenger stood and gave Alana a long, tight hug.

Alana collapsed onto the stool beside her. All she could do was stare.

Messenger patted her on the shoulder. "Everything's okay. Come with me, honey. Let's go for a walk together. I've got some folks I need to see today."

"Messenger!" Alana fought to keep her voice calm and steady. "Don't you understand? You were gone for over two weeks, and we didn't know where you were. We were frantic and … ." Alana pushed the words out. "We didn't know if you were alive."

"Well, I am sorry about all that. But believe me, it was out of my control." She looked Alana up and down. "You seem okay to me. Let's go on that walk. Looks like you could use it too."

"Okay," Alana weakly agreed. She would agree to anything not to lose Messenger again. "I'd better stop in the restroom before we leave."

"I'll hold your backpack for you," Messenger said.

In the bathroom, Alana leaned on the sink with both hands. *Messenger's back, and she's all right!* Alana realized now she hadn't completely trusted everything Jackie said. *But how could Messenger just disappear like that for so long, then reappear like it's no big deal?* Messenger obviously didn't get what she'd put them through! Even for Messenger, that was a lot to just blow off. A cold clamminess snuck up Alana's spine. She stared in the mirror. *Do I look guilty? Does Messenger already know I posted the website? Is that why she came back?* Alana washed her hands and smoothed her hair. Her head cleared enough for her to think, *I've got to get to Ed.*

She hurried over to the bar. "Ed," she said, her voice low. "Please don't say anything to Messenger about what I told you—about posting the website."

Ed stared at her, quiet.

"I know I have to tell her. Just let me do it in my own way, okay?"

His face relaxed. "Sure. Okay." He smiled. "It's good to have her back."

"I know! I can't believe it!"

When Alana returned, Messenger cut her eyes at her. "You and Ed seem to be getting along just fine."

Alana chuckled. "We did have a fight, but I guess everything's okay now."

Messenger nodded. "Ed's come a long way," she said. "So have you, honey! So have you."

Alana didn't know how to reply except with a lame, "Thanks." She fought to get her bearings, to believe her own eyes. Messenger was really back!

On their way out, Ed was busy with the coffee line but called, "Have a nice walk, ladies."

The day was sunny and clear but cold, one of those winter days in the city when the air seems cleaner and warmer than it really is. They started on their usual route through the neighborhood, arm in arm like always, dodged crowds of people pouring down the street on either side of them. Messenger's solid body beside her and her slow, steady gait soothed Alana's jagged nerves and helped her sort her feelings. *This would be so sweet*, Alana thought, *if only I hadn't posted*.

They walked down First Avenue. "Messenger, I have to say you really scared me. Even Ed was worried in the end. It seemed like you'd just disappeared into thin air. But I guess even you can't do that."

"Well, yes, I can. In my own way, that is. But moving between worlds can get to be hard on a body. Especially one old as mine." She unlinked her arm and pulled her red cap down to cover her ears.

"What are you talking about? Moving between what worlds? How?"

"I'll tell you more. But look. There's the Professor. He's one of the folks I want to see." They walked along the street by the fence to the playground and came to the Professor's office, set up today in the pocket park. Surrounded by his walls of crates stacked two-tall, the Professor stared intently at his blank screen. Papers covered each crate. And on his desk (more crates), he'd arranged his stapler, tape dispenser, and three-hole punch.

They walked toward him, and he looked up. "I see you've returned," he said to Messenger.

"Yes, I have. Where's your coat, Professor? It's mighty cold today."

"I'm swamped, madam. Believe me, I am swamped." He typed furiously, did not look up again. Alana loved to hear the old-fashioned clicks his keyboard made.

"May I come in?"

"Certainly, but I only have a moment."

When Alana chuckled, Messenger locked eyes. "Never underestimate him," she whispered.

Messenger pulled an apple out of a pocket and left it on the closest stack. "Take care. Bundle up, now. It's cold."

He glanced at the apple but kept typing.

Meanwhile, Alana snuck a look at her phone to check her site. Three thousand views. When she'd logged 1,000 views earlier that morning, she'd been excited. Now it all made her sick to her stomach. She stuffed her phone back in her pocket. They headed away from the Professor down the street. "You said you know how to move between the worlds—are you talking about different dimensions?"

"Uh-huh. Sure. Call it whatever you want. These other imaginal worlds lie in the space all around us. No boundaries. We're part of them, and they're part of us. That's not new news, but our smarty scientists are just beginning to figure it out. Moving in and out of the worlds is nothing special. You could do it if you wanted to, honey." She held her gaze.

"No way. How? I don't have any gifts like that."

"You have everything you need." She paused. "I remember that's what my teachers always told me."

Alana's eyes lit up. "Who were your teachers?"

At the same time Messenger turned from her and called, "Jackie! Is that you?"

Alana sighed. Jackie shuffled down the sidewalk in her cheetah-print booties. Today she wore a bright red coat that engulfed her tall, rail-thin body. The single dreadlock on the crown of her head hung all the way down her back. She refused to wear a hat.

"Messenger, Alana. Good morning, good morning!" Jackie cried. "You're looking good today! You're always styling."

"Oh go on! Trying to sweet-talk me! Well, I'll see you later." Jackie waved her hand back and forth as they passed, as if she were on a float in a parade. "Told you she was all right!" she snapped over her shoulder on her way down the street.

"What did she mean by that?" Messenger asked.

"Oh, I saw her yesterday when you were still missing, and she told me you were okay." Alana looked away. "But I didn't believe her."

Messenger linked arms with Alana again. "I'm sorry you were worried. That was a real shame. But not of my making." Messenger stopped and reached up to rub the space between Alana's eyebrows. "Relax, honey. There. Feel better?"

"Yes." Alana registered how very much she'd missed Messenger. She pushed away her own uneasiness about how to confess. "Can you say more about the different worlds?"

"Okay. Well, these worlds I'm talking about were all known by the Wise Ones. You know," she counted on her fingers, "Mayan, Toltec, Aztec, Native Americans, First Nations, Aborigines, many tribes of African, Alaskan, Arctic, Celtic peoples. Every culture, faith, or religion since the beginning of time had Wise Ones. The Wise Ones are in the imaginal world now, working hard on our behalf. They will help you, if you ask."

Alana's head hurt trying to keep up. "What do you mean? How can people from the past help me in the present?"

"Time is no problem!" Messenger continued. "This lifetime—other times, from the past and the future. You want to know how many different times can dance on the head of a pin? One. All time is happening at the same time! Nobody gets this. Well, Einstein did. The mystery and beauty of the worlds ... the web ... the threads ... the patterns ... the unity. The interconnection. All that is lost on most people. Or," her voice grew stronger, "those folks who want to keep the true nature of reality from everybody else have hidden it."

Alana frowned. "Why would they do that?"

"Fear. Greed. Spite. You name it."

Alana slowed her pace to match Messenger's, struggled to make sense of all Messenger had said. *She's always slowing me down,* Alana thought. *She's taught me to weigh my words, to figure out how to get answers. I made a pledge to myself to go at Messenger's pace. But what did I do? I have to tell her.* When they turned the corner onto Second Avenue, Alana suggested, "Why don't we head back to Ed's soon? It's so cold." *I'd rather tell her with Ed there. He'll give me courage.*

But it was too late. Messenger had spotted the Flower Lady. "How you doing?" Messenger called to her and waved.

The Flower Lady was all set up on her corner one block down; white plastic buckets filled with carnations surrounded her wheelchair. "Doing good! Cold today," she called back.

"Tell me about it!"

"Good to see you back! We," she glanced at Alana, then back to Messenger, "all missed you. A lot." Three customers picked flowers out of her buckets. "Listen, come back to see me later. Okay?" the Flower Lady said.

"I'll try," Messenger told her.

They watched her gather a bouquet in her hands, then stuff the stems in the gap under the arm of her wheelchair as she cut the raffia. "You all have a real nice walk!" She turned back to her flowers and whipped raffia around the bouquet the first customer had handed her.

They left the Flower Lady, arm in arm again. "You were telling me about your teachers," Alana prompted.

"My teachers taught me that in order for people to wake up and notice the patterns, they need space and time. Space in between life as they experience it and time to grasp the scale of reality. Well, that's what my messages do. They create a pause. A breath of fresh air. Maybe a Clinamen. A swerve! A change! Change *is* a liminal space. The chance to step out of your life—just for a minute—and take a look from another place. To see the patterns of your life and the lives of those around you, how they weave in and out with your own. How we're all part of it and we're all connected. How this incredible flow of connection is much bigger than it might seem and works on our behalf at all times. It works not just for those of us here, now, but for all future generations too. Connection. That's an example of a dimension for you. That's the dimension I'm working in."

"But what difference does it make if a few people get their messages or not? To the bigger picture, I mean. It all seems so random."

Messenger held Alana with her milky amber eyes. "But there is no such thing as random. Not in this dimension or any other. When anything appears random—that's its genius. You have to wake up and look with new eyes. Then the pattern will reveal itself." Messenger pulled a brown paper napkin from one of her pockets. During the process, an old ballpoint pen with a hairline crack down the side of its white barrel fell onto the concrete from her pocket. Alana picked it up and handed it back to her.

"You keep it," she said.

"Oh, that's okay."

She shook her head. "Keep it. Might come in handy."

"Thanks." Alana stuck it in her backpack.

Messenger linked arms with Alana again.

"Where were we?" Alana asked.

"Oh my, honey. How can I tell you? Okay, think about it this way. Gaze at all the problems we face in our own lives or worry about in the lives of those we love. All over Planet Earth. We have to work together to mend the fabric. Straighten out any tangles. Fix the tears. Connect the patterns. We do it one stitch at a time. At first, one stitch, one message seems like nothing. But sooner than you think the work is done, and a huge hole is repaired. That's all it takes. Paying attention." She looked around as she walked—even slower than usual. "Wait a minute," she said. "I have one more thing I need to do."

Alana wondered if she was about to receive a message, but no. It was just the lady with the Chihuahuas, all three of them resting on the bench by the school parking lot. They walked down the street to meet them. Messenger reached into another pocket and dug out a lint-covered dog bone, then tried to break it in half.

"Here, let me." Alana broke it and handed the two halves back to her. Messenger slowly bent over, laid the treat out flat on her gloved hand, first for the tan dog, then the white-and-tan one. The lady didn't say a word, but a slight smile played across her face, which was like a miracle. Messenger smiled back, then straightened. They walked to the next bench and sat down.

Messenger nodded back at the lady with her dogs. "People don't understand how fragile human beings are. I'm not talking about the big stuff. No. One sharp word creates hurt feelings, the strings of nerves plucked can make a tear. But a tear can be mended." Messenger's eyes filled with tears—the first time that had ever happened.

*Does she know?* "Messenger, I thought you said you were fine. Is something upsetting you?" Alana struggled to keep her voice light.

Messenger shook her head and looked away. "Oh no, honey. No. Just got something in my eyes. Soot. That's all. Dirt from the street."

Alana fished a tissue out of her backpack. "Here. Let me help you." She wiped tears from Messenger's cheeks and from under each eye.

"Thank you," Messenger said. She leaned back against the bench and sighed, her eyes closed.

Alana sat close to her, closer than ever before. She lowered her head onto Messenger's. They fit together like two puzzle pieces. A loneliness that Alana did not know was there filled her. Had she just made the worst mistake of her life? They sat there together for a long time while Alana struggled for the courage to speak, to tell Messenger what she'd done. *Do it now,* she coaxed herself.

Suddenly, Messenger straightened up, her body rigid. "Alana's not ready yet. She still needs to build her confidence and learn to trust more." Although these words flew out of Messenger's mouth, it wasn't her usual voice that Alana heard. It sounded low and creepy, like she was very far away or talking in her sleep or even weirder, like it was recorded.

Alana froze. All the hairs on her arms stood up. She shook Messenger. "Messenger? Messenger!"

"Huh?" Her body jerked. She blinked her eyes. "Oh my. Sorry, honey. I'm sorry."

"What just happened?"

Messenger gulped long draughts of air. "Nothing for you to worry yourself about." Her face paled, and a veil of perspiration spread across her forehead and upper lip. She shook herself several times, then turned to Alana. "You're right, honey. We need to get inside. Let's stop back in at Ed's. He'll treat us to a cup. I need one right about now." She linked arms with Alana, leaned on her, and they trudged back to Ed's.

Alana practically held Messenger up the whole way back. "Messenger, what happened to your voice? Tell me what you meant! What aren't I ready for? Who should I trust?"

But Messenger wouldn't answer her.

When they burst into the shop, Ed looked up, frowned. "What's wrong? You both look like you just saw a ghost."

Messenger hooted. "Oh my. I just gave her a scare, that's all."

Alana's worried eyes met Ed's.

"Go sit," he told them. "I'll bring you some coffee."

Alana settled Messenger on her usual stool. *What did I just witness*? she wondered. The whole episode was so bizarre, yet it dawned on Alana how strangely like her own experience—the flood of words that had filled her—it was. *Is there a connection between the two?* A sip of the strong coffee Ed placed in front of her helped. "Thanks so much," she told him.

Ed got his mop and pail and set to work in their vicinity, to keep an eye on Messenger, Alana figured.

Alana pondered both experiences and had to wonder if spending so much time with Messenger was rubbing off. She patted Messenger's hand. "Are you sure you're okay?" she asked.

Messenger closed her eyes, then slowly opened them again. "Fine. Just fine." Messenger's voice sounded perfectly normal.

Alana's gaze met Ed's and lingered.

"Don't worry about me," Messenger told them.

## MESSENGER'S GRIP ON TIME

Messenger sat completely still on her stool at Ed's. She knew what had happened. It had happened to her before. She mentally repeated her training as she breathed. Stay awake. Keep your eyes open at all times. Travel light. Speak only when necessary. Stay in the present moment. That's how you keep time flowing correctly. Without that, if you get impatient or boastful or angry or proud or even nervous, worrying if you'll be able to bear it—you're sunk. Time gets wadded up and pulls you down like quicksand. It had just happened. Past, present, future akimbo—the vertigo was murder.

She'd come back to finish what she'd started. To save Alana, to keep her safe.

She had to settle down.

Gather her strength.

Prepare for what was coming.

# ALANA AND A STRANGE WOMAN

Alana left Messenger with Ed and headed back to the subway since she had to be at Tale of the Whale by four o'clock. On her way, a strange woman with bright red hair and wearing about ten chunky necklaces around her neck grabbed Alana's arm.

"Get her out of here," she whispered into Alana's ear. Her breath smelled of coffee and dirt.

She looked so crazed, Alana pulled away, afraid the woman might hit her. "Who?"

The woman frowned, her eyes darting. "You know who! Just get her out of this neighborhood. Now! She should never have come back. Look, they're coming for her, and they mean business. She's going to be arrested if she's not careful."

"Messenger? Why?" Alana backed away even farther, desperate to create space between them. The smell was overpowering.

"The police will try and get her on insanity—danger to herself and others—that shit. Then they'll throw her in the psych ward. Believe me," she muttered, her eyes filled with tears. "She does not want to go there. No! I'm telling you—get her off the street."

Alana watched the strange woman weave in and out of the crowd. *Could she be right?* Her stomach clinched in a vise. That sense that something bad was about to happen grew and mixed with her guilt. Why hadn't she told Messenger what she'd done?

# Messenger's Composition Book

*You know the Our Father? Well, we don't say My Father, do we? Our—all of us together. We need each other to make it happen. That's how it's done. How we play best. Life is about choices. We all have free will to choose. Some more than others. When your children are all fed and you've got clothes on your back, and nobody's trying to kill you or run you out of your home, then you have more choices. But you see, it's all choice and it's all gift. One action creates a reaction. And on it goes.*

*You don't get it? Oh no—hee, hee. Your nose is out of joint because you want your own little personal message. You think it's all about you. Hah! Oh yes. You're an individual, all right. The bad news is: so are all the other 7.7 billion souls on this planet.*

*See—it's not a contest. No losers. All winners here. You are a winner, but you're not any more special or precious than the guy on the corner or the lady at the bus stop or the child halfway around the world. So don't begin that game at all. Lift everybody up. Rejoice in who you are, sure. But guess what? It's too small a planet for prima donnas. We're all part of this game—one huge, organic whole. Here, what we prize most in life—individuality, independence, freedom from the man—makes us proud. We grab our lapels and puff out our chests. Problem is, instead of our greatest strength, it's really our greatest danger because it cuts us off from each other. Anything that happens anywhere on the planet affects each and every one of us. Sometimes in subtle ways, others dramatic. Call it the ripple effect in quantum motion.*

*You've got to ask for help in this world. Get over this feeling you're here on your own. We've got to get beyond the i's—iPhones, iPads, individualism, isolationism. Anything that separates you from others, from the whole, is definitely the wrong track, which will lead us to a head-on collision or derailment of our best interests. No! We need to get beyond rightdoing and wrongdoing to that field my brother Rumi wrote about so long ago. We all need to meet there immediately. Who ever said creation, evolution was over? Who said we're done? Nope. Rumi's field is the next step and just happens to be our only hope for survival.*

*Come on. Meet me there. You can feel it. Close your eyes. Reach out and touch it. Go and live in that space, and you'll be so much more than a winner. You'll fly—like in your dreams as a kid, when you could reach your arms up high and just take off. Easy as pie. The future of Earth and all Earthlings depend on it. Won't you come? It's time to leave home. Embark on the adventure of a lifetime.*

*Oh, honey. You're going to get your message, all right. That will come in good time. For now, you've got a job to do. Sometimes you like to drive me crazy, but I reckon you're about ready. You need just a little more time that I hope I can give you. You're going to have a big surprise—a shock, even. But it'll all work out. All will be well.*

*Now it's about time for me to go.*

*Everything's going to get a little rough around here. Oh, I've seen it before, believe me! Listen, whatever happens, let them know I loved them. I did it all for love. My teacher told me—make your life a story of love. I did have a little bit of school learning, but mostly I learned from the school of hard knocks. I wanted to give my all. To say yes to everything. To pour it all out and not count the cost. So in my own way, I did. Did I do right? Did I change things? Did I tip the scales for good, even a little? I hope so. I'll never know. But that was my intention. To leave this planet with empty hands and a full heart. That was my choice. My free will.*

*Get up! Go to it! I'm telling you, our poor old planet needs you up and moving. My advice is—keep moving. Keep the ball rolling. Okay, music, chanting, twirling, rocking, shaking, swaying, dancing. You feel your groove scurry up your spine from your root all through your body; energy flows to your toes, fingertips, the top of your head, and beyond. That's power. That's what you need to make things happen. Believe it.*

*You can read about it all you want, but you've got to feel it yourself. Oh yeah. Flow. Layers and layers. You've got to get into the flow of life before it's too late. For you or for us. Connect. We're working to make things better and you need to too. You can do it. Accept the gifts you're given with love and gratitude, then give them back. That's the dance. Don't break the flow. Play your part and be grateful.*

*There is a point of no return.*

*Most of all—consider it an adventure, baby. Consider it an adventure.*

# THE LAST DAY IN THE PARK

Alana noticed the difference immediately when she and Messenger walked through the south gate to the park that morning. Police were everywhere. Granted, a few were always scattered around, keeping an eye on things. Normally, Alana would have been happy to see them. "Police officers are our friends!" she and her classmates had chanted three times each Friday morning when Officer Stanley visited her elementary school with his canine sidekick. But today she remembered the strange woman's warning about the police and felt their eyes watching Messenger and her. "The police are our friends," Alana whispered to herself, but the back of her neck tingled. *Things are getting really weird around here,* she thought. *Or is my guilty conscience just making me paranoid?*

She and Messenger had agreed to meet at the park to see if the fountain had been turned back on now that spring was almost here. They walked past the Garibaldi statue, the green and blue public recycling cans rusted out at the bottoms, and the old, half-dead tree, strange growths morphing in every direction. Just a few small smudges of chartreuse dotted its ancient branches. When she and Messenger got farther in, Alana realized why the police were here. So many more people than usual were milling around.

"Do you have any idea why there's such a crowd? Is it some holiday?" Messenger asked her.

"I don't think so." *It couldn't be the website,* she reasoned. She walked along the path, arm in arm with Messenger. *Don't make eye contact with any of them,* she cautioned herself. But she couldn't shake the notion that she and Messenger were being watched from all sides.

Alana turned back to Messenger. Her eyes bored into Alana's, intense and strong. Alana had never seen her look so sad or so old.

"Are you sure you don't know what's going on?" Messenger asked.

Was this one of Messenger's games? Did she know what Alana had posted? How? Alana struggled to read Messenger's face while she walked and talked, pretended nothing was different, everything was fine. Normal. Even though every cell in her body knew it wasn't.

The fountain was not on, but a swarm of people had formed around it—some sitting along the edge, some milling around the concrete pavement. Buzzing, waiting. Anticipation crackled in the air. Alana and Messenger approached the crowd.

"Hey! There she is!" a thin, drugged-out girl called from the side of the fountain. The crowd surged toward Alana and Messenger like a colony of ants. They were soon surrounded.

"Aren't you that Messenger woman?"

*Oh, no!* A wave of dread almost knocked Alana down. *It was the website!*

"I want a message!"

"Give me a message!"

"Lady, please. You gotta help me!"

"Does the church know what you're doing?"

"Do the police know what you're doing?"

"Who are you anyway?"

Shock shook Alana to her core. She spun toward Messenger to find her staring right at her. Her eyes met Messenger's amber ones, and Alana realized without a shadow of a doubt that Messenger knew everything. Everything.

Alana couldn't face her. She took her arm. "We've got to get out of here," she muttered.

Messenger wouldn't move. She turned to Alana, "What have you done?"

"Nothing!" she whispered.

Men and women, moms and dads, old and young people, babies, kids, beggars, street people of all ages closed in on them. Not menacing, exactly. Calling and crying and demanding, growing louder every minute.

At first, Alana was relieved to watch four police officers elbow through the crowd and push it back, away from her and Messenger. *They'll help us,* she thought. *We can get away.* But when she looked into their eyes, she wasn't so sure.

The last voice Alana remembered hearing screamed, "Old Bitch! You think you're a voice from God?" More hate lodged in those few words than Alana had ever heard in her life. The man's voice sounded tinny, like he was talking underwater.

He was tall, about six feet, bent forward, a man on a mission, resolute, with a steady gaze. Big and chubby, rather than muscular. His eyes, nose, and mouth looked too small for his large head and face. His dark hair was curly and chopped unevenly. He followed behind them, mumbled, blathered, yelled about Satan and hell. Lots about hell.

They tried to ignore him and hurried to get away. The hairs on Alana's arms stood up, and the terrible energy charging the air around them filled her whole body with fear and dread.

Then everything fell into slow motion.

"Don't think you can get away from me. Oh, no you don't! I've got the power here."

He charged. Using all his might, the man slammed into Messenger, butting her with his right shoulder. Made his hit. Alana would never forget the flat sound of contact as his body rammed Messenger's. She flew forward from the force and hung there a moment. Alana reached out with both arms, somehow believing she could catch her.

But instead Messenger catapulted forward, out of Alana's grasp, and landed face-first on the concrete pavement. She slid before coming to a stop and seemed to shrink before Alana's eyes. Her red cap had flown off, now crumpled by her side. Her completely bald head shocked Alana to the core. One shoe had fallen off, and a swollen, exposed foot hung twisted on the end of her ankle like a misshapen animal. A pool of blood stained the concrete around her head.

The man panted from his exertions, spun around toward the gathered crowd, and snarled, "Run!" It seemed to take forever for him to finish saying that word. "Run!" he yelled again. Many people did.

Then everything sped up. Still screaming about liberals and God and judgment and Satan, he charged toward Messenger, who was now curled in a fetal position. "You are nothing. Nothing!" he cried, his scruffy face contorted, crazed.

"Stop it!" Alana pleaded, trying to shield her. "Leave us alone."

But he was too fast. He drew back and kicked Messenger's prone form with as much force as his push. He grunted, kicked her in the back, then again in the head. Her poor body offered no resistance. Alana could almost feel the kicks in her own body, delivered via his tan work boot.

Before he landed the third kick, two big men from the crowd grabbed him, and within a moment, the police were on him too. They pushed him down, arms pinned behind him, his face slammed on the same pavement as Messenger's.

Alana dropped beside Messenger, not knowing what to do, afraid to touch her. "Help!" Alana cried. "Please help us." *Be okay, be okay, be okay.*

An ambulance's shrill scream cut the air. Alana jumped. Blood continued to pool around Messenger's head, smelled like dirty iron. Alana got up the nerve to try and turn her, but someone called, "Wait! Let us help." Others gathered around the body, and working together, they gently turned Messenger so she could breathe. A purple-blue egg of a welt rose on the side of her head, and nasty gashes and abrasions from the cement wept blood. Her nose, flattened at a weird angle, poured red, mixed with the stream from her split lip and mouth, and veiled the bottom half of her face. Messenger moaned slightly, but didn't move, didn't open her eyes. Alana picked up a tooth that lay on the cement beside her head.

"Messenger? Can you hear me? Can you speak?" Bystanders held their breaths with Alana, listened, but there was no response. Alana thought she saw Messenger's ribs rise and fall, but she wasn't sure.

When the EMTs arrived, they took over. Alana stepped away from Messenger. They secured Messenger's neck and laid her onto a stretcher. Messenger's face was already so swollen Alana wouldn't have recognized her. Tears dripped from the corners of each eye, made little rivers through the bloodstains.

Alana handed the medic Messenger's tooth. She longed to hold her hand, but both palms were skinned red and dirt was ground into them, both wrists were twisted, cockeyed. Alana wanted to say I'm sorry but didn't.

Two EMTs lifted Messenger into the back of the ambulance and closed the doors behind them.

Alana pulled on the arm of the head medic as he wrote his report. "Please," Alana pleaded, "Can I go with her?"

"What is your relationship?" he asked.

"I'm, I'm … ." Words failed her.

He looked up from his paperwork. "Family?"

"No."

"Only family," he snapped. "You'll have to get yourself to the hospital."

"No! You've got to let me go with her. She doesn't have anybody else."

"Lady, you're not getting the message. *Only family.*"

He turned and got into the front seat. The siren blasted. Alana had to cover her ears.

She watched the ambulance swim through the crowds of bystanders, leaving her behind.

# AFTER THE ATTACK

Alana sat on a cold aluminum bench, breathing fresh air. She stared straight ahead. After they took Messenger away, she'd run to the nearest subway, had arrived at the hospital not long after the ambulance. She'd sat in the emergency room for hours, watched one horror after another roll in through the door. But nothing was more horrible than the way Alana felt. She still couldn't believe what had just happened right before her eyes. The attack replayed in gruesome detail in her mind, and Alana couldn't make it stop. She'd never witnessed violence like that, playing out in real time. A violence she had invited. Even though it hadn't been confirmed, Alana had no doubt that whoever this monster was, he'd learned about Messenger through Alana's website.

They wouldn't let Alana into the emergency room cubicle with Messenger since they were evaluating her and the police were involved. Alana had already pestered the nurse at the waiting room desk at least a dozen times for an update, but all the nurse would tell her was, "Be patient."

Alana had been outside only ten minutes, but something nudged her back through the automatic doors and into the harsh fluorescent lights of the waiting room. At about the same time, a male nurse walked out from the back. He sat down beside Alana. "Are you here with the woman called Messenger?" he asked. He was a big guy; his chest bulged through his navy blue uniform, but he had gentle eyes. His ID tag said Rob.

"Yes, I am! How is she doing?"

"Still very out of it. Not unconscious, exactly. In and out. She has a concussion, broken ribs, a broken nose, contusions everywhere. She's pretty bad."

"But she's going to be all right. I mean, she's going to make it?" Through her worry, Alana vaguely registered how the nurse's uber-clean, hospital smell reminded her of her mom.

"Oh, sure. Don't you worry. Everything's going to be okay."

"Really?"

"Yes. Just relax. It's busy down here, as you can see. They'll probably move her up to ICU a little later, but right now—"

"ICU!" Alana cringed.

Rob paused and smiled. "That might not happen," he reassured her. "If it does, it'll just be a precaution for tonight because of her age and status. You can't go up since you're not family, but don't worry. I bet they'll move her down to a regular floor by morning. Then you can see her."

Alana finally exhaled for the first time since all this had happened. "Thank God. Some good news!"

Rob paused. Alana had the feeling he wanted to add more, but instead he said, "I'd better get back to work."

*Did something happen that he isn't saying? About Messenger or the attack?* "Are you sure you're telling me all you know?" she asked.

Rob nodded. "That's all for now." Even though she'd just met him, Alana thought she read pity in his face.

"Well, I can't thank you enough for taking the time to come out here. You've been so kind."

"That's why I'm here. Listen, why don't you go on home tonight and come back tomorrow bright and early? No offense, but you look exhausted. They're going to keep working on her down here for a while. We're waiting for some specialists to come down, then they'll probably order more tests. It's going to be a long night. I'm sure that's what she'd want you to do. Just go on home and get some sleep. Try not to worry. You've been through a rough time yourself today, haven't you?"

Tears filled Alana's eyes. "Yes," she whispered.

"Okay. Head on home now."

Alana hesitated, but what Rob had said made sense. "Can I give you my number? Will you text or call if anything changes? I mean, I know I'm not family or anything."

"I'll call." He jotted down the number she gave him on his arm. "Have a good rest. She'll see you tomorrow."

"Will she be conscious by then? I mean, I know you can't say for sure, but would you expect it?"

"I think she probably will."

Alana's heart leapt. "If she wakes up, will you be sure and tell her I was here?"

"Of course."

So Alana left. She walked out the emergency doors, intended to do as Rob suggested but suddenly felt dizzy and weak. She sat down on the aluminum bench again, breathed in and out, ordered her head to stop spinning. The cold metal helped steady her. But she realized she wasn't alone.

A group of reporters, some with video cameras, surrounded her bench. "Aren't you Alana Peterson?" a guy with thick, black glasses called, his voice loud and jarring. "Weren't you the one posting about this Messenger person who was attacked? We just want to ask you a few questions."

She sprang to attention. "No."

"Oh yes you are. I saw you all over social media. You're Alana Peterson."

"No, you're wrong. I don't know what you're talking about."

"It was you. You just posted a website about her a week ago. *The Messenger Files*. And you've been asking for first-person accounts for weeks. You know it's you!"

"No! Leave me alone."

Several others ran toward her, yelled questions all at the same time, took photos. Alana held up her arm and covered her face. When they wouldn't leave her alone, she ran off down the street, but they followed. Alana ran and ran. She couldn't tell if she was panting or sobbing. She found herself at Ed's, saw him mopping the floor through the glass, all alone since it was long past closing time. Alana burst in and fell into his arms. He didn't ask one question; he just locked the door behind her.

# LATER THAT NIGHT

Even though the damage had already been done, the first thing Alana did when she got back to her apartment was to take *The Messenger Files* website down. Later that night, since there was no chance of sleep, Alana steeled herself to go online and see what she could learn about what had happened. She sat in her dark bedroom at her little desk; the glow of the screen illuminated her face. A local crime alert listed the following information:

*Jane Doe. Victim of violent attack in park. Female, undetermined race. Approximately sixty years of age. No identification. Assumed homeless. Height: five feet two inches. Weight: approximately 170 pounds. Perpetrator obviously harmful to self and others. Victim transported to hospital by ambulance. No word yet of condition. No evidence perpetrator knew victim. May have had knowledge of reported suspicious activities victim was involved in.*

There were also some very unflattering photos of Alana hiding her face with a caption beneath: "Journalist blogger investigates mysterious Messenger." Alana cringed and immediately clicked to another link.

The police had identified the attacker as Rickie Brokoff, a member of the Church of the One True Light, a right-wing sect scary enough that the police and FBI were very familiar with them.

Their leader, Pastor Mike, also under investigation, had apparently called his followers to attack and destroy any perceived threats to what they defined as the true faith, to step out and take action, violent, if necessary, against heathens and blasphemers. To take a stand for God.

The Church of the One True Light was against just about anything you might consider socially progressive. Their website slammed celebrities who presented themselves as spiritual seekers, any writers or even religious leaders who veered the least bit from a completely literal interpretation of the Bible, which was "written by man, wholly and entirely inspired by God." Pastor Mike viewed any natural event or disaster as God's judgment against human depravity.

Alana read every single word and realized that, crazy or devout or both, Rickie Brokoff had not just chosen a vulnerable person to attack at random in the park today. Undoubtedly, her website had tipped him off. He'd probably read about Messenger's work, decided she was violating numerous laws of God. All the information Alana had provided and the growing interest in Messenger had provoked him to act. To hurt Messenger.

But then yet another shock sounded through her. *Oh God, no!* Could Rickie Brokoff be that anonymous troll who had posted on her blog so long ago about his anger with receiving a message? Had he been seething with rage ever since then, seen *The Messenger Files* website, and made the connection, read the list of places to find Messenger that Alana had included on the website to try and prove that Messenger was real? Then chosen the park?

Alana closed her computer screen and stared at the bedroom wall in front of her. Everything made sense. Posting her website had worked as a signal, a beacon. It was exactly what Rickie and his group had watched for. He'd been waiting since the day Messenger gave him his message, she realized now. All he needed was the list of places to find messenger. Then it was just a matter of time. *I handed her to him,* Alana concluded.

This was all her fault.

# THE NEXT DAY

When she woke up the next morning, Alana felt like *she'd* been thrown down and kicked around. Rob had never called. She'd viewed every hour on the clock in the glow of her phone. Tossed. Prayed. Rickie Brokoff's face, his grunts, his weird voice, his scream—"Run!"—haunted her. She watched Messenger's body slammed down on the pavement, her swollen face and flattened nose, the huge goose egg on her forehead where she'd hit. The blood. Alana tossed and turned, waited impatiently for the faintest wisps of first light, the promise that day would come soon and then she could go back to the hospital and see Messenger.

And confess.

That was the first thing she'd do. She couldn't wait. She'd mentally rehearsed what she'd say. *I'm so sorry, Messenger. I feel so terrible. Please forgive me. I shouldn't have done it. I should have listened to you and waited to post it. But I had no idea this would happen. If I had, I never would have done it. It's just—you abandoned me. At least it felt that way. But that's no excuse. Please forgive me. I'll do anything.* Somehow, she was determined to make everything right.

Alana headed out of her apartment, took the train, and stopped at the Flower Lady's. "Terrible, horrible scourge," the Flower Lady muttered, teeth clenched. She added a few more red carnations to

Alana's bunch, then tied the stems with raffia. "Give her my love. Ed and I will be over after lunch-hour rush, once I sell the rest of these. Won't be long, thanks to you." Alana passed Ostap having a smoke on the street, and he told her he'd come by the hospital later.

In the bright, spring light, almost blinding but so welcomed after all those monotone gray winter days, Alana felt her spirits lift. She glided through the hospital's glass doors. The elevator was open, waiting. She smiled at the people who shared the ride—a young man gripped a pink balloon, a little boy in his other arm wore an "I'm the Big Brother" T-shirt covered in bright red letters. Happy, expectant faces. They carried gift bags, a tray of food from the cafeteria. Everybody looked up while the elevator climbed.

Alana got off on the eleventh floor. She'd asked for Messenger's room number at the visitors' desk and was thrilled to learn she wasn't in ICU. She wound her way back toward room 1144. As she walked down the fluorescent-lit hall, she realized this was the first time, since the very beginning of her search, that she actually knew where Messenger was.

She turned the corner, knocked gently on the door. When there was no answer, she opened it. A chill ran through her. Morning sun shone through the double window, but the neatly made bed was empty. The room smelled freshly cleaned. Alana stared at the room number again, checked the note she'd made on her phone. No—1144, this was the right room. Her throat closed up and sick panic rose. Had she died? In the night, all alone? Alana ran out the door and back down the hall, grabbed the arm of the first nurse she saw.

"Where's the woman who was in 1144?" Her voice shook. She could hardly get the words out.

The nurse sighed. "Can you believe she snuck out on us?"

"What? But she had a concussion. Broken ribs. She needed tests."

The nurse shrugged. "Don't I know it! She had no business doing that. Somebody most definitely helped her break out, but we don't know how." The nurse's long brown hair hung down in her face, and she flipped her head to the right.

"Broke out?"

"Yep. She wasn't even conscious when the night nurse saw her last. She was one inch short of ICU. She would have been in there, too, if it hadn't already been full last night. So what do they do to us? Put a critically ill patient on our floor, on top of all the others we've got to tend." She flipped the hair again. "It's nuts! She had to yank the IV out of her arm, unhook every single monitor. Not to mention the fact that, with broken ribs, she'd be in terrible pain. It just doesn't add up. Someone would have to basically carry her out, the shape she was in."

"Did anybody come into her room?"

"The night nurse said she saw this skinny old lady in some wild getup, tall but no bigger than a minute, dart out of the room and down the hall before anybody could stop her. But the nurse told the police there was no way that old lady could carry her out. It had to be someone else."

Alana breathed, willed herself to stop shaking, but it didn't do any good. "She's really gone."

"Yep. Only thing she left was a message on a little scrap of paper on the bedside table. 'Thank you very much. Okay—bye.' The police took it. They're out looking for her now."

"Good luck," Alana murmured.

The nurse flipped her hair. "I tell you—these people. We work so hard to pull them back from the brink. But you know what? She'll be right back in the ER, worse off than ever. What can you do?" She flipped again. "And who's paying for it? You and me. That's who. The responsible ones! We've gotta take care of everybody else. Government takes it out of us. They just don't get it."

"Why didn't somebody call me?" Alana demanded. "Rob said he would."

"Who?"

"The nurse. Rob. Big guy, really nice. Down in the emergency room."

"You must be mistaken. There's no Rob in ER."

"Oh, come on. He talked with me last night when Messenger was still down there. Rob!"

"Nope. No male nurses in the ER right now."

*What?* Alana gave up. Nothing made sense. She couldn't talk with this nurse a minute longer. She shoved her flowers into the nurse's arms and managed to get down the hall. She rode down in the elevator, alone this time, sped out the doors and back to her aluminum bench. It reeked of nicotine, even though a sign read, Tobacco-Free Zone. Alana sat, steadied herself, gulped air. She scanned the area for reporters who might be lurking but saw none.

Where was Messenger now? The police wouldn't find her if she didn't want to be found, Alana knew that much. At least Messenger wasn't dead. And she was apparently conscious. Who had broken her out? Jackie? But how? It didn't really matter. Once again, Messenger was gone.

*She's left. She's left me again,* Alana thought. And her guilt, that choking, sick feeling in her stomach and throat overtook her. She'd disrespected Messenger's wishes. Betrayed her. A total breach of trust. Messenger had loved her. Yes. That was the only word to use.

All of Alana's flimsy justifications fell away, and she couldn't collect herself. Alana had always thought that was a funny expression. Her guilt, fears, regrets, sadnesses, anger, heartache, plans, strategies—all circled around her head like a baby's mobile over a crib. She could almost see them dangling. Try as she might to bring some order to them, to grasp one and run with it, she couldn't. The worries gathered, circled her and the bench, so she couldn't move, decide what to do, where to go, whom to ask, where to begin. She held on to the aluminum bench for dear life, growing colder by the minute.

# Alana's Notebook

## Seven Fears

1. *Is Messenger all right?*
2. *Why did she leave the hospital?*
3. *Who helped her? Jackie? Who else?*
4. *Is there permanent damage? Brain damage from the concussion?*
5. *Where is she? Did somebody kidnap her? Somebody who wanted her gone?*
6. *IS SHE GONE FOR GOOD?*
7. *Will Ed forgive me?*

## Seven Conclusions

1. *IT'S ALL MY FAULT! I caused everything that's happened. SHE TOLD ME NOT TO DO IT. I should have listened, should have anticipated how things could turn out. I knew something bad was going to happen. It was just a vague feeling, but I knew it. And ignored it.*
2. *Messenger is gone but undoubtedly still suffering from her many injuries.*
3. *Darker forces may be at work here.*
4. *Jackie is involved.*
5. *If the messages stop, a light in this dark city (in this dark world) has gone out. Messenger's work for positive change with the messages is set back. No—halted!*
6. *The Clinamen won't happen now. I've ruined it.*
7. *NO, Ed won't.*

# ALANA TAKES STOCK

After a few days, when they figured she wasn't going to say anything more about Messenger, the reporters soon lost interest and left Alana alone. For them, after the violence had played out, Rickie Brokoff was identified and charged, there was no story. It all added up to just another act of urban terrorism, violence committed by another young, angry fanatic. The authorities hadn't revealed a direct connection between Alana's website and the attack, but Alana knew in her bones the truth.

Messenger was gone. Each day, Alana prowled the streets, the doorways, stoops, storefronts, benches. Still hoping. She strained her eyes, longed for that dot of red. How many times had Alana walked these streets with Messenger, tried so hard to ask the right questions? To keep her talking about her messages? Where they came from? What they meant?

Alana scoured the internet for traces of Messenger, for posts about any message from a strange angel. Nothing. She tried to check in every day with the Flower Lady, the lady with the Chihuahuas. Ostap. The Professor. She asked all the crusty kids outside the barbershop every day if they'd seen Messenger. Even the neighborhood cops to see if they'd seen her or had any news. Jackie seemed to have disappeared again too. Alana figured she was with Messenger, wherever that was.

Alana had considered all the people in the neighborhood her friends too. But since the attack, a new awkwardness filled her whenever she was around them. Some, like Ostap, were very clear about their feelings. Whenever she saw him on the street, he wouldn't acknowledge he knew her, wouldn't speak, and walked right past her.

The Flower Lady confronted her soon after Messenger disappeared from the hospital. "You have no idea what you've done! We all put our necks out for you, not just Messenger."

"How? Tell me!"

"No, I've already said too much." She turned away and stared into her buckets of flowers.

Ed's kindness was the only exception. *Ed!* He should have been the most hostile, since he was probably closest to Messenger and knew all about Alana's role in the attack. But no. Alana would never forget how natural it had felt to fall into his arms when all those people had chased her from the hospital.

One morning, after he'd served her yet another free coffee, she said, "Hey, Ed. You know the other day, when all those reporters were after me?"

Ed filled a filter-lined basket with freshly-ground coffee. "Yeah?"

"Listen, thanks again for helping me. For locking them out."

"No problem."

She studied him. "Why are you being so nice to me? You know everything I did."

"I'm always nice to you." Ed focused on the basket.

"No. I'm serious. Everybody else around here's giving me the cold shoulder, and who can blame them?" Her voice caught. "But not you."

Ed met her eyes. "I have no right to judge."

"What do you mean?"

Ed shook his head and turned away.

Alana gathered her things and left. *That's so Ed,* she thought. *Drop a cryptic remark and then refuse to explain.* As she walked down First Avenue, Alana realized again how little she knew about

Ed's life or his past. He'd only reveal little tidbits here and there. But his response made her determined to learn more.

After another hour of fruitless searching, Alana returned to Ed's. He was busy with the drink line, so she settled down on her stool, rubbed her eyes, fought her exhaustion. *Messenger, where are you?* she cried inside. She stubbornly held on to her dimming hope that if she worked and searched hard enough, she would find some clue, some way to make things right. Beyond her guilt, which she owned, Alana fought her old angry, hurt feelings, which bubbled up unexpectedly and brought tears to her eyes. *I guess I thought Messenger would try and find me. Or at least say goodbye. Or leave me a message after all our time together. It doesn't look like she's going to. What would I say to her if she were still here? What message would I give the Messenger?*

Alana dug her notebook out of her backpack and jotted this letter to Messenger:

*Dear Messenger,*

*I was so wrong. I'm sorry I didn't listen to you and posted the website. I'm sorry about Rickie. I'm sorry about all of it. I meant well. (Did I?) I'm just so very sorry.*

*I know I probably drove you crazy, stalking you all over the neighborhood, asking questions, bothering your friends, demanding your time, taking you away from the job you had to do. I just want to say thank you for all you taught me. I still don't understand most of it, but I see the world differently because of you. Though you'd never know it from the choices I made—from what I did.*

*This may sound lame, but I do see it now. Believe me. You never gave me a message, like all those other people I interviewed. But that's okay. Just knowing you was my Clinamen. It changed my life.*

*Thank you.*

*Love,*

*Alana*

That night, Alana dreamed she was in a hotel. She stood in a long hall with rooms on either side of it, ugly green/brown carpeting on the floor. Way down the hall, a person turned a corner and walked toward her. Alana knew it was Messenger because of her slow, steady gait, even though she was very far away. Alana ran down the hall to meet her, but Messenger suddenly turned in the other direction and disappeared. It was one of those dreams where you can never get where you're trying to go, no matter how hard or fast you run. The hall seemed to grow longer as Alana ran. "Messenger!" she cried. "Stop! Wait! Help me."

All she heard in response were Messenger's giggles. Running down the hall on the ugly carpeting, Alana found feathers and pennies that fell out of Messenger's clothes, like a trail of breadcrumbs. But even though Alana searched all the way down the immense hallway, as far as she could see, Messenger was gone.

# GUILTY

The next morning, on her way in, Alana spied four or five feathers on the sidewalk—one red, the others gray and white—weird for the city. She found several pigeon feathers too. And a penny on the subway steps and one on First Avenue, both heads up. She collected each one and put them carefully into her backpack.

Alana got coffee at Ed's and sat at the end of the coffee bar before making her rounds to search. She knew she should head out but sat there instead and watched Ed wash dishes.

When Ed looked up, she realized tears were dropping down her cheeks into her coffee.

"Alana." Ed stuck the blender pitcher into the draining rack and handed her a brown paper napkin.

"Oh, Ed. I feel so lost without Messenger. I know you do too."

Ed nodded.

Alana wiped her eyes. "If I could just tell her how sorry I am for what I did. Somehow make it right. I just feel so guilty."

Ed leaned his elbows on the bar and clasped his hands into a fist. "You want to know about guilty?" he asked. "Let me tell you."

She braced herself while Ed paused, as if he had to force the words out. "How about feeling guilty because nothing's more important to you than your next drink? I lost my job over it. I was a contractor until I fell off a roof. The only reason I didn't break my neck was because I was so drunk. And young. I'd completely lost my way. I mentioned my ex-wife to you before. I lost her. Well, that wouldn't have lasted anyway. We were just kids when we got married. High school sweethearts."

Alana interrupted. "Lots of marriages fail, Ed."

Ed kept his eyes down. "No. Let me finish. My wife was three months pregnant. The doctors had heard a heartbeat and everything. But she started bleeding in the night. The doc had told her to go to the hospital immediately if that ever happened. So," he sighed, "she woke me up from the chair where I'd passed out. The TV on, blaring. I was still drunk. Very drunk. I knew I shouldn't be driving, but this was an emergency. Well, I wrecked the car on the way to the hospital, rear-ended an SUV with a trailer hitch on the back. Caused the guy right behind me to plow into us. As drunk as I was, I'll never forget the sound of that grinding metal. The whiplash on impact." He looked straight at Alana. "My wife didn't have her seat belt on. She didn't want to put any pressure on her stomach. So she was thrown to the floor of the car. She lost the baby."

"Oh no." Alana covered her mouth. "What happened to you?"

"Nothing. Just bruises. Again, because I was so drunk."

"Did you have to go to jail?"

"I just barely missed jail time. I deserved it, but I had a good defender. No prior record. That was a long time ago, and they were more lenient. I did lose my license for a year. Had to complete a lifetime of community service hours." His voice was quiet. "My wife never got over losing the baby. Never got over what I'd done."

"So sad," Alana said.

"You haven't heard the saddest part. I still didn't stop drinking! Even with AA. Hours and hours of counseling. I tried and tried to stop, so many times. I was really a wreck. Until Messenger came into my life."

"Messenger?"

"Yeah. That's the project I mentioned. I told her everything—like I've just told you. Every day she'd come in, and every day I knew she was going to ask me, 'Ed?' That's all she ever said, but we both knew what she meant. I'd shake my head. And I wouldn't drink. I didn't want to disappoint her. I'd visualize her eyes whenever I was tempted."

"How long since—"

"One year, nine months, ten days. But who's counting?" He laughed.

Alana took a deep breath. "Wow, Ed. I'm so sorry. Thanks for trusting me enough to tell me. But what are you going to do now that Messenger's gone?"

Ed gripped his fist. "Messenger might be gone from here. From us. But I know she's somewhere. She'll still know. She'll still care."

Alana nodded. She covered his fist with her hand.

"Things happen. Yes, you made mistakes. But, Alana, you didn't mean to cause it, just like I didn't … ." He looked into her eyes, and she saw her own pain there. "Terrible things can happen to people we love. We can wish every single day of our lives that we could take it back. But sometimes, you can't."

# WHAT NOW?

Ed's was still Alana's home base when she wasn't working at Tale of the Whale. One of the other waitresses had gotten a better job, so Gus had let Alana take her shifts. Otherwise, she was at Ed's. Alana felt closer to Messenger, sitting there on her usual stool, than in her own apartment. Even though it had been weeks without word, without one lead, even when she had to face Messenger's empty stool, Alana clung to her hope that it might be like before. That Messenger would come back.

One morning, Ed told her, "Alana, it's been a long time now." He wiped the counter in front of her and handed her a cup. "I think she's gone for good."

Alana's spirits plummeted to her feet. If Ed had given up hope, should she? Alana unfocused her eyes and pondered Ed's advice. "I won't give up," she finally told him. "I can't."

His smile reminded Alana of her mom's oncologist's. "It's hard. I understand."

Alana tried to drag herself out the door to make her rounds, but she couldn't gather the energy. She sipped her coffee and watched Ed wipe down the clean counter one more time.

The next morning was cloudy and felt colder than the actual temperature. When Alana reached Ed's, the drink line already flowed out the door, and people filled all the stools at the long table along the windows. It was okay. She'd come back later. She began her rounds, turned down Fifth and slowed her pace. The cars parked solid down both sides, one side parallel, the other on an angle, blocked her view. When she got to the playground, she spied the lady with the Chihuahuas perched on her usual bench, a dog on each side. The lady wouldn't make eye contact as Alana approached, wouldn't answer her questions (as usual), turned her back. But the dogs wagged their little rat tails and yipped. Alana figured they hoped she'd have a treat for them, like Messenger always did. They hadn't forgotten.

Alana walked past them and settled on the farthest bench of the three, Messenger's favorite. Today, after all this time, Alana realized she'd never once seen any kids play there. She felt the knot in her stomach that wouldn't go away, no matter how deeply she breathed. She raised and lowered her shoulders, worked the kinks out, leaned against the bench's hard, wooden back. She stared up and noticed small green buds forming on the tree's branches, waving now, since the wind had picked up. Curled brown leaves from last fall blew toward her, and street grit stung her eyes. She wrapped her green scarf tighter around her neck.

A voice inside her advised, *Alana, give up! Stop torturing yourself. Ed's right. Messenger's gone.*

Alana remembered how, even before she'd met Messenger, when she'd first seen Marty's photo, a chill had shimmered through her. Then, a warmth, an excitement welled up. That same inner voice had whispered, *This is it! You've been waiting for this your whole life. Your big break!*

*Yeah, right. You really made a mess of everything.*

Alana traced the circles in the cold, black wrought-iron bench arm with her finger, her cuticles chewed and picked to shreds the last few weeks. She knew Messenger would say that every single thing that had happened to her since they'd met was part of the whole—a much bigger whole. But Alana still had so many questions. *Am I the crazy one after all? Was it something I needed to believe in instead of a credible story?* Messenger always said the messages came through her. From where or from whom? Alana had never understood. Messenger admitted she didn't even know the answer to that question. So many strange happenings, so many unbelievable coincidences playing out in real time, in real people's lives. It was real. All those people who posted had believed it. Could they all have been wrong?

Alana couldn't explain all the strange things that had happened to her since she'd met Messenger either. They just kept coming. But one thing Alana did know for sure—her blind ambition was dead. Yes, she'd had big dreams. For achievement. Fame, even. Also dead was her darker aim, her lame attempt to get her dad's attention, to show him. To be noticed. To make him rethink the decisions he'd made long ago, when he'd left.

Now, after everything that had happened, it was all about Messenger. *What was she to me?* Alana wondered. *A friend? A teacher? Ed said she was like a mother to us—and that was true. All that and more. Of course, she was just fun to hang out with. Something always happened when she was around.* And hanging out with Messenger and all her friends had revealed a truth Alana had run from for a long time—how alone in the world she was. After Messenger came into her life, all that changed.

This bench beside the playground, the streets and shops around here, the same people they tended to see while sitting here or strolling together. Ed's coffee shop, of course. The smells there, of freshly ground coffee, pastries warming in the toaster oven, even the clean smell of the soap in the restroom. Ed's cleaning solution in the bucket. This is where Alana belonged now, more than anywhere else on earth.

Mary would never understand. None of Alana's old friends would. She herself wouldn't have understood six months ago, that she'd find what she'd always wished for here. A home. All of these people in the neighborhood were her people now. She'd have to find a way to regain their confidence, to win them back. And with Ed, maybe there was something more. Her heart warmed to think of him. But the center of it all—Messenger—was gone. What Alana wouldn't give to see her face, to hear her voice, one last time.

Alana remembered all the laughter. She'd never heard anybody laugh like Messenger did. She'd felt safe with her, like Messenger was a grown-up. Like she'd seen some things. Like she had something for Alana and they had a purpose to accomplish together. Alana gazed out across the street from their bench. How many times had they sat there together? She remembered the very last time, when Messenger had been upset and Alana hadn't understood why. They'd sat closer than ever before, and Alana had rested her head on Messenger's. Alana thought about how, at the moment of her greatest frustration with Messenger and the project, she'd made herself let go. She'd realized if she wanted things to work with Messenger, she had to surrender, to do things Messenger's way. It had worked, for a time. Until Alana had ruined it. *Maybe I should do that again,* she thought. *Stop trying so hard and just let go.*

A car horn jerked her back to the present. Alana finally noticed what had been parked at the curb, right in front of her all along. The green MINI-Cooper, license plate CLINAMN. Alana's heart lifted, and she jumped up. "Messenger!" she cried, hoping, praying to see her red cap, her amber eyes, to hear her laughter. She tore up and down the street, searched each face she passed, glanced back toward the benches.

But they were all empty.

# YOU'RE READY

The coffee shop door flew open, and Ed looked up.

"Messenger!" He ran around the bar, threw his arms around her and lifted her up. "You're back! You're all right!"

"Ooooh-whee! That was quite a ride." She laughed and hugged Ed back. "Yes. See? I'm just fine."

"Have you seen Alana? She feels terrible about what happened."

"I'm on my way to tell her goodbye."

Ed's hopeful face fell. "You're leaving?"

She patted his cheek. "Uh-huh. I'm sorry, but I don't have much time. I've got a train to catch and a daughter to find."

"Oh. A daughter? You never told me."

"I know. And that was wrong. But," she smiled, and her whole face lit up. "I'm telling you now." She settled herself on a bench at the bar.

"I'm going to miss you."

I'll miss you too, honey. Listen to me. Keep counting the days, and you'll be fine. You're fine now. You've got this."

"You've helped me so much," Ed choked out. "Thank you," he added simply.

"No, Ed. You're the one who did it all. I was just here to cheer you on. There's more I want to say about Alana, though."

Ed poured Messenger a coffee and took a sip of his own. "Alana? What?"

Messenger just smiled at him, so broadly he had to smile back.

"What?" he repeated.

"I want you to do something for me. She's going to need you, Ed."

"But I can't get involved with her or anybody else." He glanced around and lowered his voice so only Messenger could hear. "You know I haven't been sober long enough."

Messenger spoke slowly and calmly. "It's been almost two years. You can't use that as an excuse."

"I guess," Ed admitted. "But how can I help her when every day is still a struggle?"

"Nobody can help anybody else in the way you mean, Ed. Change them. Fix them. Nope. Never works. I'm not telling you anything you haven't learned these last two years."

Ed sighed. "I know. It's just hard."

"I'm only asking for two things. One: keep an open heart when it comes to her; really be there for her. And two: understand that your own happiness, your freedom, is tied up with hers."

"Are you saying Alana and I have a future together?"

"Well, I'm not saying you don't. What I'm trying to tell you is *everybody* is tied up with you. We're all working together. It's not all about you, Ed. Don't make that mistake."

"Of course. I know."

Messenger touched his arm. "Stand with her, whatever comes. Don't shut down. Keep your heart open. Trust it. She's going to need that from you. And honey, believe me. You're ready. You're more equipped this very minute than you give yourself credit for."

"Really? You believe that?"

"Yes!" Messenger cheered. "I'll believe it for you, if you can't believe it yourself. You know the drill."

"Focus on today."

"Yes, that's right."

"But what's this all about? Why will she need me? Is something going to happen to her? Why—"

"Just promise. Do that for me."

Ed shrugged. "Okay. I owe you that much, after all you've done for me. I guess I can pay it forward and be here for her."

"There you go! I don't think you'll mind it too much." She winked, picked up her coffee, and rolled off the bench. "Besides, wake up! You've been doing it already this whole time. There's no reason to be afraid! She feels the same way about you."

"What did she say?"

"I don't need words! When I look into her eyes after I catch her looking at you—that's all I need to see."

Ed blushed.

They both looked over to the window because Jackie had her nose against the glass and was tapping at them. She put her hands on her hips, then waved for Messenger to come out. Messenger laughed. "Got to go now."

"Is Jackie going with you to find your daughter?"

"Nope," Messenger answered. "You'll be seeing lots more of her. Remember, Ed, what you just promised. And don't forget—you've already got everything you need."

Ed followed her to the door. She reached up and hugged him again.

"Wait," he reached for his wallet. "Can I help you?"

Messenger put her hand on his and shook her head. "No. Nothing. Just your promise."

"Okay. You got it."

Messenger calmed her heart and walked through the door, out of the coffee shop. Despite her resolve not to, she found herself turning back around.

Ed stood there. He raised his hand.

She nodded. Took it all in. Turned away. She struggled to put one foot in front of the other and not look back.

# IN THE ALLEY

Alana headed down Fifth Street toward First Avenue and approached the entrance to the alley. She hadn't been back down there since the day they viewed Messenger's ruined altar. *That was another hint of what was coming. Another warning I ignored,* she thought. She still regretted not taking a picture of it. She'd give anything to have it now.

She stood at the entrance, then decided to walk in and see if she still heard that strange buzzing. Sure enough, as soon as she stepped into the darkened alley, the same sound filled her ears, just like before. There was static in the air, an electrical charge she could feel. Above the buzzing, she was sure she heard faint footsteps coming from farther down.

Her skin went cold. "Hello?" she called over the buzzing. "Who's there?"

*Should I run?* All the nerves on the surface of Alana's skin tingled as she strained to listen to what were now two sets of footsteps echoing in the alley from down the way. She froze, eyes widened, braced herself.

Messenger and Jackie walked around the corner! Messenger's face shone in the darkened light of the alley, and she held her arms out wide. "Alana!"

Alana's heart leaped, and she threw herself into Messenger's embrace, felt her substance and weight hold her tight. Alana's tears streamed as she sobbed into Messenger's red cap. "Oh, Messenger. I'm so sorry I posted the website. It was all my fault. That monster Rickie found you through me." Choking tears made it hard to get the words out. "I didn't understand, didn't know what he would do. I'm just so sorry about everything."

Messenger gently pulled away and patted Alana's shoulder. She dug in a pocket and handed her a brown paper napkin from Ed's. "Oh, honey. It's okay. Forget about all that." Messenger looked just like she always did. Multiple coats, red cap, face open and shining—like the attack had never happened. She waved her hand as if to brush away anything between them. "Everything's okay now."

"You're all right?" Alana swabbed her eyes and blew her nose.

"Sure, honey. See?" She stretched out her arms and turned all the way around. "Good as new."

"But how did you get up and out of the hospital like that?"

"I helped her," Jackie chimed in. "She couldn't have done it without me. And Rob."

Messenger chuckled. "Now that is the truth, Jackie."

"Wait," Alana said. "You two know Rob?"

"Uh-huh. He's our friend. The police were getting too nosy, so I had to get out of there quick, you see," Messenger explained. "Jackie snuck in, and she and Rob helped me."

Alana studied Messenger's face and body more carefully. She couldn't see one bruise. No stitches. Her nose was straight and looked perfectly normal. Relief filled her entire body.

"I don't have much time," Messenger said, "but I've got some things to tell you before I go."

Alana's heart sank. "Go? Where? You can't leave again! Please! I've been looking all over for you since you left the hospital! I've missed you so much!"

"I know, and I'm sorry about that. But I have no choice. I'm not going to be a Messenger anymore."

"What?"

"No. It's decided. My time as Messenger is over."

"No! You can't quit. What about all the people who need messages? What about the Clinamen?"

"Don't worry, honey. You don't think I'm the only Messenger? Oh my, no. I'm just one of many. We're all over the place. Name a city—you'll find Messengers there. But then the real story is: We're all messengers for each other. Everybody on this earth. Everyone can be a messenger for someone else. That's the flow for you!"

Alana objected, "But not like you."

Messenger smiled patiently. "No. We're not there yet. But we're heading in that direction. Then, the Clinamen will come. As soon as enough people know it, feel it deep down in their bones and get moving. Speaking of moving, I've got some traveling to do." Her face brightened even more. "I've got a daughter to find."

Alana's hand flew to her mouth. "What? You have a daughter?"

"I do. She's grown now. Twenty-eight."

"My age."

"Uh-huh. I had to leave her with my mother. After the messages started coming, these people—the Watchers—found me and explained what was happening. They said I had to work to help create the Clinamen by delivering my messages. But I couldn't do that and still live my old life. See, people like us have had to hide."

When Messenger said "us" a chill ran up and down Alana's spine. *Who is "us"?*

"I've told you before how dangerous good news can be. We couldn't risk bringing danger to our loved ones. We had to leave our families and our homes."

"How old was your daughter when you left her?"

Suddenly Messenger looked older and sadder than Alana had ever seen. "She was just a baby. A toddler."

Alana's eyes widened. "How could you do that?"

Messenger dropped her head. "It was terrible. The hardest thing I ever did. But those are the rules for Messengers. You leave everything, strike out on your own." Tears filled Messenger's eyes. "Was it really necessary? Probably. To keep our loved ones safe from what happened to me in the park. But it was a big price to pay."

"Too big." Jackie shook her head.

"It was wrong. Now I've got to make it right."

"Yes, you do!" Alana automatically agreed, then realized what she had just said. Her head swam with each new revelation. "This is a lot to take in. Who are these Watchers you're talking about?"

"Well, Jackie is one of them. She's my main Watcher."

Jackie stood up straighter and nodded.

Messenger continued. "And there are others, but I don't know who they are. For my protection and theirs."

"What do the Watchers do?"

"They help, protect, and defend the Messengers, of course. They guard and watch for upcoming dangers. They warn you when trouble's coming. Then step in when necessary, to help."

"Well they sure did a lousy job with Messenger!" Alana blurted out.

"Listen, girlie. We did our best, but Messenger is stubborn as a mule and you—"

Messenger touched Jackie's arm. "The Watchers did warn me. They did all they could. But I chose to ignore their warnings."

"Why would you do that?" Alana asked.

"For the Clinamen. I want things to change."

Alana pressed. "You allowed Rickie to attack you to bring about a Clinamen?"

"No," Jackie snorted. "What she's not saying is: She wanted to protect you after you posted that website like she told you not to. Every crazy, threatened, twitchy, violence-loving nut in the city would have come after you if she hadn't come back and taken the heat."

Tears flew into Alana's eyes. Her stomach felt like Jackie had thrown a punch.

"Jackie!" Messenger put her arm around Alana. "Now, now. Don't beat yourself up. It all worked out."

"I'm so sorry, Messenger. I'm just so, so sorry. You've got to understand. I was desperate. I didn't think you wanted to work with me anymore. I thought you were gone for good. And I guess a part of me hoped it might somehow bring you back."

"It brought her back, all right!"

"Please," Messenger said. "Let me finish explaining."

Jackie crossed her arms and looked away.

"You should have trusted me, Alana. It was all timing, you see." She patted Alana's back.

"How?" Alana wiped her eyes.

"Energies were building. It always happens before a Clinamen. Action, reaction. This time, they were very negative energies. Destructive energies. It was only a matter of time. You just hurried things along."

Alana's eyes filled with more tears. "I know. I'm sorry."

"It was the next step. Unplanned, of course, but the next step. Anyway. Everything is changed now. My work was important, but it's time for me to find my daughter and make things right. Hopefully, if she can let herself love me, maybe she can forgive me. There's no forgiveness without love. The love part has to come first."

Alana tried to take in everything Messenger had said. "But where is she? Where are you going?"

"The Watchers have kept an eye on her too. They tell me she's in Virginia."

"What? That's where I'm from."

Messenger nodded.

"What's her name?"

"Bree." Messenger said it like a prayer.

Raw panic rose up in Alana and spread throughout her body. She couldn't lose Messenger again. "Let me go with you. I could help you find her."

Messenger touched her shoulder, then massaged between her eyebrows. "No, honey. This is for me to do. But don't you worry now. You won't be alone. Jackie here," she pointed to Jackie, who was studying her fingernails, "is going to stay with you. She's going to help you finish what we started."

"Finish what? Are you talking about finishing the book?"

"No. It's much bigger than that. Anyway, it'll all be clear soon. Until then, trust me. Wait. Work with her."

"Jackie? Are you kidding me?" Alana's eyes widened in disbelief.

Jackie smiled her creepy smile.

Messenger laughed at both of them. "Yes, Jackie. You're going to see another whole side of her."

"Listen," Jackie interrupted. "I'm not exactly thrilled about it either, but … ."

Messenger shook her head. "You two will do just fine together."

"But why didn't you tell me about the Watchers and your daughter and all these secrets from the beginning? When I'd ask you?"

Messenger gazed lovingly into Alana's face. "As I've said so many times, honey, timing is everything. Before, you wouldn't have believed me. You had to learn it for yourself. You had to research. Conduct your own investigation. Then you had to begin to experience it. Experience is the best teacher. You're ready now. Even though you don't know it, you are."

"Ready for what?" The panic thickened. Her heart thundered in her chest, and she swore the buzzing was getting louder.

"Oh, you'll see. And don't worry. You won't have to do it all alone. You'll have Jackie, but you're going to have Ed too. You two will work great together."

"How? What do you mean? Will Ed help me get the word out about the messages and how they're helping people?"

Alana could tell by the smirk on Jackie's face that she was enjoying Alana's confusion. "Sort of," she teased.

Alana turned to Jackie then Messenger. "Why won't you two just give me straight answers for once?"

They laughed so hard it echoed through the alley. "In time, I promise you, Jackie will answer all your questions. But you've got a job to do now."

"What are you talking about?" Alana could hardly force the words out, her jaw felt locked.

"That's all I can say for now, honey. I'm sorry, but I've got a train to catch."

Alana dug in her heels. "But what if I can't do this job you're talking about? Or don't want to?"

Messenger smiled patiently. "Nobody's going to make you. You have to choose it. But let me warn you. Even after all I've been through, I still know this is true." Her eyes seared Alana. "You've got to bring forth what's inside you. Everybody does. That's the way you've got to go. Because if you don't, it will destroy you." Her voice rang out strong. "Remember this when the going gets rough."

Alana had a million questions but all she said was, "Don't leave me." The tears she'd controlled returned full force. The shivering started.

Messenger put her arm around Alana and turned. "Will you give us a minute?"

"Sure!" Jackie answered. She didn't move.

"Alone," Messenger added.

"Oh, okay. I get it. But you know you've got to go soon." Jackie clicked down the alley away from them.

Messenger turned back to Alana. "Oh, honey. You're going to be just fine."

"No, I won't," Alana muttered. "Can I contact you?" she asked, even though she knew the answer.

"No, but don't worry. I'll be in touch. And I'll be back. Helping in a new way, that's all. You'll see me. Just not all the time, like before." Messenger reached up and placed her hands on Alana's shoulders. She touched her cheeks, held her eyes in one long, loving gaze.

Immediately, Alana's shaking stopped.

"I have to go now, honey. We don't know when or how the Clinamen's coming. We just keep doing what we can. But know this: You're ready. You've got everything you need. Like I said, we're all messengers for each other. Look for it in every face you meet. Every single one of us is important in the scheme of things. Trust it. In every joy. Or in every trouble. When you say, 'Sorry for your trouble,' you mean it more than you know. They are your troubles too. Yes! And the Helpers will aid and guide you. They're always available. There are worlds you don't even know about—but you will. All working together, moving us forward toward the Clinamen. Believe in the power of love. It's for us, and it'll work with us. It's the thing everybody wants because it's the only thing that's real."

The buzzing had grown so loud Alana wanted to cover her ears. "Messenger! What is that buzzing?"

"The energy of Mother Earth. Calling to us. I'm so glad you can hear it."

"Yes! I heard it both times we were in here before." Alana looked down. "I just didn't tell you."

"I know," she said. "That's okay."

"It wasn't this loud before. What does it mean? Is something about to happen?"

Messenger gently wiped the tears from Alana's cheeks. "Yes, honey," she said so quietly, Alana could hardly hear. "Yes, it is."

# ALANA AND ED'S CLINAMEN

Alana burst into the coffee shop. "Ed, I saw Messenger! She's fine! I don't know how, but she's just fine!"

Ed looked over with sad eyes. Had he been crying? "I know. She stopped by here on her way to find you."

"Ed, are you okay?"

"Yeah, sure." He bit his lips. "Where did you see her?"

"I just happened to walk down the alley on Fifth Street and met Messenger and Jackie coming from the other direction. They seemed to know I'd be there, somehow. Lots of what they said didn't make sense, and of course, they wouldn't answer most of my questions. But Messenger told me she was leaving to find her daughter. I get that." Alana remembered the many hundreds of times she'd pictured just such a reunion with her own father.

"Did you know she had a daughter?" Ed asked.

"No! Did you?"

Ed shook his head.

"She also told me she wasn't going to be a Messenger anymore."

"Oh, wow."

"Yeah, but she wouldn't say why. She did explain that Messengers used to have to leave their homes and families. That's why she left her daughter. But she thinks that rule is wrong and wants to change things. There are Watchers who help and protect the Messengers.

Jackie's one of them. She's Messenger's main one. But there are other Watchers all around." Alana paused, deciding how much more to tell him. "She also mentioned that there's this job I'm going to have. It has nothing to do with the book. What she told me really didn't make sense. It's almost too crazy to be believed."

Ed smiled. "Try me."

"I think Messenger was hinting ..." Alana paused again, thinking. "No, I'm not ready to say it out loud. I'm just figuring it out myself."

Ed stopped her. "It's okay. Take all the time you need."

Alana studied Ed's open face. He looked like a different person. She forged ahead. "Whatever this job is, she told me you would help me."

"I know," he said. "I promised her I would."

Her eyes widened. "What else do you know about it? Tell me!"

"Messenger only said that you'd need my help. That we had a future, I guess you'd say, a job to do together too."

"I know you've kept things from me in the past. If you know more than you're saying ... ."

Ed held up his hands. "That's it, but let me tell you what I do know. Messenger loved you. Even though I think you drove her crazy sometimes with all your questions."

They laughed.

"Whatever is going on, we know that Messenger's intentions—her plans—are good. I bet everything will fall into place. And when you do figure it out, whatever you need, whatever it takes, I'll help you."

"Thank you." Alana shook her head and laughed. "Are we both crazy?"

"Probably." He sighed and studied the counter. "I just have to figure out how I'm going to make it without her."

"I know!"

"No. It's more than that."

Alana wrinkled her forehead.

"Remember how I told you she checked on me every day to see if I'd taken a drink?"

"Oh, I get it. Yeah. But like you said before, she'll still know. She'll still care. Anyway, I can do that for you."

Ed looked up. "Really? Thanks." He came out from behind the counter and stood beside her. "Even though Messenger's gone, Alana," he smiled his crooked smile, "you've still got me."

"We'll help each other."

Ed met her eyes, and he did not look away.

At that moment, all the pieces fell into place. Everything that had happened from that first day Alana walked into Ed's, even before she'd met Messenger, until now. It happened in a split second, just like Messenger had said it would. A Clinamen. Before, Alana had been on her own. Now, it was her and Ed. Together. Facing whatever was coming. Whatever job she was going to be called to do.

She wasn't alone anymore.

# ON THE TRAIN

Messenger stared out the window of the Amtrak train headed south. Rain slashed the plated glass, then beaded up. She let herself jostle along in time with the beat of the car as it sped down the track. She smiled and sucked on the dark chocolate she'd just popped into her mouth, held the crumpled red foil in one hand. The message had told her, "Follow your dreams."

Had she done her part to create the Clinamen? To make things better for those coming along behind her?

She hoped so, but it was too late now. She was finished. It was done. She'd done her duty and fulfilled all her promises. Love, so deep, was still alive inside her. She would find Bree if it was the last thing she ever did. Alana—with Jackie as teacher and Watcher and with Ed by her side—was almost ready. They'd had to rush things, make do with the time they'd had. But all was well. A fresh start. A new way. She'd do just fine.

# ALANA MAKES A DISCOVERY

That evening, Alana worked her dinner shift at Tale of the Whale, then headed back to Astoria. She got off the train, walked down the nasty steps from the elevated station, black with soot, the pigeons settled for the night, cooing in their filthy, rusted corners. When she passed the funeral home on the next street, she noticed signs of spring in the garden. In the streetlights, she could see dashes of yellow green dotted the dead stems and branches, the grass, and the pots lining the fence, even though it was still so cold.

Inside her apartment, Alana got a glass of water and settled at the small desk in her bedroom. She shook her head. She felt like she'd been riding roller coasters all day. Messenger returning. Then leaving again. Everything Messenger had told Alana before she left. All the questions left behind. Knowing for sure that Messenger was really gone for good. Alana's sense of connection to Ed (Ed!), to Messenger, to whatever this crazy experience meant filled her. Not regular thoughts in her brain but a dawning within her echoed through her body and landed between her heart and her gut. A calm feeling she'd hardly ever known. Peace. That was it. Even though none of her problems had left her. Now, in this moment.

Peace.

Alana noticed the ballerina, lying on her back on top of her desk. Alana picked her up, held her by her straight leg. She noticed the silver painted toe shoes had mostly rubbed off. All the spokes on her tiara were broken. But she still held her left arm high in the air, her fingers stretched up to the sky. That hopeful gesture always made Alana's heart lift too.

Alana laid the ballerina down and picked up her drab green backpack, unfastened the clasp. She pulled out trash, brown napkins, lots of chocolates she didn't know were there. She wished she'd given them all to Messenger. She fished out the old ballpoint pen Messenger had given her. The feathers and the pennies. She'd meant to show them to Ed. She felt for her thick notebook, now almost completely full, where she'd jotted ideas, lists, notes, stream-of-consciousness hopes, fears, doubts, plans—anything that had come to mind since the beginning. She laid it down on the desk beside all her other mementos.

She held her backpack on her lap and hugged it to her. The nagging feeling that something was clearly there, from Messenger's words, the dreams, the coincidences, her strange knowings, the license plate. The buzzing. How do you explain it? Connect all the dots? What Messenger had implied—Alana still couldn't let herself go there because it was absolutely insane! No. Impossible. More than Alana could fathom or that Messenger would reveal. *You are crazy, Alana*, she told herself.

But when she lifted the backpack off her lap to put it down on the floor by her desk, she noticed something. *Why is it still so heavy?* she wondered. She felt around, then unzipped the inner back pocket, a section she never used. Inside, she discovered a black-and-white marbled composition book, smudged and coffee stained.

*What's this? Where did it come from?* Suddenly, it dawned on her. The composition book she'd given Messenger so long ago! *When did she put it in here?* Alana wondered. She felt her fingers tingle. She opened the cardboard cover and flipped through its worn, grimy pages full of writing—Messenger's writing. Every single page was full. Alana flipped back to the beginning, to the words of the very first entry.

There, Alana read, *Call me Messenger.*

# Alana's Notebook

## Ideas Jotted While Reading Messenger's Composition Book

*FORGET ABOUT THE BOOK FOR NOW.*

*While writing Messenger's story is important and something I will do, isn't it more important to get the messages out? Start the sharing? Isn't this technology at its best—a way to get good news to people all over the world at the same time? To form a community over time and space? It's worth a try.*

*What if I expand my website, keep collecting messages, and put them and the recipients' stories online, so anybody, anywhere can read them? If Messenger's right, and there are messengers at work in every city, every country, all over the world, they could also be added. Who knows how many messages there are altogether?*

*More people could be touched by reading the messages and the stories behind them—feel encouraged, feel braver, feel more love surrounding them, no matter what's going on in their lives. It could work. ISN'T THAT THE CORE OF HER MESSAGES? THE UNIVERSE IS RUN BY LOVE? Messages from Messengers from all over world and their stories would prove it.*

*What have I learned about the truth? Or about myself? I clearly know I'm not special, and it's not about me or what other people think of me anymore. I can't stop here because I have a job to do. I'm all in. What do I really know about Messenger? Why was she here? Why was she giving out messages to people? What bigger aim did she have? How will the Clinamen happen?*

*Mystery. It's all mystery.*

# Messenger's Composition Book

## Last Entry a Gift to Alana

*Awww. You're such a wonderful girl. You still don't get it all—but that's okay. You'll figure everything out when the time comes. Through experience—the best way to learn anything. At least everything that can be known. You'll get your mojo back and start rolling with it.*

*HAH, HAH! Don't you see? It's been right under your nose the whole time. Now the gig is up! My work is complete, but yours is just about to begin.*

*What you don't know is this—I left a gift in your backpack. In that big inner back pocket. I put it there when you went to the bathroom at Ed's the last time we walked together through the neighborhood. When you do find it, you'll sit down and read it from cover to cover.* IT'S THIS COMPOSITION BOOK YOU ASKED ME TO KEEP. *Bet you thought I forgot about it.*

*And that's when something else will happen. While you read it, you'll sit down with your pen in hand and a nice fat pad of paper, waiting for inspiration, for structure, asking for a way to create something out of chaos, to make sense of your experiences. That's what you'll think you're doing anyway.*

*You'll feel your feet. The energy will fill you—like a buzz. You already know what it feels like. Just like the buzzing in the alley. The beat! Up from the floor and down from above into the top of your head. Words will fill you, swirl, dance. If you sit very still and let them, they'll eventually form a pattern, then catch your attention. You'll begin.*

*SURPRISE, HONEY!*

*Your first message will come.*

# Acknowledgments

Journeying with *Messenger* has taught me this: trust your team.

First and foremost, heartfelt gratitude to my tireless agent, April Eberhardt. Her faith in *Messenger*, efforts, enthusiasm, expert advice, and circle of resources proved invaluable. April invited me to join her La Poterie community, where I first workshopped *Messenger* with master teacher/writer Kristen Harnisch, reveled in Cynthia de Moucheron's spectacular hospitality, and met fellow writer Diane Dewey, an unflagging believer in *Messenger.* Also, through April, my collaboration with brilliant editor, Annie Tucker, greatly enhanced the book. Thanks to all.

*Messenger: A Novel in 16 Episodes* podcast, wouldn't have happened without the support and creative talents of Rachel Pater. Thanks also to our phenomenal podcast team of Brandon O'Neill, Wells Hanley, and Lance Koehler and to all our faithful listeners.

The day *Messenger* found a home with Warren Publishing was one of the happiest of my life. Admiration and gratitude to publisher, Mindy Kuhn; to gifted editor-in-chief, Amy Ashby, whose skill and understanding knew no bounds; and to Lacey Cope, marketing director and media expert.

Thanks so much to Marissa DeCuir of Books Forward and her dedicated team—Elysse Wagner, Erica Martin, and especially to Corrine Pritchett, my brilliant publicist and Jeizebel Espiritu, web designer extraordinaire. Landing in their experienced hands was a comfort and delight.

My entire life I've been blessed with master teachers, especially Susan Hankla, Cynthia Bourgeault, John Philip Newell, and Joy Paoletto. Through their writings, teachings, and the wonderful people I've met in their respective communities, my life and *Messenger* have been enriched. And special appreciation to Audrey Stech, who prayed this project through.

My family has anchored me always. Huge thanks to my sisters and their families, to my extended Keller, Garber, Hepner, and Whitehurst clans, and to our family of dear friends. To Wilson, Joy, and Tucker, who helped in more ways than I can count—eternal gratitude.

CPSIA information can be obtained
at www.ICGtesting.com
Printed in the USA
LVHW092332101021
700109LV00004B/7/J

9 781954 614437